More Praise for
NO ONE RIDES FOR FREE

Also by Larry Beinhart
Published by Ballantine Books:

YOU GET WHAT YOU PAY FOR
FOREIGN EXCHANGE

NO ONE RIDES FOR FREE

Larry Beinhart

BALLANTINE BOOKS • NEW YORK

Library of Congress Catalog Card Number: 85-15386

ISBN 0-345-37294-8

This edition published by arrangement with William Morrow and Company, Inc.

Manufactured in the United States of America

First Ballantine Books Edition: April 1993

CONTENTS

I

ATTICA

FOR THE DEFENSE: Paul Dean Whitney, Harvard 1940, number three in his class and Law Review. Assisted by Paul C. Chillgren III, Harvard '49, number five, Law Review; and Andrew Lande Depue, Yale '73, number seven, Law Review. As strong and classy a defense as any guy could ask for.

The team from the Manhattan D.A.'s office, the world's most prestigious place to public prosecute, was headed by Franco DeMattresse (Columbia '69, number fourteen), backed by Leonard Ginsberg (N.Y.U. '79, number four, Law Review) and Roosevelt Long (N.Y.U. '82, number twenty-seven). What they lacked in class and connections, they made up for in raw aggressiveness.

On the bench: His Honor Paul Stewart McCarthy, Brooklyn Law School. Night.

The client was clearly guilty. But the court world reflects the real world through doubled lenses that concentrate and distort with equal intensity. The rules of society, faults in the fate line, random events, skill and incompetence, precedent and the sins of omission all collide with anxious irrationality to produce nothing consistent. There was no reason, therefore, to expect or predict a verdict of guilty.

In spite of that, the verdict was "Guilty."

His Honor P. S. McCarthy pronounced sentence: "Three to five. Attica."

The entire defense team went into a state of shock even deeper than that day in 1957 when the first Jew had been admitted to the firm of Whitney, Whitney, Stanley and White. You could have heard a pin-stripe drop.

The prosecutors with their street smarts, wise-guy ways and ugly urban accents, already elated over victory, were shocked. Even the courthouse spectators, aficionados of aberration, were shocked.

But most deeply shocked of all was the defendant.

Attica. A nightmare. Attica. Why not say hell? Why not say Auschwitz? He was sixty. Was that old enough to save his pale white ass from rape? Big black street-fighting bodies were going to slam his office-pale, office-soft body against tiled walls in naked showers. Big fat fists. Heavy feet. Vindictive laughter as they bent him over to violate him and make him vile. Giggling and guffawing with the Joy of Destruction (fifth sequel to *Joy of Sex*, sixteen weeks *N.Y. Times* best-seller list). Attica. Nightmare. Bedspring knives in the hands of P.R. punks. "Gimme yo' cig'rettes, gimme yo' money. I pop yo' eyeballs, pop."

This was a white-collar crime. First offense. This was a lawyer. Upper-middle-class, middle-aged attorneys do *not* go to *Attica*. Did John Mitchell go to Attica? Dean? Haldeman? Erlichman? Attica was for the animals. The judge, he crazy, putting the pigeon in the cat cage. The Jungle Bunnies gonna eat him alive. Tear him up. Suck his blood. Then pluck his feathers, just for the fun of it.

"At-ti-ca! At-ti-ca! At-ti-ca!"

"Never. No. I'm not going to go!" the defendant yelled. He looked over at his former partners, they who had instigated this barbarity. "I'll get you all for this. I'll take you down, and that cock-sucker Charlie too!"

His Honor P. S. McCarthy banged his gavel. The defense

restrained the defendant. When the court quieted, the judge
continued to expound, as is the judge's privilege and duty,
on the ratiocination that had led him to this particular judg-
ment. His logic was clear and precise. His reasoning was
cogent and comprehensible. That too was unusual.

His Honor said: "I send guys up the river for stealing a
fifteen-dollar radio. This guy stole eight million dollars. He's
going to Attica."

The defendant's mind was screaming with rage and fear.

The defendant Edgar Wood (an Ellis Island variant on
Woiczkowsky) had been the attorney for Over & East, Inc.,
the giant conglomerate nicknamed "Takeover & Eat" on
Wall Street.

The chairman of the board was Charles Goreman. This
inspired more nicknames, for preppies thrive on nick-
names, and every Wall Streeter is a prep school boy, none
more so than the alumni of DeWitt Clinton in the Bronx
or Franklin Roosevelt High in Detroit. Thus: "Gore &
Glory: The Takeover Trail of Over & East,"[1]"Takeover
& Eat, Still The Same Old Gory,"[2] "Charles 'Blood &
Gore' Goreman—Swashbuckling King of Speculators,"[3]
"Mergers & Manipulations—The Whole Gory Story,"[4]
"Captain Gore—The Last Pirate,"[5] "Gore Among the
Bluebloods: A Social Takeover in the East."[6]

The world sucked Wood down, and the hand that should
have saved him, the hand of Charles Goreman, did not reach
out. They had been together since before the beginning.
Wood was Goreman's personal attorney, as well as counsel
to Over & East. He was on the board. He was on the boards
of several subsidiaries. Together they had built an empire.
Together, like Don Quixote and Sancho Panza, like Roy
Rogers and Trigger, like Sergeant Preston and his lead dog
King, like the Lone Ranger and Tonto. Now the white man
had come for Tonto, and the Lone Ranger said, "It's every
Indian for himself. Got it, Tonto?"

[1]Fortune: S. 17 '73.   [2]Forbes: Ja. 8 '79.   [3]Wall St. Jrnl.: 11/6/75.
[4]Barrons: Jn. 6 '77.   [5]People: F. 17 '79.   [6]Women's Wear Daily: 3/5/81.

Wood saw, as in a vision, like a man going down for the third time, the road to salvation. The paving stones of the path were carved from vengeance, which made it sweeter still.

"Call the SEC," Wood told Whitney.

"What?"

"The SEC," Wood repeated. "Tell them I'm ready to deal. Tell them to keep me out of Attica and I will tell them everything that I and 'Gory' Charlie the Goreman did to turn Over & East into Takeover and Eat."

"Edgar, we have not exhausted by any means our normal, legal options." Whitney was somewhat patronizing. Patronization is an attorney-client privilege. "We can appeal both the sentence and the verdict."

"Listen to me, Whitney." Wood spoke like a man whose balls were being shaved by a burred blade. "Do it my way. The SEC has been after our ass for years."

"Listen to me," patronizing and patient, Whitney went on, "this is New York State Criminal Court. The key words are Criminal and State. The Security and Exchange Commission is not a judicial agency; it is a regulatory body of the federal government."

"No. You listen. We're going my way."

"I know you're upset; you're shocked by the verdict and even more by this obscene and unprecedented sentence. You are an excellent attorney, Edgar, but you are not a criminal attorney. We are. That's why you hired us. And we will go into Appeals Court with both guns blazing and we will knock the heck out of this business. Just you wait and see."

The bile churned upward like oil in a cracking plant; his blood pounded with neon Broadway rhythms: "At-ti-ca! Re-venge! At-ti-ca! Re-venge! At-ti-ca!"

"Whitney, go suck your own ivy-league, blue-blooded dick."

"What!" said Whitney. Only colored defendants and fellow Groton alumnae ever spoke to him like that. Even then, only if they had graduated in the same class and said it with a smile.

"This is what you are going to do. You will call the SEC. You will tell the SEC that I will testify to every dirty deed, every back-door deal. I will show them where the bodies are buried and the closets to open to find the skeletons. They will be delirious with joy. The first SEC investigation of Over & East was in '63. I stopped them. They've come back at us almost every goddamn year since, and every goddamn time I stopped them. Believe me, Whitney, bet your D.A.R. membership on it, those boys are going to sit up and beg."

"You're upset, Edgar. You don't really mean this."

"You can also tell them that I will give them, as a special bonus, Charlie 'Gory' Goreman on a big silver platter. With an apple in his mouth and subpoenas up the ass."

"Edgar, take a couple of days to think about this. We have a lot of alternatives. Believe me, I can get you out of this. At least keep you out of Attica."

"Yes, you probably can . . ." Wood was almost dreamy now; his mind had come through a climax; he was post-orgasmic and his words came floating to Whitney, ". . . yes, you probably can. But it won't hurt Charlie at the same time . . . that's the beauty of my way. Don't you see the beauty of it?"

"There is no rush on this. I'm sure the judge will grant a continuance of bail while we appeal. . . ." Whitney regarded Wood critically while he spoke. His client looked calm and something close to content. Whitney wondered if he'd gone over the edge, and, if so, how long it would be before he returned.

"Not necessary," Wood's voice floated. "Call them after lunch, and they'll be on the two-thirty shuttle, plenty of time before the court closes. They will say: 'Please, please, Your Honor, this man is oh so very important to us. Please let him come and visit our Nation's Capital instead of that awful place upstate. We would like him to come and chat for a year or two or three."

"I'm not sure," said Whitney like a Cardinal gently chiding a subtle heresy, "that the SEC is qualified to plead as amicus curae in New York Criminal Court."

"Paul, my boy . . ." And hearing his Christian name Whitney understood it was irrevocable. When a patient calls his doctor by his first name, or the defendant the attorney, it means the dependent has taken his destiny out of the hands of those gods and into his own. ". . . do what I say. It's simpler than dismissing you and finding other counsel just to make one call."

Paul Dean Whitney was upset. He hated it when a client made decisions. Hated it even more than riding the subway. He was so upset that he began to search his pockets for change before he realized that Washington would be a credit-card call.

2

SQUASH

CHARLES "CHIP" FORTE Riggins, a Yalie from his side-
burnless cheeks to his Pumas with custom insoles and back
to his square jaw, was born to sail, play squash and work for
a Wall Street law firm. All of which he did. He was a young
associate at Choate, Winkler, Higgiston, Hahn & Moore, all
of whose names are on the masthead with "d'csd" next to
them. You know you're in the presence of real class when
every single name in the name is dead. It means the firm
itself is so revered that the mention of a living attorney can
only demean it.

No one has ever come to any firm conclusion about what
I was born to do. I started playing squash because it was
free. A friend at N.Y.U. taught me the game and fixed me
up with a fake ID card. By the time he was thrown off the
faculty, for reasons he never coherently explained, and my
free-play days were gone, I was strung out on the game.

It always gave me a special glow and left Chip feeling
disoriented when I beat him.

I beat him and he left his clothes in a sullen heap in the

locker room and went into the steam room wearing only a huff.

"What kind of cases do you really handle?" he asked me. He spoke without looking in my direction in case his eyes should accidentally drift to my genitalia.

"Anything that pays." I thought for a moment, remembered that he worked for all deceased people and tripled my fee. "Seven hundred fifty dollars a day, for my time, plus costs which can include additional people, which I mark up. No OT on my own time, but any day that runs longer than fourteen hours, I charge two days."

"Your rate is not a problem," he said, being very serious. "I want to know what sort of work you do."

He wanted to play "Say the secret word and you win a duck." There was an answer he wanted to a question I didn't know, and the reward would be a job, which I needed. I hate the game.

"We're squash buddies," I said. "Nobody can be truer and more steadfast than squash buddies. If you were married I would say you want me to prove that your wife does awful things with small animals so you won't have to pay alimony. But you're not married. I don't think it's you that's in trouble, because I don't think you know how. So. Let us cut the crap; tell me what the problem is and I'll tell you if I can help."

"It's not for me. It's for . . . let's say a client. But I don't want to waste your time if it's not in your line."

"Of course it's for a client. You're an attorney, Chip, remember."

"Yeah. Look . . . uh hah . . . I don't know how to say this. You're not the smoothest guy in the world. I mean I don't mind. That kind of thing doesn't matter to me. And if you're the right guy, it won't matter to . . . them. So I'm just trying to save everybody time and embarrassment."

"What the hell. I don't need your insults. I don't need your job. You're lucky to get me."

"Then how come," he said, "I've had to pay for the court the last two weeks?"

You can't fool a squash buddy. Even when your touch on

the drop shot is picture perfect, he knows when you're broke. And the s.o.b. still wanted to play "Say the secret word."

"Awright, you wanna know. My work could be characterized as tough-guy eclectic. I chase bail skips. I discover disreputable dirt for divorces. I track down white-collared corporate crooks . . ."

I saw his eyebrow twitch. It was practically a clue. I was very, very close to the secret word.

". . . some of my best cases have been beating the embezzler before he beats it to Brazil. I've done some very quiet stuff for politicians. I offer discretion, loyalty, superior intelligence and half a law degree."

"Half a law degree?"

"Yeah," I said, "I'm a law-school dropout. That has all the utility of being a beauty-school dropout, except I still can't do my own nails."

"Where," I knew he would ask, "did you go?"

My answer, I also knew, would clinch it. I didn't have the right kind of name, the right style or the right kind of look. But once in my life I had been in the right place.

"Yale," I said.

He sat back and pretended to ponder.

At 7 P.M. the next evening I got out of the subway at Wall Street.

I wore a suit and a rental tie. I had re-shaved at six and trimmed the burns. The woman I lived with had ironed my cleanest shirt. They were gonna love me.

The receptionist sat beneath a large, amorphous and contemporary painting that symbolized, I think, gray. I asked for Mr. Riggins. When I did not have to wait because he was in conference, on a conference call with a client or on long distance, I realized that he was really in a fit.

He looked me over and found me adequate. Not good enough to praise. Not bad enough to complain. So he led me on through the rabbit warren of Associates' territory. A clean undistinguished factory of the mind, still busy as the associates put in unpaid, but highly billed, overtime to prove their dedication to the holy, and very well paid, grail of partnership.

We ascended through an internal stairway to Partners' turf. The law firm provides associates with office furnishings; partners buy their own. It is one of the finest ways in the western world of demonstrating class distinction. Partners may even put in custom doors. Like a scout entering Indian territory, Chip's awareness of danger increased geometrically with each sign and marking.

"Hey"—I put my hand on his shoulder—"I won't embarrass you. I'll be a credit to my race." His look implied that it was improper to joke when surrounded by forces so capriciously hostile. "Really," I back-tracked, "I won't even make jokes. I will act like this is serious, which I'm sure it is. I will act with probity and correctness."

"Good."

We straightened our ties and he led me to a corner office. Corner office is, of course, top of the heap. Think of it! Two views! Only four rooms per floor have two views! And the furnishings. An acre of Persian carpet. In mid-acre, an antique desk. An ornate surface with no drawer space, a desk that says functionless. Pure, unadulterated status desk. There were no law books. No bookshelves. When you saw this man, all this said, you were not paying for books, for dusty research, for filings or record keeping. When you saw this man you were paying for the privilege of seeing him.

There were only two chairs. One was behind the desk. No one had to explain that Chip was not included. He offered me up to this High Lord of the Legal Admiralty, gave me one last pleading look and left.

Lawrence Choate Haven was about sixty-five. His suit was two months of my rent. His nails were manicured, his hair precision cut, his tan wealthy but not ostentatious. His posture was a credit to his class or he was wearing a corset. His middle-name name belonged to the Choate in the firm's masthead.

He explained that he had checked my references. I looked humble. He had found them adequate. I looked grateful.

"When we have been called upon to utilize investigative services in the past we have used one of several large, established firms. Accountability is an important qualification in most instances. However, like all positive qualities, accountability has its obverse side. It means that a system is operative, and a system means that a significant number of nonessential personnel, management, clerical, accounting, et al, are involved.

"In this instance we have a situation in which discretion is more important than corporate accountability. If I were employing you on behalf of Choate, Winkler, I could not permit myself that option. This, however, is a personal matter, and I am indeed free to exercise that option."

The man spoke not only in complete sentences, but in complete paragraphs. A vanishing art. I was impressed.

The partners at Choate, Winkler had not gone out and recruited Mr. Wood because of his stunning legal qualifications and sterling character. He had happened to them.

Leisure Time Industries had started as a record company and grown into toys, games, concert promotions, resorts. Anything that could be called leisure and some things that could not. One of their subsidiaries made squash rackets. But they had a moment of weakness, and Charles Goreman, who could scent weakness like a hound can smell a bitch in heat, made his move. Even though LTI was actually larger than Over & East, it became clear early on that O&E was going to win. Rather than have a long drawn-out battle, full of blood and gore, LTI changed course in midstream and allowed a friendly merger. Choate, Winkler handled the approach and everyone made out like bandits.

Especially Choate, Winkler. Part of the deal was that they then became the corporate attorneys for Over & East. By handling the losing side, they came out with a client twice the size.

Part of that deal was that Wood was given a partnership in Choate, Winkler, Higgiston, Hahn & Moore. Thus everyone's back was adequately scratched. A spiral daisy chain at a financial Plato's Retreat, where everyone made out.

Over & East continued to play Takeover & Eat, the legal fees rolled into Choate, Winkler, and Wood's partnership share started in the $750,000 range and only went up.

Then, one night, eighteen months back, a junior accountant was going through the books at Choate, Winkler. Junior discovered something that every other accountant had missed for eight years. He worked all night, checking, double-checking. Impatient for dawn, he worked through the following day, checking what had to be checked during working hours.

When Junior was sure, he talked his way into the office of Lawrence Choate Haven and laid the bomb on that pure, unadulterated status desk. Edgar Wood was a thief. Worse, he was using the law firm as a conduit.

At that point, Junior had traced $4,873,927.64 that had come out of Over & East, through Choate, Winkler, Higgiston, Hahn & Moore, to existing but nonfunctioning subsidiaries of Over & East, and from there to suppliers, which were, in fact, Edgar Wood. Subsequent investigation brought the sum to a tad over $8 million.

"Perhaps," Haven said, "I acted precipitously. All too often a pall of silence falls, a veil is pulled across the face of the truth. The principals are more concerned with protecting their public relations than in punishing the perpetrators. But I felt at the time, and I still feel, that that is the wrong approach. It virtually rewards the culpable and puts the burden of restitution on the stockholders, or, in our case, the partners. They cringe in the fear that the public will conclude that because there is one malefactor that the entire organization is capable of malfeasance.

"It is a form of cowardice and an abuse of the public trust.

"Choate, Winkler, Higgiston, Hahn & Moore has been in existence for over one hundred and fifty years. In all that time, nothing of this sort has ever occurred. Nothing has ever blemished our name. Now that it had, I felt that we would only be stronger for strong action. The other senior partners agreed with me, if for no other reason than that someone must set standards.

"We decided to prosecute vigorously."

So they had. They went directly to Robert Morganthau, Manhattan district attorney, that very day. Before they informed Mr. Goreman. Before they informed Over & East. Before they confronted Mr. Wood.

That way, there could be no backing down. And there wasn't.

"It set off a chain of events that I could not have foreseen. Although Edgar Wood had embezzled money, I could not imagine that he would involve outsiders in the matter and, worse, violate the attorney-client privilege."

Edgar Wood, corporate counsel to Over & East, personal attorney to Charles Goreman, had been privy to anything and everything. But that knowledge was protected. It was not his to share. The attorney-client privilege is the foundation of a lawyer's relations with clients. It is the rock. It requires the attorney to never disclose the client's affairs. Requires. It is not an option like cruise control or white-wall tires.

Everyone now anticipated a new attack on Over & East by the SEC and the law firm retained to meet the challenge was Douglas, Cohen, Bartholomew, Neffsky and McDonald. The reason, according to Choate Haven, was that Choate, Winkler, et al, was potentially party to the SEC action and to a number of suits involving Wood and Over & East.

I had heard of Douglas, Cohen; they were the gunslingers of the three-piece-suit set. The Choate, Winklers of the legal world could handle the day-to-day corporate business of corporations, states and even nations. But when the fat was in the fire, when the feds discovered the smoking gun, when the vice-president was indicted on vice charges, they called in Douglas, Cohen.

They were so good that the names in the masthead actually belonged to nondeceased people.

But even they were having problems. They wanted to know what Wood was saying. The SEC, who had hidden Wood away and was taking his testimony in secret, claimed, so far successfully, that they were not part of the judicial system;

they were a regulatory agency, and not subject to the normal process of discovery. To add insult to injury, the SEC was leaking the choice bits and pieces to the *Wall Street Journal* and the *Times*.

"They are the attorneys of record. But I, as a private party, have a responsibility, because my conduct, however proper and correct, may be leading to injury to parties whose well-being was entrusted to me."

"Yeah, I can find the guy," I said. "I can find him. Maybe Mr. Wood and I, we could have a conversation. But I don't think he will summarize his testimony for me. I have sources at the *Times*, but I bet they don't know much more than they're publishing. I can butter up a secretary or a steno down in D.C. . . . but I don't think that's going to answer your questions, not over the long run anyway, and this is an on-going thing. So we're talking about going further than that."

"If you are implying that you might act beyond the bounds of the law, I certainly recommend against any such activity. I would be hard put, no matter how grave the situation, to countenance your commission of an illegal act while performing as my agent."

I looked at him and shrugged.

"Can you do the job or not? You seem to have doubts."

I stood up. "I can do the job. I'll get you results. If the price is right." I stepped over to the window. The wind whistled and cracked from tower to tower and whipped tendrils of cloud against the glass. "Expenses could run quite high. Out of town and all that," I said over my shoulder.

"This is thirty-five thousand dollars," he said. That turned me around fast enough. Instead of a check, a $5.98 pressed-paper attaché case had appeared on the deep-glow wood of his status desk. It had to mean cash. I went to the desk and opened the case greedily. It was cash.

The case contained, in addition, those odds and ends, like photos and a dossier on the man, considered useful by most investigators. Nice, but it was the long green that held my attention.

"In addition, there will be a like sum when you hand me

an accurate summary or transcript of Mr. Wood's testimony.''

"That'll be all right," I said.

3

SHUTTLE

I LIFTED WAYNE up in the air. He giggled and grinned. I did too.

"I'm gonna be away for a while," I told him.

"Are you going on a mission?"

"Yes," I told him solemnly.

"Wow," he replied. "Do it to them before they do it to us."

"I will," I promised, and put him down. He grabbed his school things and tore out the door. "See ya," he yelled as it closed.

"Will you be good while you're in Washington?" Glenda asked me when I walked back to my coffee.

"Whatever do you mean?"

"There is a certain school of thought, among men, so I have heard, that out-of-town doesn't count."

"The line is, 'Under five minutes and out-of-town doesn't count.' "

"I don't want a line, I want an answer. Are you going to be good?" She said it with a smile, but the tension was real.

She loved me. She took good care of me. She helped pick up the pieces when they were strewn all over hell and Avenue C. Or at least she stood by me, gentle, accepting and patient, while I picked them up. I figured I might be good. I figured that was a real serious possibility.

"Sure," I said, looked her in the eye and smiled.

I found my attorney, Gerry Yaskowitz, in the hall of New York Criminal Court, which is where I always found him. He had just finished a plea bargain for a midlevel heroin dealer and just started an argument with the Korean manager of the Far-Out Far-East Big Apple Health Spa. The spa offered "the ultimate in relaxation, calming exotic atmosphere, lovely Oriental hostesses to serve you in the Oriental manner, best of satisfaction guaranteed." The Korean was giggling and offering to pay in barter.

"You cheap son of a bitch," Gerry said. "Do I look like the kind of guy who needs it that bad?" The Korean giggled even more. "OK. You cheap son of a bitch, I want my fee, in cash, up front, and you can throw in the barter on top."

At that point I interrupted.

"Tell me, Gerald, what kind of trouble can I get into if I do a little bugging, maybe a B and E?"

"Depends. Who and where?"

"The SEC, probably," I told him.

"Are you getting stupid again? Are you back on drugs? You want my opinion, my expert legal advice, backed by many sleazy years in a sleazy racket, namely the law: Don't. Do not do it. And I am going to send you a bill for that advice, because it is very serious advice and worth money."

"Yeah, well, I have just accepted a whole lot of bread, and to do what I have accepted it for may, just may, require that."

He looked up and down the hall, pulled me close and said, "In the first place, be very careful. In the second place . . ." he scribbled a name and number ". . . here, a good well-connected D.C. criminal attorney. Remember, I was not an accessory before the fact."

Gerald was right. It was only money and not worth my

license, which is my living, and certainly not worth prison, which I truly dislike. I doubted very much that there was any completely legal way to get what Choate Haven wanted, and it was not so much that I was willing to do anything for money but that the risk itself intrigued me. Dumb.

While I packed a kit that included a variety of microphones, cameras and picklocks, I filled in my partner, Joey D', on what I was doing.

"Yeah, fine," he said, "just don't do anything stupid while you're down there. You know you have a good thing going with Glenda. That one, she's a real lady. And you got a good thing going with the kid. Don't go fucking it up." All that and he hadn't even heard me call Sandy to say I would soon be in D.C.

"What is with you?" I said.

"Ahh, you just gotta restless look about you lately, and most guys, when they go outa town . . . Just don' go looking for trouble."

I really wished I had a trench coat to hunch up on my shoulders when I walked out the door, turned and said, "Trouble is my business."

I caught the last shuttle down to the nation's capital.

Sandra Klein met me at National Airport.

We looked at each other. Past and present fused, and history swirled around us like curlicues of confetti. She was just lovely, serious, bright, one of the few moments of good sense I showed back in the burn-it-up and break-it-down years. We were magic makers in a long-distance romance with nothing but love and laughter every time one or the other of us got off a jet. Sandy was a writer and therapist. Unlike most members of either breed she was sensible and shrewd. She knew there was no future in the condition I was in, and possibly in who I am. She did the eminently sensible thing. She left me.

Catalog time. Taking accounts. Reading minds. From our very first glance, we never had to speak to know.

She looked relieved. I had worried her once. I seem to do

that to a lot of people. But I looked healthier, happier, younger than I had, than she expected. And calmer. But the same years had hurt her, and the aging was sharp, as if five years ago had been the peak of the bloom. And she had trouble. I didn't want that. I wanted her to be the happiest woman in the world.

She smiled at me for thinking that last thought and reached over and touched my cheek. Then we both turned away to make the mind reading stop. She started the car and neither of us spoke until we were over the dirty gray Potomac. She asked if I would have dinner with her and I said sure.

I really did have a legitimate reason for seeing her. Choate Haven had made up a list of Wood's habits and tastes, and said, "If I know Edgar, he will never, this side of incarceration, give up his automobile or his compulsion for *nouvelle cuisine*." When Sandy's first book came out she had been on the talk show, cocktail party and reception circuit. I figured she knew the "in" eateries. I explained all that to her, and she said she would help.

When we were together she had talked about the search for a "life partner" with the clarity and sense with which others approach career choices. She was intuitive, loving, lusty when appropriate, a genuine adult. I had been sure, then, that she would choose well. She was not only on my personal best all-time top-ten list, I had her slated as most likely to succeed at marriage. I was sure, now, that when she opened the door of her apartment we would be alone.

We were.

I didn't ask where her husband was. I guessed out of town. I didn't ask when he would be back. I guessed not that night.

"Do you want something to drink?" she asked. "Or would you rather not."

"Oh, I take a glass now and again. It's only a problem when I'm doing that other thing too . . . and I don't do that shit nooo more."

"I'm glad," she said and she looked it. "I used to worry about you. . . . And now . . . you look good."

I reached out and touched her face, the way she had mine in the car. She reached up with both hands and pressed my hand first to her cheek, then to her lips. Then she was in my arms, eyes wet, face pressed to my chest, holding on.

One part of me was paternal. The other remembered all too clearly the way she orgasmed. That rising, rising moan of rhythm. And separate parts of my body remembered, each by itself, the different ways we used to get there. . . .

I pushed back from her and looked her in the eyes.

"I have been living with a woman for four years, that's practically a record for me. . . . Not only that, I've been faithful for three, which is certainly a record."

I held her close, her hair soft against my cheek, her tears moist on my chest, loving her as much as I ever had. And relieved as hell that I was not the one she had chosen, not the one to have made those tears.

The Watergate is conveniently located, tucked into a curve of the Potomac between Georgetown and the marble of government town. It holds some of my fondest memories, as it does for most Americans, and it was where I spent that night alone.

Still, the first thing that Glenda said when I called home the next morning was, "How is Sandy, and don't tell me you haven't seen her."

"Fine, and happily married," I said, awed by the range of her radar. Then Wayne stole the phone and saved me from protesting too much. He didn't want to go to school. He wanted to go out and play in the rain. "I like puddles," he said. Also, he wanted to join a squash club, just like me.

I called my congressman, John Straightman. He was willing to see me right away. That was very gratifying.

Particularly since I didn't even vote in his district. Four years previous, his connection had been picked up with three keys of coke. The search and seizure was correct, the warrant was good, Miranda was read and New York's finest were not on sale that day. The dealer figured he could trade the congressman for at least a reduction to a misdemeanor.

The D.A. had mixed feelings. On the one hand, all that potential publicity. On the other, the congressman had a lot of friends. Perhaps if the dealer had handed the D.A. a rock-solid case all wrapped in ribbon, there would have been no indecision. As it was, it was only a lead. To do something real with it, the D.A.'s office would have to set up a sale, with witnesses, wires and the rest, and avoid entrapment and the other technicalities that can blow a case.

One of the prosecutors had been a classmate of William Contact, the congressman's chief aide. The D.A. allowed as how a leak along that line might be all right.

Willie got in touch with me. The dealer was out on bail. I was able to get the right kind of introduction to him and tempted him down to Atlanta on the promise of a four-kilo buy. He was busted in Georgia and found out the Atlanta cops didn't give a damn about some story about a Yankee congressman's evil ways. The New York case was stashed in the pending pending file, and the dealer got a whole chunk of his life scheduled for a Georgia work farm.

I was ushered in to see the man moments after I arrived. He told the receptionist to hold the calls and greeted me fulsomely. Full smile, full, firm handshake, with the elbow grasp thrown in. I realized that he was afraid of me.

"Relax," I said. "You paid me to do a job. It was done. Now forget about it."

"Is that your code?" he said in a tone meant to be jocular.

"Yeah," I said deadpan. "But you can do me a favor."

"What can I do for you? Name it, you have it."

"I want some information," I said. Straightman lived in ellipses and could hear omissions ring the way most of us hear church bells toll. He understood there was no need to know what his left hand was doing.

"Let's get Willie on this one," he said, taking me by the elbow and leading me to his left hand who had a connecting office. "I'll let him know he's to give you full cooperation. If he doesn't give satisfaction, get back to me."

We smiled. Proud that we had handled so many delicate issues so quickly and discreetly and with so little said. He handed me over to Willie, repeating his full-cooperation routine.

Willie greeted me with genuine enthusiasm. We were on the same level in a way. We did our deeds based on other people's needs, particularly when they ran to the gray areas and beyond. Maybe the only real difference between us was that he was staff, I was free-lance.

To Willie, someplace to talk meant someplace we could not possibly be overheard. We got into his car, but even that was not considered suitable, though I thought it was pretentious of him to think he was important enough for people to bug his car. The Watergate, of course, was not a place that anyone paranoid about listening devices wants to talk, so we ended up at the Jefferson Memorial, walking through the trees around the Tidal Basin.

It had been raining when I left New York. In D.C. the sky was slate-gray, drifting between a dreary mist and drizzle.

"The SEC," I told him, "is taking testimony from a guy named Wood, Edgar Wood. What I want to know is simple. Where is he? What's he saying?"

"I have a friend over at Justice."

"No. Justice won't be in on this one. There's a glory shortage these days, and besides, keeping it in-house protects the investigation."

"How's that?" he asked.

"Wood is an attorney and he's talking about his former client. If he were talking to somebody at Justice, or any other law-enforcement group, his testimony would be flat-out illegal. It would also be open to discovery and he could be deposed."

"Interesting. Very slick," Willie said admiringly.

The wind came from the east, throwing the rain at a slant. We edged around the sheltering curve of our tribute to Thomas Jefferson. When we were facing west the angle of the wind and wall gave us a dry spot. Willie took a "bullet" out of his pocket. He manipulated it around so that the cocaine in the bottom dropped into the little cup of the crossbar. Another twist and the cup faced up into an aperture at the top. A quick practiced set of gestures that ended with a deep snort. He repeated it for the other nostril. Balance.

He offered me some.

I wanted it. When I took it I would want more. No matter how much more there was, eventually I would have to deal with coming down. I concentrated on the ashes of coming down.

"Thanks anyway," I said. He shrugged and helped himself again.

"Let's say," Willie said, chemically inspired, "let's say I number among my friends a congressional aide whose boss likes to make an issue of corporate abuse. Without naming names . . ."

"Of course."

". . . let's say my friend approaches the SEC. His congressman, he says, is interested in corporate abuses of securities regs. Even that, like he wants to strengthen enforcement capability. You know, he wants to start hearings, but he needs a juicy case, something ripe."

"It sounds real time-consuming," I said.

"In a rush, are we?"

"Yeah."

"I'll do what I can."

"Go to hell, Willie. Find a way to do it. Waltz over, use your boss's name. Over & East is a New York corporation; the Exchange is in New York; if it affects the Apple, it's your business."

"The regulatory agencies are tough. They're insulated. You gotta, you know, coax 'em."

"OK, I'll give you an easy one. To start with. I want to know who's on the investigation. A guy named Brodsky, Mel, he has his name attached to the press stories. Find out if he's the man. If he's not, find out who is."

"You got it," he promised. "Gimme a couple of days."

"Let's do this on New York time, shall we, not D.C. time. It's not even lunch yet. Get it for me by the end of the day."

"Fuck off," he said.

"OK, how long, Willie?"

"As the guy on the toilet seat said," Willie said, "as long as it takes."

"Don't make me push you, 'cause I will. It wasn't so long ago you and your man had your asses in a sling. Do it before your bottle runs dry."

"OK, OK, you want it, you got it."

"I'm at the Watergate," I told him. "And get me addresses, phone numbers, all that."

"I'll move it as fast as I can," he promised and shook my hand as if it meant a lot. I turned and walked away. He called out, "Hey, don't you need a ride?" But I kept walking.

"Take care of yourself," he called wistfully.

I waved over my shoulder without turning and walked down toward the river. The sky was muddy and the muddy gray river was coated with scum. The job could be routine. Not really so different than planting a little listener to prove that the unloving and unloved spouse was doing a rub-a-dub-dub and a humpty-bumpty with anonymous strangers so there would either be lots more or lots less alimony. Or than finding out the thief was inside and was the son-in-law. Or locate the runaway to find out that she should have gotten the hell out of where she ran from.

But it could get closer to the line. I hated prisons. I understood Edgar Wood's panic. I understood every punk in the world who sold out his friends to stay on the outside. Something ached in me to play touch and go with the line that had bars on the far side. It was the same yearning ache that lurched inside me when Willie Contact offered me the cool white cocaine. It was in my testicles and lower bowels. There was a sensation, as if the devil stood behind me. When I turned to look, there was nothing there, not even my own shadow.

4

THE LINE

"THE WORKING TITLE of my book, the new one," Sandy explained, "is *Over the Line*, but only the title seems to be working at the moment, so, yes, take me away from my typewriter and tell me about Edgar Wood and I'll help you look in restaurants."

The subject of her study, an inevitable one for a shrink in Washington, was why someone who had everything would risk it all committing grossly illegal acts just to attain what he obviously already had. Wood definitely fit that category. It was a wonderful coincidence. Now both of us had a completely justifiable desexed rationale for being together.

"A question like that presupposes," I said, "that man is rational, that crime is an aberration. That aberration is an aberration, and it's not. It's the real norm."

"Is it?" she asked. "You go over the line. But I think you do it to find out where it is. And it puts you in conflict. In a way it helps you to identify with the people you're after. But it hurts you, because when you bring punishment, you think you should be punished too.

"But, I bet, not your Mr. Wood. He thinks his prosecutors

are persecutors. The kind of people I'm studying are people who are really making it. The eminently successful personality who, it would seem, has, or can get, everything without crossing the line. One thing that marks them: David Begelman who was head of Columbia Pictures and stealing nickels and dimes; or John Mitchell; or Secretary of Labor Ray Donovan who's been named by Genovese family bagmen; or Ed Meese who rewards the people who lend him money with government jobs, is that none of them sees the line. Even when they're caught, their viewpoint is that they were merely doing business as usual.''

"You can hear that same old song from every two-bit con at Rikers or Attica, it's no big thing.''

"The way you go over the line,'' she snapped, "most often is with women. Maybe because that's where you don't know there is one. But that's boring and you're not the type I'm interested in.''

Some of that wasn't true. But I didn't argue, a sign of wisdom and maturity.

"Another thing,'' Sandy said, still trying to transform simplicities like greed into the complexity of a personality profile, "is that they're all overachievers. Watch out for overachievers.''

"Your husband,'' I said. The psychologist psyched, the Freudian had slipped and it showed. We always understood each other too well.

"We always understood each other too well,'' she sighed, smiling. "Maybe I should have let you marry me.''

"That's why you didn't.''

Lawrence Choate Haven had provided me with photos of Wood. A Washington clipping service had photos of Mel Brodsky from his promotion to litigator. Sandra had made a list of the capital's twelve most ostentatious restaurants based on my theory that no man making the kind of money Wood earned gets into a position where he has to steal $8 million unless he has the most obvious and ostentatious tastes. The

maître d' at the Four Seasons recognized Wood. I tipped
what I call lavishly. He did not appear impressed.

The maître d' at Leone d'Or, though a little *haut* for my
taste, put the two photos together as dinner companions.
Which told me that Wood was in the D.C. area and that
Brodsky was at least one of his interrogators. When I called
Mr. Brodsky at the SEC he was not in, but they offered to
take a message. I asked if he would be in later. They didn't
know. Tomorrow? They didn't know, but they could take a
message. I concluded that Mr. Brodsky was off, wherever
they kept Wood, merrily deposing.

Sandy drove me back to the Watergate. I expected to be
dropped off, but she climbed out and let the valet take the
car.

The elevator was crowded and warm. Sandy opened her
coat. In Miami, in August, the mangoes come into season.
Their erotic shapes hang so heavy the branches curve down,
they're so rich and ripe, that it's possible for a man to get an
erection looking at a tree. Sandy's breasts remind me of
mango season, or vice versa, and the three middle-aged,
midwestern men in the elevator practically turned corners
with their eyes in a desperate search for cleavage. They had
three wives who were not fruit fanciers.

"I've never seen you in action before," Sandy drawled;
"you have some good moves, and I'm looking forward to
more." She topped it off with an extra swing in her walk
when we stepped out. She was angry about something.

Her anger stayed with her while she waited through my
phone calls. Willie Contact had Brodsky's address and phone
number, in suburban Maryland. Willie acted like he was a
hero to come up with so much.

I called Joey D' in New York. The man might be old, but
he moves on New York time, and he would get me more by
the hour than Willie did by the day. I asked him to find out
what kind of wheels Brodsky had, the plate number, and his
credit status. He asked me if I had seen Sandy.

"Yes," I admitted, looking at her.

He grunted.

"She's happily married, or at least thoroughly married, and has no interest in me." She mouthed the word "liar," and I continued, "But she has been of great help, strictly in the investigative sense."

He promised to get what I needed by five and hung up.

"A great scoundrel has reformed," Sandy said bitterly, "and the women of the world don't know what they're missing."

"In all the time we went together," I replied, "I never saw you angry."

"You never saw me married."

"I can understand my marriage going wrong," I said. "I blamed it on her, of course, but I don't think any woman would have been entirely satisfied with my attitude. You know, when she would ask which was more important, her or my work, I would actually say work. Then she would ask if I would always be true. I would say, I don't know. Just because they were honest answers is no excuse."

"A great scoundrel sees the error of his ways! Da-dum da-dum!"

"But you're smarter than I am, and any man who got you is lucky to have you."

"The man that got me," Sandy said, "sometimes thinks that marriage is a prison."

"Prison," I said, "is not a metaphor. There is nothing that is like a prison."

"And he thinks freedom is anything under twenty-five with quick-release pants." She glared at me. "You should understand that. That's not far from your style."

"Is it gonna help if I go to bed with you," I slapped back, "or is it gonna help if I don't?" Then I was sorry and said, "Would it help if I told you you're one of the most marvelous women I've ever met? Special. Lovely. That I want you desperately. That when you talk, I listen because I trust your intelligence. That when you left me it was ashes in my mouth. Because that's all true. That's the way I think of you."

She nodded "yes," then she said, "Have you ever noticed

that life is a damned cliché? Frankly I'm insulted by that; I thought I was too good to live a cliché.''

"Sandy, life is worse than a cliché. It's a country-and-western song.''

5

COWBOYS

MEL BRODSKY HAD a wife, Priscilla, and two children, ages two and four. He had a six-year-old Buick and a one-year-old diesel Rabbit. The Buick was blue; the Rabbit was yellow, and he still owed money on it. He lived in an attached townhouse in a development just outside Gaithersburg, Maryland. $78,00 was still due on that.

If he wasn't a stay-at-home guy, he was in big trouble.

The development was called River Oaks. I assumed that meant that it had neither, but I was wrong; there was one oak by the sign marking the entrance. The development also had a school, supermarket, rec center with two pools. It was its own little world of commuter living with a choice of garden apartments, townhouses or tract homes. It was only ten or fifteen years old, and aside from that one oak, there wasn't a tree thicker than my thigh.

Oak View Lane was a curlicue up a hill that ended in a cul-de-sac. Three separate flanks of attached townhouses formed a U around it. Two parking slots were assigned to each of the twenty-two homes with six extras assigned to visitor parking. It was the sort of place where a stake-out would blend into the background like a Hassid at the College of Cardinals.

Fortunately, all the little lanes with arboreal names gathered together into one main street, and that street was the only way out. It led to the state highway. The far side was, as yet, undeveloped scrub growth.

The next morning I was back at 5:30 A.M. with a pair of cheap binoculars, a poncho and a thermos of the strongest coffee I could get. I found myself a homey spot on a high rock hidden in the trees.

The false dawn came at 6:30 and with it, the rain.

I pulled the hood of my poncho up over my head as the fat drops began to drip through the branches. First they were intermittent. Then they became regular and steady. Plop, plop. Plop, plop, little thwacks on the top of my hood. Then faster and irregular. Plonk, plop. Plop, plop, plop. Plonk.

I didn't mind that somehow, gradually, a small puddle was gathering inside the poncho where I was sitting and that I felt like a wet-diaper baby. I didn't mind too terribly that my shoes were not exactly waterproof and I was growing a squish inside my socks. I could live with an occasional enterprising droplet that evaded the poncho and found my eyes or neck. I was even willing to find it amusing when I had to urinate, holding up the poncho with my elbow, holding my urinator in one hand while keeping the binoculars up and pointed to the road with the other. But the plops on my head turned seconds into minutes, minutes into hours.

Brodsky was a lazy bastard; the yellow Rabbit didn't come out of the warren until 9:30, and I hated him for every one of the plopping 14,400 seconds of the 4 hours.

He made up for it, slightly, by being an easy tail.

He took 270 to the Beltway like he was going to the District but continued around the city, then took us southeast on 66 and 28, into Virginia.

About fifteen or twenty miles out, he turned off the interstate and onto a country road. The landscape was downright rural. I lost him around a curve and down a hill. When it straightened out and I should have seen him, there was nothing but Rabbitless road. I raced ahead, but after ten minutes all I found was a sense of being lost and too many places where he could have turned.

There had been one narrow turnoff in the section where I lost him. I went back to it. Fifteen minutes down that road and I came out four miles from where I came in. But a detective must be dogged and determined. They didn't call Bulldog Drummond "Bulldog" because he was short and squat. No sirree bob!

I took the cutoff again. There were six lanes or driveways off it. The trees were thick along the shoulder and I could see only two houses. Neither of them had a yellow Rabbit.

One of the lanes was overgrown. I turned and went cautiously into it. Hidden behind the trees was the shell of a farmhouse that had been gutted by fire, then finished off by vandals and the weather. My rental car was nicely hidden there, and I decided to check the rest of the area on foot.

Thirty minutes and four houses later, I found the yellow Rabbit. It was nestled in beside a sleek green Jaguar with New York plates.

The light of the day had a lean blue-gray cast. It made the yellow-tinged light from the incandescent lamps indoors seem warm, inviting and homey. It was a solid old two-story house built of stone and wood. A whiff of smoke drifted from the big stone chimney. It was a nice place to hide, and a long, long way from Attica.

I drifted around the house, staying close to the trees. They told me, in grade school, that Indians could walk through the woods without ever, ever making a sound. Not even the crack of a dead twig underfoot. Not even a squish as they pulled their moccasins back after they sank to their ankles in the mud. Back in grade school I believed them.

I made my way, squishing and twig snapping, up to the house's blind side, then around under the windows to the living room.

Wood sat hunched over. He spoke haltingly as a small tape recorder turned languid reels on the table. He sipped from a large crystal brandy snifter. After each sip he stared into the glass, looking for an answer that he knew wasn't there. Eventually the staring took over from the talking. He sat silent. Water dripped from the eaves down my back.

It had gone irrevocably wrong for Edgar Wood. And looking in at his face, as gray as the rain falling around me, I wondered when, not if, I would find my way to taking the wrong kind of fall.

Still, there was the thirty-dollar bottle, the logs glowing like sentiment in a frame of Old Dominion stonework and the fifty-thousand-dollar car outside. Those thoughts restored me to a healthy glow of cynicism. Judge McCarthy would keep sending guys up the river for stealing fifteen-dollar radios. Guys like Wood would simply retire, with luxury sufficient to compensate for any sense of shame they might feel. All was right with the world.

I couldn't hear what they were saying. But by the next day or the one after, there would be an extra ear in the room, and I would find a place to put an extra set of reels to record what the ear heard, and Lawrence Choate Haven would have a copy as clear as Mel Brodsky's.

I made my way back to the woods and along the road to my deserted driveway.

Which wasn't deserted.

A lean young fellow with a gun lounged against my rental car. A nice new silver Cadillac Coupe de Ville was parked about six yards away.

It must have been the twig I snapped.

"Hi, guys," I said and waved cheerily.

The lean fellow smiled his best "gotcha" smile. He didn't look like a rising young attorney from the Securities and Exchange Commission, so I held my arms away from my sides, hands open and facing outward. I really felt it was best if he felt unthreatened.

Having little else to do, I went through the options in my mind. I could flee. I didn't think I'd even get as far as a fifteen-yard penalty. I could go for my own gun. Except that I didn't have one. I could fall on my knees and beg and plead.

I decided to keep beg and plead as my ace in the hole. If they got really nasty, I would whip it out on them.

He beckoned me forward. I kept coming, slow, open-handed, pleasant.

A window on the Coupe de Ville slid down, electrically smooth. Another gun peeked out. My lean buddy gestured me to assume the position on the side of my car. He patted me down, thoroughly, professionally. But that still didn't make me think he was a member of one of our many law-enforcement agencies.

He opened the back door of the Caddy and gestured me toward it.

There were two men in the front seat. When they looked at me they began to argue.

"He's gonna get the backseat wet." The accent was Spanish.

"So what," his partner replied in the same accent, "you want to get out in the mud?"

"Hey, this is custom leather upholstery, the real thing."

"Fuck it, he messes up the upholstery, get another car," the second man said. It clicked because the attitude matched the accent. I had heard it from some very heavy hitters in the cocaine trade; the accent was Colombian. My reaction to the recognition was twofold: confused and scared shitless.

"Get in," the first said. I did and tried my best not to drip.

"What do you want with the man in the farmhouse?" he asked, not unpleasantly.

It was too soon for truth. I couldn't think of a good lie fast enough. I would have tried wise-guy, but the cocaine cowboys I have known have been excessively touchy and quick-tempered. I didn't answer.

The gun that I had first seen through the window now rose over the back of the seat. It came up as slow and big, fat and round as a harvest moon.

"Someone hired me to find him."

"Go on," the man without the gun said. The man with the gun gazed at me lazily. All I could hope for was that he really did care about the upholstery and wasn't ready to trade in for the new model.

"And to find out, if I could, what he's saying." What a pushover I was. I knew they wouldn't respect me in the morning.

"Don't," he explained.

"OK," I said.

"Get out," he said. That was it? That was all? All those guns and not even a meaningful conversation. I got out.

There was more.

My lean buddy gestured me to lie down on the ground. I couldn't think of any reason why not. I lay facedown. A stone dug into a rib. The rest of the ground was soggy mud. But there are worse things than wet and dirty. Then I heard the front door of the Caddy open. Someone got out and walked over to me. I could feel his presence. Then he knelt with one knee in the middle of my back. It was time to use my ace in the hole. I got ready to hit him with a good beg-and-plead when I felt his gun pressed against the back of my head. It left me speechless.

He had a question. "You understand?"

"I understand," I said and got muddy twigs in my mouth. The gun shifted.

Then he fired. The world exploded in my ear. Dirt and stone splattered against my face like blood and bone. My body jerked in reflex and fear. The side of my head pounded. But I was alive. He had fired alongside my skull and I could feel the scorched trail through my hair and scalp.

"Good," he said with charming simplicity, and stood up.

I heard him walk back to his car. The front door slammed shut. Then the back door closed. The noises were faint through the ringing in my ears and the pounding of my blood.

I thought I heard the big wheels start to move out through the sodden track. I was afraid to look. But I did. I watched the Caddy roll smoothly and smugly away, its real custom leather interior still dry and clean. The plates were District of Columbia diplomatic. I got the number.

Dear God, it's great to be alive.

6

SIX

I CALLED LAWRENCE Choate Haven on his private line, as he had requested, and told him that I had found Edgar Wood.

"That's quite expeditious," he said and asked where he was. I told him and began to explain my plans to put in a sound system. He didn't want to know about that.

"Was Wood ever involved with Colombians?" I asked.

"Colombians?" He sounded as genuinely baffled as if I had asked about South Moluccans.

"Yeah, like Peruvians or Ecuadorians, but one country over."

"To the best of my knowledge, Edgar Wood had no clients who were from Colombia."

"What about cocaine? Was Wood involved in cocaine?"

"Absolutely not." Choate Haven sounded as if he were defending his own integrity, or the integrity of Choate, Winkler, Higgiston, Hahn & Moore, whichever was greater, as if he didn't know that he could waltz down his decorator corridors and, with only one ear cocked, hear the wind in the straws as dozens of young associates snorted their way to Paradise Lost.

"Wood was a thief," I reminded him. "And cocaine and money go together like Abélard and Héloise, or Cagney and Lacey."

"It is certainly true that Mr. Wood is severely flawed; that is a matter of record and not to be denied. However, I cannot conceive . . ."

"That he would violate," I interrupted, "the most basic ethic of his profession, maybe the only ethic of his profession . . ."

"In my opinion," he said with a voice that made clear who the client and who the employee was, "the nature of his flaws, and they are great, is not the sort to lead to involvement with narcotics. Certainly there has been neither evidence nor indication of such an involvement."

He went on, in full paragraphs, and I began to understand that it was really not something he wanted to hear. It was something I could keep to myself until such time as it was necessary to share.

My initial reaction to the encounter with our Latin neighbors had been one of elation, even though I think that someone who enjoys pain, busted kneecaps and bullet wounds is a certifiable psycho-sicko. As for death, as far as I've been able to determine, I'll only get to do it once. So I want to save it for last. Like dessert. Maybe I'm an adrenaline junkie.

By the time I checked in with Joey D' back in New York, I was coming down, like any other junkie on any other kind of rush, and he could hear the stress, the fear and the anger in my voice. He asked if I was all right, and I guess my yes didn't have conviction.

"Look it, kid, did you shit in your pants?"

"No."

"Did you let go your bladder?"

"Gimme a break," I said. "Whaddya think I am?"

"Then you did all right. You came out alive, with all your parts, plus your pants clean and dry. Can't ask for more'n that."

"Is that the measure of a man where you come from, Joey?"

"It'll do, till this women's lib thing blows over," he said. "Listen, you thinkin' of maybe gettin' some backup?"

"Yeah, sure, what am I gonna do? Call in Uncle Vincent?"

"It sounds to me like you got different things going in different directions down there. And nobody can watch their back and front and keep moving all at the same time. That's why the army, they got different guys taking point and the rear."

"You know what the toughest thing is gonna be," I said, thinking out loud, "it's gonna be checking out those Colombians. They had dipple plates. So when that Caddy goes home, home is gonna be an embassy, or something like that. The thing to do, normally, is to sit out front, take some pictures, show 'em around to the kind of folks who might know something about them. So there I am, me, my rental car and my telephoto, just relaxing on the street. Except I'm outside the embassy. So embassy security will right away notice me. Unless D.C. cops, cruising Embassy Row, find me first. Then phones are gonna ring and here comes the FBI; and if the FBI are there, can the CIA be far behind? Meanwhile, the ambassador is on the red phone to the state department."

"We got a lotta money on this job, right?"

"Oh we surely do," I said, warmed by the thought.

"So don't be scared to spend some of it. Share the wealth. Like for instance, you get a guy who is into surveillance, someone who has a panel truck that says 'Shmuck the Plumber, No Pipe Can Resist Us' like that, that can sit there all day."

"And you of course have someone in mind," which by then I knew he did, and I knew that whoever he recommended would be Italian, have no imagination and have been doing whatever they did longer than I've been alive.

"Yeah, I have someone in mind."

"And another good idea," I said before he had to suggest it to me and make me feel stupid, "is that I get someone to back me up when I go back to the farmhouse."

"Yeah," he said, and gave me the names and phone numbers he had in front of him.

Gene Tattalia's company was called Ace Investigations, as imaginative a name as I expected. I sighed but went to meet with him anyway. He proudly showed me a snapshot of the truck he used for just this sort of situation. I was pleasantly surprised. It looked exactly like a phone company van. When I found out that it was a real phone company van that he rented from a phone company dispatcher, I was genuinely impressed. It was something I had to respect.

It took him less than ten minutes to discover that the Coupe de Ville was registered to the trade mission. I agreed to his rates, which were high, we shook hands and he promised to start surveillance the next day.

I looked at the powder burn on the side of my head and the small cuts from flying rock on my cheek in the hotel-room mirror, and I could see that the distance from life to death was somewhat shorter than I usually like to think it is.

When I called home, Wayne answered.

"It's E.T., Mom," he screamed to wherever Glenda was. She might have been no farther from him than the inside of my skull was from the burn and he would still have delivered the news at max volume. "He's phoning home."

"What," I asked him, "if it's not E.T.?"

"Awww, who else could it be?"

"Maybe it's Dick Tracy."

"Mom, Mom, it's the dick tracer," he yelled, giggling madly with the notion that he had said something at least vaguely dirty.

Back in my early twenties all my friends were single, except Don O'Malley. O'Malley lived with a cozy little wife, on a cozy tree-lined brownstone street in Brooklyn Heights. They had two kids at the rug-rat stage crawling and climbing over furniture and guests with equal interest. His wife actually cooked home-cooked meals and baked bread and made homemade pies. Whenever I visited, I felt like a miner, fresh from the hasty wood shacks and frozen wastes of the Yukon, coming in from the dirt, the muck, the cold. Into a real home, made warm and bright by a woman's love, snug with happiness and growing life.

I felt the same whenever I came home to Glenda and Wayne. Even if she didn't bake and we split the cooking. She was shelter from the storm.

My own marriage was only a two-year stint, but our divorces coincided. We drew closer, as victims of similar disasters do. Then I discovered that the cozy little place in the Heights was, and had always been, filled with hostility, anger and sexual frustration. O'Malley stuck it for ten years for the idea of marriage and for the children. He visited prostitutes when the need for a substitute for love overwhelmed him.

Glenda got on the phone. She asked me how it was going. I told her I had spent the morning in the woods playing cowboys and Indians.

"Wayne is more mature than you. I'm living with two six-year-olds, not one."

"Five and a half and a quarter," I heard Wayne yell, insisting on the precision that people do who have few enough years behind or ahead to make those distinctions.

Glenda was not my wife, which I regard as a positive statement. Emotionally intelligent, mature, she fought fair and was sensible about more things than not. Generally she was as eager to make love as I was, often more so. If she had a headache, she would lie and say she felt fine.

She could not, however, stand the idea of my being unfaithful. She didn't even like the idea that it might be difficult for me to be faithful. She operated on a different emotional logic, and for her fidelity was as natural and normal as lunch.

Some people think of that as a man-versus-woman thing. Maybe it is. Yet no woman I've ever been involved with has treated it as a philosophic-psycho-gender issue. Nary a one has said, "Oh well, men are just like that, I understand." The dialogue is always formed from curses and tears.

This time I wanted the center to hold, so this time I was trying it out their way, or her way. It was working out OK, more or less.

Sandy could look at the powder burn on my head and my

chopped-up face and the nearness of my mortality, and together we could use that as all the excuse we needed. We could make a sweet and sweaty storm of thrusting, crying bodies. Would I feel better for it? The voice inside said, "You bet." The voice was probably correct and the hotel placed the phone right next to the bed. But if I picked it up and dialed, it might be more dangerous to me than the man with the gun.

7

XJ-12

IN THE AFTERNOON sun, it was easy to read the signs on the twin pickups parked alongside the suburban residence in Alexandria—Polatrano & Sons. The papa Polatrano, an ex-cop named Franco, was waiting for me by the front door. He had put in his twenty years, retired with a pension and started a landscaping business. It kept his big body fit, made a fair sum of money, and alternately soothed him with the pleasure of growing things and bored him. So he free-lanced at a variation of his old trade.

He carried a canvas bag, and when he got in the car offered me coffee from the thermos inside.

"I favor a .38, standard police .38," he said as we rode. "But every year, the punks, they get more and more firepower. So I got me a rabbi."

He pulled a short, stubby machine gun, an Israeli Uzi, from the same bag that carried his coffee and doughnuts, offering it up for admiration.

"I call it Rabbi Begin. I respect that man. He's tough. He was a guerrilla fighter against the British. They called him a terrorist, of course. Well, this"—he patted it—"is my own personal terrorist."

Gene Tattalia's stakeout had gone well; forty-eight hours after our conversation I was looking at contact sheets of my Colombian friends. A few hours after that, I had blowups of my favorites. Now I had him doing two things, finding names to go with the faces and keeping an eye on them to make sure they stayed in the District while Franco and I went into Virginia.

I checked with Gene from a pay phone a few miles before the farmhouse. The bad guys were still in town.

Still, I found a different parking place. It was a two-mile walk, at least, but walking is healthy. Certainly as compared to being shot at. The rain had finally blown out, the late sun glowed and I noticed the trees were beginning to bud. Ah, spring.

Brodsky worked Wood during the day. Wood did not seem like the type to cook for himself, so I guessed that he would go out for dinner most nights, if not every night.

When we arrived, the Rabbit, boxy and bright in yellow, was beside the Jaguar, so low and sleek in British racing green. Each was a definite fashion statement.

Franco and I settled in behind a screen of brush to wait. If Wood left, I would go in, Franco would guard the outside. If Wood stayed, we would return the next night, then the night after, until the way was open.

When Mel left, Edgar escorted him to his Rabbit. In the stillness I could hear Wood asking, obviously again, for Brodsky to join him for dinner. Brodsky refused, citing the wife and babies waiting in Gaithersburg.

Wood stood and watched the little diesel drive off, his face dead. When he turned and looked at his own car his expression changed.

One night, several years ago, I had been in bed with Simonet, a high-fashion model. When she had four or five good reasons to assume that I was too exhausted for anything but a sleep as sound as death, she slipped from the bed and moved silently to her living room. It was her favorite place, an unobstructed wall covered with a mirror. I watched her watch herself. She examined her skin for pore size and her flesh for tone, missing nothing from her toes to the underside of her buttocks; pirouetting and pouting, gloating and biting her lip, she went around, back, and beneath, stroking the sleekness of belly, tentative at the danger zone under the chin, proud of the purity of her inner thighs. It was as if she was watching her past, present and future all at once. Which she was. Nothing that had happened in the hours between the sheets had aroused the intensity that her mirror reflected.

Which was how, with less grace and drama in his gestures, Edgar Wood looked at his automobile. Mud marring the British racing green was a personal insult, smudges on the interior finish were faults of character.

He went back into the house. When he came out, he had changed from his suit to chinos and an old shirt. He carried a flight bag in one hand, a vacuum cleaner in the other, and an extension cord trailed behind him.

He placed a towel on the ground, then pulled his cleaning equipment from the bag—mink oil, furniture polish, saddle soap, rags, whisk broom, dust pan, brushes, chrome polish, sponges, buffing pads—like he was preparing for surgery.

I sighed with impatience. This was going to be as tedious to watch as it was to do. Franco offered me some coffee from his thermos. It was laced with Sambuca. It was good.

Wood spent almost three hours, just on the interior. I thanked God that the sun was almost completely gone and he wouldn't be able to do the exterior.

He went inside. We waited. We sipped the last dregs. At last he emerged. Even from a distance I could tell that his clothes were custom-made. Probably on Savile Row, where they create the same kind of understatement that Rolls-Royce creates. A simple announcement that nothing in the world costs more. His face had a hint of pink from reshaving and his shower-fresh hair was neatly combed. He stood for a moment and spoke to the air. "Oh, to be in England," is what I think he said.

When at last he started the car, he sat and listened, head

cocked, to see if all twelve cylinders were in tune. It sounded good to me, all that money just ahummin' away. Wood eased it down the driveway. When he reached the road we could hear him bear down on the accelerator, and the car roared off into the distance. The sound died. I stood up and went into the house.

It was a piece of cake. A kitchen window was open and I didn't even have to play games with locks. I opened the plate over a light switch; the transmitter clipped to the A.C. where it could be a power parasite. The mike went where a screw had been.

My recording system was a pair of Panasonics put together so that when the tape ran out in the first it started the tape in the second. Both were sound-activated, and both were modified to run at one-fourth normal speed. A C120 cassette, which normally ran sixty minutes per side, now gave me four hours per side. They did not flip automatically, but that still gave me an eight-hour run. The debriefing sessions seemed to run no more than six hours, so even with the starts and stops of garbage noise I figured it would do the job. A backup battery pack was attached so that both machines could pull from it. The arrangement meant that someone would have to come once a day to change the tapes and, as needed, the batteries. It was cheaper and less conspicuous than setting up a full-bore listening post with a full-time attendant.

We checked the rig with me in the farmhouse and Franco outside. It worked. We put it in a waterproof box, buried the box in a shallow grave with a topping of dead leaves and ran a wire up a tree as an antenna.

Then we strolled out of the woods to our car, where no one was waiting with a gun or some other form of ugliness.

There's nothing like a walk in the woods on a cool evening to build up a man's appetite. We had spotted a restaurant in a small shopping center. It was called Scotch & Sirloin. I liked the name because both items require so little preparation that I could reasonably expect the place to serve at least one of the two without screwing it up.

I heard sirens as we approached. I looked at my speed-

ometer reflexively, then out my rearview, and realized that
the siren wasn't for me. When we came around the curve we
saw bubble-gum lights coming from the opposite direction
heading the same place we were. I didn't think much of it
and drove in after them.

There were four squad cars, lights flashing, and all sorts
of busyness at the far end of the lot where almost no cars
were parked. Curious, like any rubbernecking civilian, I
strolled over.

Wood's body lay on the blacktop, facedown and crumpled. Even from behind the hasty police barricade I could
see that something like a pipe or a tire iron had crushed the
back of his skull. I looked around the lot for his XJ-12.

A uniform and a detective were talking to a waiter. I sidled
over to catch what I could of the conversation.

"This guy says the victim has been coming in for about
three weeks. Usually alone," the uniformed officer said.

"What about a car? Does he know what kind of car the
guy drives?" the detective, on the same track I was on, asked.

"A nice car, a real nice car," the waiter said. "A Jaguar,
but a regular kind."

"You mean a sedan?" the detective said.

"Yeah."

"Does he park it way over here, usually, I mean?"

"I don't know what he does usually. I only seen it once."

"Was it way out here?" the detective asked.

"Lots of times, a man got himself a high-priced machine,
he likes to park it where nobody opening a door gonna scratch
at his paint," the uniform said.

"Yeah, I think we got a car theft with a mugging. But let's
look around, see if we can find it."

I noticed that some of the cops were scanning the crowd
of onlookers. There were fifteen or twenty of us by then. It
says, right on page fifty-eight of *Practical Homicide Investigation*, "Obtain pictures of the people in the crowd. Often
witnesses . . . including possible suspects, will be watching." I wasn't either, but neither would what I was doing
there bear scrutiny.

I took one last look at the corpse. The wallet, rifled, lay near it. The ring was off his finger and the silver links were gone from his French cuffs. The collar of his custom shirt and Savile Row suit were stained with blood. His shoes were scuffed from the fall. His pants were soiled on the inside when his body released urine and excrement, soiled on the outside by oil and trash of the day gone by.

The killing made the morning edition of the *Washington Post*. The tone of the story was muted schizophrenic. The reporters clearly wanted to make something out of "secret federal witness assassinated"; the cops were hanging tough with "mugging and robbery, similar to several in the area recently"; and the editors were remembering that a *Post* reporter had won a Pulitzer for journalism that ought to have been awarded for fiction.

The story must have also made the *New York Times* because Choate Haven called me. Case closed.

"I can still get the transcripts," I told him, greedy for the bonus.

"There is no need. Whatever Mr. Wood told the SEC will be revealed soon enough, and while his testimony may lead them to further investigation, any litigation must rest entirely on the record and the record alone, not on facts skewed by an angry man bent on 'getting even.' "

"Do you think he was killed for what he was saying?" I asked.

"The average man in the street imagines corporations involved in every sort of skullduggery, possibly because they have not the opportunity or training required to examine the situation realistically. As counsel to Over & East I am privy to all aspects of their operations, and I can assure you, for the record, that based on the reality, based on the facts, that sort of speculation is frankly ridiculous. If Mr. Wood were alive and testifying, I suspect that, as is usual, Over & East would spend more on legal fees than on any penalties or fines."

Edgar Wood, a random chew in someone else's hunger.

To die for one's deeds is called glory. It doesn't matter if the death is soiled and the deeds are tawdry; you can still, like Jesse James, get a song out of it. If you think there is a sea god and Poseidon is drowning you, for reasons of personal malice, you can go under knowing your death is your own. We long to link the effect to a cause that is ourselves; there is dignity there. Wood was just dead.

Unless, of course, it had been the Colombians.

It really was not my business anymore. What was my business was that Choate Haven had requested neither a refund nor an accounting. I did not remind him. There was enough left that bottom-line-wise, dollar for dollar, pay per hour—that is, by every rational measure—it was my best case, ever.

8

PATCHEN

When I first met Wayne he was about two. Not knowing a whole lot about kids I decided to treat him like a dog, and it worked out real well.

If you treat a little kid or a dog like a regular person, you create tremendous frustration. For example, if you take either one for a walk and expect them to go straight ahead at a steady, even, purposeful pace, you have a very serious problem. What is natural to either animal is to run ahead, then dawdle back, check out the gutter on one side, the store fronts on the other, and when they meet another of their own species they have to go through some very strange, check-each-other-out rituals. Except when they don't.

Yelling at either one to train them to heel makes sense. Getting nuts because they don't see going for a walk the same way you see it just hurts all the parties concerned.

Wayne was now approaching the midget stage, sort of like a regular person, but smaller. I think we found each other instructive.

There is a dark side and a light side in all of us. That is

something I learned taking Wayne through the entire *Star Wars* trilogy twice.

The force inside has its own urgency. It creates a pressure to act and does not care what shape those actions have. It is amoral, without concept of self-perpetuation or self-destruction.

In D.C. I felt its presence awakening, like a rush from the adrenals. It was not the offers of drugs, a woman and violence; those things are always there for the picking. It was the feeling that I wanted the kick of crossing the line. That I was young, tough, resilient. That the legs had life enough for fifteen rounds and I could take the body blows and be back up before the mandatory eight-count was done. Forgetting that the last time I went down, it had taken over two years to remember what getting up means.

Two divorce cases and one job fingering the inside man in a series of garment-center thefts later, I decided to spend some of the money I made down in D.C. We sent Wayne to get spoiled by Glenda's parents and we went upstate to Mohonk.

We ate huge breakfasts, dressed for dinner as required and generally behaved like gentry except for some of the positions in which we made love. I hiked; Glenda strolled. My favorite was the dawn hike: quick march up the mountains to watch the sun rise, then back down for a plunge in a lake fed by springs and melted snow. When I hit it, my testicles snapped back and my heart pounded like it had a hit of amyl nitrate. I also started taking rock-climbing lessons, pitons and all of that, and tore the pads off two fingers after a slight error.

"If you want to go run up mountains and clamber over rocks like a child, jump in icy water and enjoy the feeling of a simulated heart attack, go right ahead. I will meet you back at the hotel for tea," Glenda said, and actually meant it.

Any other woman would have made my stay half miserable with "We came to be together, why don't you stay with me," or worse, attempted to keep up, through blisters, strains and sprains, never murmuring a curse of pain and only letting the sacrifice show in her eyes and written in the invisible ledger where women count the debts that men, unknowing, grow to owe them.

The week after we returned to Manhattan, Choate Haven called.

Edgar Wood was survived by a daughter, a wife and a mistress. The trustee of the rather considerable estate was the trust department of Choate, Winkler, Higgiston, Hahn & Moore. The mistress had been dismissed as a facility too distant to use when Wood went out of town. She would not have figured in the estate in any case. The wife was pre-estranged and when death came she decided that she was more content as a widow than as the wife of a living thief.

"Edgar Wood's daughter, however, is young and impressionable. She has reacted to his death in a neurotic and even obsessive manner. It may be guilt. She was out of the country, in Ibiza I believe, at the time of death, and due to problems with overseas communications and in locating her, she did not learn of the event until after the actual funeral.

"The police reports, which we have obtained for her, make it quite clear that this was a mugging, plain and simple. Apparently there had been several similar incidents in that area in the months directly preceding, though none of them resulted in death. I have gone so far as to speak to the local law-enforcement representatives, and I have assured myself that they take the case with utmost seriousness and that they have gone into the matter with unusual thoroughness.

"In spite of that, young Miss Wood seems to feel that not enough is being done. She has suggested that the police are covering something up. To be quite frank, some of her statements and accusations have been, shall we say, extravagant. In view of her bereavement we have all tried to be tolerant of these hysterical outbursts."

I could visualize that. A half-dozen pin-stripers standing in a grave and tolerant circle around the screaming, spoiled daughter of the rich dead Wood. A JAP in hysteria, swinging her Gucci bag at increasingly patronizing old WASPs. And once in a patronization mode the WASP is a stone wall. As the WASPs grow blanker, her frustration rises and rises until it is total and she begins to tear at her own clothes, the Italian silk halter and designer jeans. The denim will not rip but the silk does, and at the sight of breast the pinstripes call for sedation all around.

And there I was. Sedation.

"Although I and the other trustees regard the use of a private investigator as, in all probability, a waste of money, the estate is considerable and Miss Wood can certainly afford to indulge her feelings.

"We have had clients spend their money on far sillier things, believe me."

Humor, from Choate Haven. I was so shocked I chortled along with him.

"As you are somewhat familiar with the case, I thought perhaps you would be suitable."

"Should I mention that?" I asked.

"That's hardly necessary. And I think you should report through our offices. You will find that more convenient, less taxing, and naturally your reports will carry more weight that way."

"Part of my job, or all of it," I said, "seems to be to reassure Ms. Wood that everything that can be done is being done. I think she will find it more reassuring if she can deal with me directly. Of course I will communicate anything and everything to you, as her attorney, as well."

"Excellent point," he admitted.

"There's one more thing. Has the SEC moved against Over & East yet?"

"No, and I don't understand the significance of the question."

"Well, sir"—he responded well when I said sir—"if they have, it would make the Wood transcripts subject to discovery. If we had copies of his statements it would tell us that either no one or someone had a motive to silence him. I agree with you," I rushed to add, "that we will, in all likelihood, find nothing. But it is the testimony situation that is obviously the basis of the daughter's fears and suspicions. If we want to quiet them and bring her back to reality, we should meet that issue head on.''

''I see the point you are making, and you may be quite right. If the SEC proceeds with litigation, I shall try to obtain relevant portions for you.''

This time I got paid by check. There was a two-week advance. After that, we would review and decide if it was worth continuing. I also got a copy of the police report and the daughter's phone number and address.

When I called her she sounded calm and businesslike, and had a pleasant voice. We made an appointment for the next day, Saturday, at 3 P.M.

Then I got hold of Ol' Chip and made a squash date for 1:00.

In celebration of another overpriced job I bought myself a new Head racket with competition gut. These small indulgences can be thrilling.

Though he lost, three games to love, both sets, I could see that he was pleased with me. Every interchange between an associate and a partner is a test. Had I failed, after being recommended by Chip, it would have been Chip's head on the block. Apparently Choate Haven had never given him any feedback, either way, until by rehiring me he expressed his satisfaction through action. The relief was enormous, and Chip was feeling a rush of gratitude that verged on warmth.

Chip's field was Trusts and Estates, and the steam room seemed a good place to pick his brains. I asked him if he was involved in the Wood estate.

''Good Christ, no!''

''What's all the emphatics for?'' I asked.

''That name,'' he laughed, ''at Choate, Winkler, Higgiston, Hahn & Moore, that name is like Leon Trotsky's name at a D.A.R. meeting or Ronald Reagan's at an S.D.S. meeting. Is there still an S.D.S.? Something like that, anyway.''

''Really?'' I prompted.

''Really. Wood is . . . a traitor to his class. A worm in the apple, the serpent in the garden and socialized legal services all rolled into one. Associates who worked for him go around telling anyone who'll listen how much work they did for other partners. And partners, they say things like 'Edmund Who? Oh, you said Edward, natural mistake, I hardly knew the man.' The guy who had the space next to him wants to change his office. We're not talking even guilt by association here, we're talking guilt by proximity."

"So all your work is straight and safe. Administering the allowance of profligate children four generations down from robber baron forebears, doling out the treasured assets of sweet old biddies from Park Avenue."

"Actually, no."

"No?"

"There can be drama and excitement in Trusts and Estates."

"No!"

"Yes! You would never guess who retained us to put his financial affairs in order and to care for the financial future of his family, now that he is in the slammer for life . . . Ricky Sams."

Ricky was hot stuff. There was a semipermanent space reserved for him on page five of the *New York Post*. With photo. He got almost as much coverage as Hero Cops. Once the kingpin of heroin in Harlem, he was now the finest federal witness since Joseph Valachi. In the world of canaries, Ricky was the Diva.

"Tsk, tsk, all that dirty money."

"Not," Chip said calmly, "the way we handle it. Taxes and back taxes are paid. Actually the IRS is being remarkably fair about penalties and such. I suspect they prefer this to having everything disappear into the Caymans, Panama and Lichtenstein. Of course," he said with deep and abiding virtue, "if that was what Sams wanted, we would not be involved."

"Of course," I grinned.

"Actually," he mused, "it's kind of funny, I guess, just how straight everything is. On the up-and-up. Which reminds me, everything I've said is a matter of public record.

I have divulged nothing protected by the attorney-client privilege. I am no Edmund Who.''

"Right. You're a good guy," I said.

"And I would have beat you if it weren't for that goddamn
new racket.''

Like something shipped up on a riverboat from New Or-
leans, there is a section of buildings on the south side of Tenth
Street, between Fifth and Sixth Avenue, connected by an
ironwork balcony. The north side of the street, where Christina Wood lived, was all big, impressive, well-cared-for
brownstones, with fancy doors, stone and ironwork. All in
all, one of the prettiest streets in a city that often lacks for
prettiness.

I rang her bell. There was no answer. My watch said 3:03.
Well, I had been warned. I leaned against the stoop and
opened my *Times*, passing the time like any well-bred New
Yorker.

At 3:08 she showed up. She wore headband, sweatshirt
and shorts. She glowed with fresh sweat, youth and health.
A tall woman, vibrant with energy and muscle tone.

"Christina Wood?" I inquired.

"Oh, damn, I'm late. I'm sorry, I really am. Come on
up.''

She opened the mailbox with a key tied to her running
shoe, took the apartment keys from the mailbox and opened
the inner door to the building. She lived on top and it was a
walk-up. I followed her, watching all the way. Her shorts
rose over her cheeks. I gave thanks to sportswear designers
and the inventor of stairs.

"I'm really sorry, I just had to go out and run . . . this is
embarrassing. Do you mind if I take a quick shower? Would
you like a drink while you wait? Juice? Beer? Anything?"

"Beer," I said.

I sat down and said beer thinking scotch and there by God
Was my woman just as I had always known she would be
And I went over to her and she said come home with me

Like that . . .
Climbing the stairs behind her, watching . . .
Wondering how God could have gotten it all into this little
          tail . . .*

There was no reason for resonance, but the chord was struck, and it echoed down the corridors of my life, plucking out the poem that I read to the girl with black hair and blue eyes on the hill above the river when I was nineteen and moonstruck and life was blueberry pie.

I drank my beer and hoped the ringing would die down. She came out of the shower in jeans that were not too tight, with a bra beneath a plain cotton shirt, without makeup, and her hair toweled dry. There was no attempt to be provocative, but the ringing went on.

"Miss Wood," I said.

She said "Christina," and there by God was my woman . . . "Fine," I said, "I'm Tony" . . . just as I had always known she would be.

She said my name, and I was glad to hear it in her mouth.

"Your attorney, Mr. Haven, asked me to look into your father's death."

"After he was forced into it. Do you know that?"

"How was that?"

"They didn't want to do it. To them I'm just an hysterical child. I hired another law firm. They claimed that there was a conflict of interest; I knew there was a conflict of interest. They persecuted Daddy, not prosecuted, persecuted. Now they represent the estate and they're blocking an investigation into who killed him. I still think it's not right for them to represent the estate, but as long as they do what I want in the important things, then I'm willing to let it go."

"Legal battles are expensive."

"They sure are, and until the estate is settled, which could be years and years, I can't really afford that either," she said. Her eyes were green, soft green, sea green.

---

*"He was alone (AS IN REALITY)," Kenneth Patchen, *Collected Works*. All following quotations, the same source.

"I'm glad that the estate is paying then; I feel better if my clients can afford me."

"I'm not sure I am," she said with real suspicion in her voice. "Who are you working for, them or me?"

"For you." Forever and always.

"So where do we start?" she asked in a businesslike way. It was only the two of us in that room there, and it was only doing business that could save us. So we did.

"We've both seen the police report," I said. "It's straightforward; they did their job. Autopsy and forensics are pretty complete, very complete. They questioned who there was to question and came up empty. Now we need a reason to look past that, to look for more." Just because she had a beautiful bottom was not supposed to be sufficient reason, but sometimes it is.

She asked me if I knew the circumstances that had brought her father to Virginia.

I did, and I said so. "But do you know of any specific reason, any motivation, any place to start?"

"Everyone wanted to be rid of him."

"Who is everyone?"

"Everyone, dammit, all of them. All those senior partners, at that high-and-mighty stuffed-shirt law firm. Someone had besmirched their sacred name. Sacrilege, sacrilege. Or maybe he didn't steal all that money by himself. It was a lot of money, it went on a long time without anyone noticing. Could Daddy have done all that alone? Yes, I admit it, it's part of the record. He was innocent until proven guilty and they did prove it and my father was a thief." She tried to hold her face rigid. She swallowed. "Poor man. He always, always tried too hard."

She got up and rushed to the bathroom. I did not hold her while she cried her eyes out. I sipped my beer and waited while she washed her face.

"I'm sorry," she said when she came back.

"Don't be, it's OK," was all I said. There had to be men in her life to say everything I wanted to say. Had to be.

I had finished my beer. She went into the kitchen and

brought out two more, one for me, one for her, and I had had her figured for designer water with a twist of lime.

"I'm ready," she said after she took a swallow.

"Good, go on."

"I started to say, maybe he had someone else. I mean, it must be hard to steal eight million dollars all by yourself." She almost giggled. Her moods were shifting fast. Somewhere between the grief-stricken daughter and the businesslike young lady, waiting behind them both, was the wayward child who could not be located in Ibiza. And she was delicious. "I mean, think about stealing that much money, and all by yourself."

"Anyone else, besides this unknown party?"

"You don't think much of the idea, do you?" she said resentfully.

"I think that if there was someone else, he would have traded him in, used him to plea-bargain. I mean this is a guy who tried to save himself by testifying to the SEC."

"Maybe, but maybe not. He only turned on the people who turned on him."

If she wanted to preserve a thread of decency in her father, that I didn't think he was capable of, all I could do was admire her loyalty. "Anyone else?" I asked.

"Goreman," she said, "Charlie Goreman. Daddy hated him at the end. He owed Daddy a lot. He owed Daddy everything, and he didn't lift a finger to save him."

"How's that?"

"I don't know the details, but I know that Daddy saved him during the war; he said that Uncle Charlie wouldn't even be alive today if it weren't for him."

"Uncle Charlie?"

"That's what I called him when I was growing up. He doted on little girls or something. And he was close to the family."

"That makes it sound like he would be the last person to . . ."

"I don't know. If you think about it, Charles Goreman went awfully far, awfully fast. Can anyone get that far that fast and be totally legitimate? Maybe Daddy knew something about him. I heard he threatened him at the trial.''

''Were you at the trial?''

''No,'' she said, and drank her beer quickly.

''How come?''

She leaned away from the question and said, ''And it could have been almost anyone of that top group over at Over & East. Daddy knew almost everything about everybody. Maybe someone else had a big dirty secret that they were afraid my father would talk about. There are so many people it could have been.''

''Maybe you're just trying to make his death meaningful,'' I said.

''I thought about that—I'm so angry, I want to blame somebody or something. I had an uncle who died, and my aunt kept saying it was the doctor's fault, that the doctor screwed up; and I've heard people talk about it was God's will, but they never sound like they believe that. . . .

''But if he really was killed on purpose, to keep him quiet, then it would be a smart thing to do to make it look like a mugging. If I were going to kill someone and I don't think I could and I wanted to be smart about it and not get caught, a good way would be to make it look exactly the way this did, the way this does. Sometimes paranoids have real enemies.''

''The last time I thought there were people out to get me,'' I said, ''there were.''

''Thank you,'' she said.

''But what I still need is a place to start looking for a motive.''

''When he was arrested, and during the trial, and particularly when they sentenced him to that place, he was making statements, threats. . . .''

''Yeah, I know about that. And a lot of people have said a lot worse about me, and it's not something to worry about unless the guy who makes the threats has the goods and the guts to back it up. So if someone was worried enough to kill your father, it was because your father had the goods and they believed that he had the will to use it. And nobody seems to know what that could have been.''

"I'm sorry, I don't know. I'm sorry."

"By the way," I asked, "was your father involved in anything in South America? In Colombia?"

"Not that I know of. Why?"

"What about cocaine?"

"Daddy! Cocaine!" She sounded as incredulous as Choate Haven had. "Oh Lord, no way."

"Not even strictly as a money thing?"

"Why are you asking?"

"Would he?"

"I can't, I guess I'm not allowed to say no." Her lovely face broke again and she turned to the bathroom.

"I'm . . . sorry," I said to her retreating back.

I heard the splash of water as she rinsed her face. "Why? Why did you say that?" she said when she came out. "Is it to finish, finish destroying what's left of him?"

"Look, I'm sorry. It was a stab in the dark. A couple of years back I ran into a case, a guy was killed the same way, pretty much, by some Colombians over a coke deal, and they tried to make it look like a mugging and stole the guy's car."

"Is that true? Is that really why you asked?"

"Really why I asked? Because I have nothing to go on and that might have been an idea, and until I find something else I'm taking wild shots."

My business was done. There was no excuse to stay. There was an illusion weaving thick through the air that we had other things to say and do. Sea-green eyes, an emotional vibrato in her throat, long flanks so live they glowed, dark hair livened with sunstreaks and a great ass, I told myself, were shallow things. Not with a structure so solid, so real and so fine as Glenda and Wayne made of my life. It was a foolish time to be foolish. As it always is.

9

LIGHTNIN'-STRUCK TREE

THE ONLY TRACE of Edgar Wood in the Virginia farmhouse was his crystal brandy snifter and the bottle of VSOP with one good shot left. I sat in what had been his chair, swirled his brandy in his glass.

"Tell me, ghost, what was your secret? Was it worth killing for? In your estimation was it worth dying for? Did you tell it to Mel Brodsky? Or were you saving it for last, your ace in the hole? Tell me, Mr. Wood, did you know how beautiful your daughter is? Looking back on it all, if you had to choose between another ten or twenty or something years and eight million dollars, which would it be?"

I sipped at his brandy, giving him plenty of time to answer. But he was, as I had suspected, as silent as the grave.

"I gotta talk to a bunch of people about you, Edgar. I like talking to your daughter best, but I gotta talk to the police, I gotta talk to Brodsky, and I'm not sure where I'll find the leverage for that; and Charles Goreman, even more leverage. And the Colombians. To tell you the truth, I feel real shy about that. Maybe 'cause I don't so much want to talk as to hurt them, or maybe I'm scared of them . . . see, there is a point where you and I, we coincide. Fear and vengeance, that's a swell meeting of the minds.

"So long, Edgar," I said, finishing his brandy, "our first and last meeting of the minds. I gotta go to work now."

I wanted to retrieve my microphone and recording rig, expensive little toys that they are. Everything was intact, the waterproof box had done a hell of a job though the batteries were shot. I was also intensely curious to know if someone else had left something similar about the premises.

I looked in the phones, inside the air conditioner, under the radiator cover, behind the pictures on the wall—not one of which was worth looking at unless you like English hunty-doggy-horsy—and through the largest collection of *Reader's Digest* condensed books I had ever seen. I looked through anything that had an underside, an inside or a backside, including all 112 dusty panels of dropped ceiling.

I looked until there was nothing to look at but the walls. I rapped, and the bruising on my knuckles convinced me they were real plaster and solid. The molding was some sort of hard wood under the paint. I could tell because someone had lifted it and I could see where the paint was chipped. . . . Oh!

A minute or two of gentle prying and there she was. A very nice job too, the transformer clipped directly into an A.C. line and no battery to wear out.

I took mine. I left theirs in place. Then I went to meet Captain Robert E. L. Deltchev at Culpeper County Police Headquarters.

I had visualized the place as a southern courthouse and county jail, reeking of dark cruel secrets, petty power politics, injustices racial and otherwise, lit in 1940s Warner Brothers Neo-Realism. But the station was merely overused, overcrowded, 1950s strictly brick and functional. An Anywhere USA cop house.

The cop at the glassed-in front desk looked to be forty-five minutes past mandatory retirement. The cable-and-jack phone system he was plugged into was twenty years past it. He had a wad in his cheek that he chomped with bovine regularity. Between chaws he told me, "Captain ain't heyah."

"When will he be in?" I asked.

"Don't rightly know," the cop said, then started answering the phone and plugging the lines into the right, or wrong, extensions. That went on for some time and he ignored me without any apparent effort.

"I have an appointment," I said. He nodded and blew a bubble. That disappointed me; I had really hoped for tobacco.

"Maybe you could call him. I bet he has a police car, and I bet it has a radio. And remind him that he has an appointment."

"Don't rightly think so," he said and went back to the switchboard as lights and bells went off.

I waited. Several other people came and went, cops and civilians. The oddest group was led by a very large man in uniform with pockmarked slabs for a face who blew in like a destroyer on patrol. An intense-looking woman dressed as a New Jersey housewife and what had to be a plainclothes cop bobbed along in his wake. Ten minutes later, they came charging back out.

After they left I asked the cop at the desk once again, "When and where am I going to find Deltchev?"

"Why didn't you speak to him while he was here?" he answered, then started on a new piece of gum.

"When was he here?"

"He just left."

"Either I've seen this movie before or I read the book," I mumbled.

"What book's that?"

"Is Deltchev coming back?" I growled.

"Mostly he does," he said, working up to a new bubble.

"I'm going out to get some coffee; can I get you some more gum?" I said.

"That's right nice. That really is. I like that double-bubble grape flavor," he replied and even offered me a nickel. I took it.

It was authentic southern coffee, which resembles real coffee only in that they both start with water and are normally served warm. If a New York coffee shop palmed off the stuff on an N.Y.P.D. cop, they would be promptly and rudely busted for fraud. And although there were cows in Virginia—from what I had seen of Culpeper, probably right in town—the white stuff they gave me to put in the warm, tan liquid was a powder built in Ohio. They did not have Danish. They had sweet rolls. I don't really know what wheat gluten is, but I think that's what the rolls were made of. And sugar.

Now that I knew what Deltchev looked like—a pock-marked naval destroyer—I waited outside where I could wonder where the scent of magnolia blossom had gone to.

Three hours after I arrived, and three more cups of warm tinted water, Deltchev steamed in again. He was still with the same group, and I tailed along like just another piece of jetsam caught in his wake.

When we all got trapped in a traffic jam trying to enter the door of Deltchev's office, he became aware of my presence.

"Who are you?"

I introduced myself and reminded him of the appointment that was now three hours late.

"I do not have the time to spare at this time," he announced.

"Look, Captain, I flew down from New York to talk to you."

"I bet your arms are tired." The slabs of his face crooked briefly into a smile so we would all know it was a joke.

"It's by water, by running water," the woman who looked like a New Jersey housewife said.

"Look, Captain," I said, "I have been waiting here for three hours."

"She has to concentrate," the other guy, the one in the polyester plainclothes cop suit, said.

"Don't bother me, son," Deltchev said.

"We're prepared to give you all the time you need," the other guy said to Deltchev, "but not for these interruptions."

"You hear that, you hear what the man said?" Deltchev

said to me, pointing a finger somewhat smaller than a kielbasa at me. "Now desist these interruptions."

"Don't wave your finger in my face. . . ." I snapped.

The man in plainclothes stepped between us and shoved me. I didn't want to hit a cop in a police station. There are some forms of stupidity that even I find excessive. But I did say, "If you fucking touch me again, I'll break your fucking arm."

Unlike Deltchev, he was pretty close to my size and I might have been able to do it.

At that point still another party entered the fray. A slim, neatly dressed black man, who I also took to be a cop, stepped between me and the pusher.

"What's the problem?" he said calmly.

"The fucking problem . . ." I started to explain.

"Tillman," Deltchev bellowed, "you take care of him. Dan, come with me. We have things to do," and he swept into his office, the other two following in his wake, Tillman staying with me.

"Detective Tillman," he said with the same aplomb, "what can I do for you?"

"I came down from New York to see Captain Deltchev; I had an appointment. I've been waiting three hours."

"Are you from the media?" he asked.

"Media?"

"I guess not," he said. "Who are you?"

I told him, I even gave him a card. I explained why I was there.

"Too bad you're not from the media," he said.

"What's going on?" I asked.

"Come on into my office, I'm the one who's really handling the Wood thing now. I'm sorry," he said, as I followed him, "you came at a bad time. We have some little girls missing, three of them, and we found the body of a fourth. The captain's a little preoccupied."

He gestured me to a seat while he opened a file cabinet and took out the paperwork. I complimented him on what a good report he had written up and what thorough police work they had done.

"Is there anything," I asked, "any dangling thread, any detail that didn't fit, or maybe just a sense of things that didn't find its way into that report?"

"Right now it looks a whole lot like the report reads. I'll fill you in on a little background though. Lately, we've been getting a big rise in auto theft. It seems like it's been moving out from the city, all around, over in Maryland too. They like to work shopping centers, particularly where there are restaurants. Not McDonald's or Burger King, real restaurants. You figure a guy goes into a restaurant, you got an hour or two before he's out. That's time enough for the car to be good and gone and at the chop shop. It seems like it's organized, because there's a pattern and because they're picky about it, BMWs, Volvos, Mercedes, Saabs, the smaller Caddies, Lincolns. The high-price spread. I'm figuring a lot of it goes straight to parts. Do you have any idea what a replacement engine for a BMW goes for?

"We had one victim, three months ago, was having dinner with his wife. He says, 'Oh, honey, I left my wallet in the car.' But what he really was doing was sneaking to the pay phone to call his extracurricular lady friend. But from the pay phone he sees these two perpetrators messing with his brand-new Seville. Being at the phone anyway, he calls police emergency. By then, the perps have already got his door open, which doesn't take but a couple of seconds, so he goes tear-ass out of the restaurant screaming; they jump away from his car and they tear-ass out in the car they came in. Less than a minute later the patrol car comes into the lot, but they're long gone, and the victim doesn't have a license number, or even a description of the perp's auto."

"What about them, does he have a description of them?"

"Young, big, black, and dat's all, folks."

"What about muggings or assaults?"

"We have about three, real similar. Two of them hit on the head from behind. Now either we are talking about the same people, or they all went to the same training program, or if it is murder designed to look like car theft someone did their homework real well."

The door burst open; another black cop, in uniform, charged in, saying, "I gotta talk to you, Bill."

In his unflappable way, Tillman said, "What is it, Jimmy Lee?"

The other cop looked at me, but Tillman said, "Go on."

"You know Nora Anne Johnson, owns the grocery place, up Davis Road?"

"Uh huh."

"That's a good woman, churchgoing, hardworking. She's in my patrol area, or what oughta be my patrol area, except that I'm down the other end of the county looking for a lightnin'-split tree near runnin' water—yestiday it was standing water—while she is being robbed. Now Nora Anne she works hard for her nickels and dimes, she works hard. So she doesn't want to just plain give that money away, and they done shot her. They done shot her. I have a pretty fair idea who done it to her, I do. But the Captain, he got me looking for that lightnin'-split tree, so I can't do my real job, which is looking after the peoples in my patrol area. Now can you do something about that man!"

"Jimmy Lee," Tillman said, his voice all patience.

"Shit, I know you can't. I just had to go blow off steam to someone."

"Jimmy Lee, just try to get it on the record. Make your request official. On paper."

"You think . . . captain gonna have my ass."

"Only in the short run. In the long run, if you go by the Book, the Book will stand by you. Just do it right and thank God for Civil Service."

"You have any media friends?" Tillman asked me when the patrolman had gone.

"What is going on here?"

"The Captain has got a psychic. All the way from New Jersey. She's got a whole scrapbook of all the bodies she has found. And that fellow that was shoving you, he is—I don't know what he is—but he used to be a cop and now he just follows her around. You been in New Jersey; is that how they do things there?''

''It's not something I do a lot, go to New Jersey.''

''Do you have any idea of how many man-hours he is wasting on stuff like Jimmy Lee was talking about? And how much real work does not get done? I do. I have kept track.''

''It seems to me that the mugging of Edgar Wood is a little different than the others,'' I said.

''The difference is that someone died. Way it works is kids start boosting cars for joyrides. Borrow one, run it around a little, leave it like there was no harm done. Then they figure out that they can use the very same skills to do themselves a little cash good. It's easy. No one does hard time for a first offense. They get probation. Second time they get popped, if they're still on probation they really got something to lose. So they get caught in the act, they grab the first thing handy. It's a piece of pipe 'stead of blackjack or sock filled with sand, and there is a dead man lying on the ground. Now that, that fits the facts. I won't be stubborn or tight-minded, but until there is something, something, that tells me different, that's the direction I'm running.''

His phone rang. ''Yes sir . . . no sir . . . as soon as possible . . . I'll get right on it,'' he said to the phone. When he hung up he turned to me. ''If the media was to get a good hard look at this thing, maybe we could get back to police work. I mean the real media, not the *Enquirer*, they already gave Captain Deltchev an interview. 'Police Captain Amazed by Powers of Famed Psychic,' the headline is gonna say. Idiots.''

''You know that Wood was a federal witness, testifying for the SEC?''

''Yeah, I know that.''

''Do you know that the farmhouse he was in was wired for sound?''

''What are you saying?''

''I'm saying, Detective, that I went up to the farmhouse where they were keeping him, and I found a listening device which I don't think belonged to the SEC because they would have taken it with them.''

"What were you doing up there?"

"Looking around like I'm supposed to, handing over anything I find out to the local constabulary like I'm supposed to, even when they keep me waiting half a day."

"Where is it?"

"Are you going to do something about it? Is it the something you needed to reopen the investigation or to push it in some new directions?"

"Yes, I do believe it would be; of course our man power, the man-hours we can devote to it, is, at present, strictly limited. Due to most of our cops being assigned by cosmic forces."

"Oh," was all I could say.

"However, were some big-city news organization, print or television, to get ahold of the situation and put it in perspective, which is a little to the left of far out, then maybe I could do the work you and I urgently desire me to."

"I might know some people."

"What I'm going to do, I'm going to take it on good faith that you will try with whatever contacts you have. In the meantime, I will go on up to that house, have a look at this device you described, pull prints if I can, run a trace on the thing if I can . . . all of which I would do anyway, because I'm a cop and here to do a job . . . but because of your good intentions, I will share that information with you."

"I have this feeling, if I can speak frankly?" I said.

"Go on. You may."

"That when, and if, Deltchev goes, Bill Tillman might become the first black captain of detectives in Culpeper history."

"Well, I don't think things would move that fast, though it wouldn't hurt. But I tell you what, whether it works that way or not, it would put a stop to something dumb. And I hate dumb. If I was ever to eradicate crime from this world, which I won't, I would go after dumb next."

"Ahead of racism?"

"Racism is part of dumb."

"I think I like you, Detective," I told him.

"Do you know where they're from in New Jersey? The psychic and her sidekick?" he asked. "They're from Nutley."

10

OWSLEY LIVES

BUREAUCRATS *HOLD THEIR* secrets like bankers clutch the float. Secrets are coin of the realm, they confer status and power. They give the bureaucrat what he wants most, a sense of self-importance.

I sat in my lonely motel room. How then was I to pry secrets from this man Brodsky? The problem seemed insurmountable. Then my eye fell on the Gideon Bible. Could that text answer my question? Were solutions to the problems of today in that book? A strange feeling came over me as I reached out, as if another power were moving me. The Book came into my hands, then almost by itself it opened to this passage: "He who taketh a wife giveth hostages to fortune." The Bible, in its wisdom, was pointing out not just the potential for blackmail, but for extortion as well.

The thing to do was videotape Brodsky in bed with a broad at the E-Z Sleaze Motel, preferably on a water bed. One thing I had learned from divorce work was that wives go extra nuts if their husbands commit their infidelities on water beds.

The other possibility was to kidnap one of his kids and trade it for the transcripts. There had been no children in my marriage, though there had been two dogs, and I stayed the entire second year for their sake. Then one night we sat down and talked. They let me know they could carry on without me. Several years later I met one of them in Central Park and he acted like he hardly knew me. It was my relationship with Wayne that had taught me how far someone will go to protect a child, and he wasn't even mine.

If I simply walked up to Brodsky, the worst he could do was say no. I could still do something horrid afterward to change his mind.

On the off chance that he would simply say, "Yes, read 'em!" I went to the Brodsky domicile at what I assumed was after dinner. I had nothing to offer but my boyish charm and a bottle of Johnny Walker Black.

Mel himself came to the door when I buzzed. This was the first time I had seen him up close. His hair was reddish and receding. His eyes were blue. Not sky, or steely, or ice or Paul Newman blue, just blue. His skin was fair and would sear his first hour on Miami Beach. He was shorter than me and a little overweight, but he carried it pleasantly. He looked like he could smile a lot, if provoked.

I introduced myself as myself, showed real ID and asked for a few minutes of his time.

"What is this?"

"Look, Mr. Brodsky, it's complicated. Why don't you invite me in? If you like scotch, we can crack open this twelve-year-old and I'll explain. Then you can throw me out if you want."

"Mel. Who's there?" came a voice that had to be the wife.

"A man giving away scotch," he yelled back, and let me in.

"That's good," came the same voice. She walked into the foyer in slacks, a loose blouse and bare feet. I noticed for the first time that Mel was barefoot also. She was taller than him.

"A private detective," she replied to my introduction, "how charming."

The living room that I was led into was furnished in non-designer homey, basic comfortable combined with child-proof. Mel got ice and glasses, I broke the seal.

"What's it about?" he asked.

I stalled. Mrs. Brodsky was quick on the pickup. "Is this something that would be better if I weren't here?"

"I don't know," Mel shrugged.

"Yes," I said. When I'm about to ask a man to violate the confidentiality of his position, I prefer to do it without the ace number-one symbol of propriety, a wife, around.

"Very well then," she said, not at all put out, "I'll take my drink and go to bed. When you're done with my husband, send him to me, please." I liked her.

"Mr. Brodsky, you were taking testimony from a man named Edgar Wood."

"Call me Mel."

"OK. Call me Tony. There's not a hell of a lot of point in beating about the bush. I'm investigating his death."

"You look vaguely familiar," he said. He looked at me, searching for a time or place to put with my face. I looked back, joining the search, and saw nothing familiar.

"The family hired me. They think the mugging was a way to cover up a deliberate murder."

"I can't figure out where I know you from. Are you from D.C.?"

"No," I said.

"Hey! Did you go to law school?"

"One year, Yale."

"Hmmmm, I went to N.Y.U. How about college?"

"Stony Brook," and slowly came the dawn.

No way I would have recognized him. They called him "A.K.A." and that sort of reddish receding hair had been full, curly and huge. Not an Afro, but hardly straight. It had been a tangled halo of glee around giggling eyes and a mouth that gleamed with chemical light. "A.K.A" stood for Acid King Also.

"Tony C., last of the Brooklyn greasers," he drawled.

"Ohhh, wow!" we both said. It was really awesome. A

blast from the past. It was the first time I had said "Oh wow!" since the Republican ascension of '68.

Re-mem-mem, remember when, oh re-mem-mem, when the world was cleanly crazy and fresh to be rebaked. It was always sunrise when, walking a girl back in the afterglow, you ran into A.K.A. drifting through the trees. Or sunset when we built a bonfire on a fogbound winter night, below the sand cliff among the rocks of Long Island's north shore. Firelight and sunlight would catch highlights of red and gold in his aura and his body would move with the awkward grace of a teddy bear that had delusions of being a wood sprite.

"You are wondering," he said with a grin like the old grin, "how I got from there"—his hand wafted through the air pointing at some location in the ether—"to here. Since you are wondering, I will tell you.

"I had a vision. Now most folks, when they have a vision, visionize the world of the spirit. See God—with whom Tom Landry has a personal relationship. See the Cosmos. But I already had a thing going with the Cosmos, as it happens. It is it, and it am I, it's really very pleasant. So my vision was a vision of the mundane."

I nodded like it all made sense.

"I had dropped out of school. On the way back to the east coast from the west coast on my way to Tangiers, I found myself in Grand Central Station. Either we were to embark from there or someone had suggested that we go look at trains before they became extinct. It was rush hour, on a Thursday.

"Suddenly, as if a celestial dam had broken, they began to come in a flood. In real gray flannel suits. Remember those days, when clothes were uniforms, they made statements? They were Identity. Anyway, we were blown out on some truly righteous Purple Owsley, and suddenly I saw all these people with love. The myth was that they were oppressed gray automatons caught in the Kafka K of Amerika.

"I blew through the myth. They were people. Functioning, having homes, man-woman relating, having-raising-loving children. And I saw that hippie, soldier, gray flannelier, philosoph or coach, if you were living a human life—it was all the same.

"Suddenly I felt free. I was free. I could conform.

"I ran out of the station, through the crowds, to find the nearest Brooks Brothers. There it was, on Madison Avenue. Tripping my brains out, I made my way to the tie department, to find out if it was really true, if it was all possible. They had beautiful things, wool, silk, cotton. Some exquisitely dull. Some foolishly playful. I knew, at first glance, that on those racks was my tie, waiting."

"Oh wow," I said for only the second time in one and a half decades. "So you bought the tie, went straight, and gave up drugs," I concluded for him.

"Oh no. Oh yes. Oh no," he clarified.

"Oh no? Oh yes? Oh no?" I asked.

"I stole the tie."

"Of course." I should have thought of that.

"I was gonna write a book, called *Steal This Tie!* but then Abbie wrote his."

"A great opportunity preempted."

"Yeah," he sighed, still regretting it.

"You went straight," I prompted.

"Oh yeah, I went back to school and really got into it. I realized in a vision . . ."

"A different vision," I interrupted.

"No. No. Same vision, in Grand Central. I saw it was all a game. I saw that I could play."

"But you didn't give up acid?"

"Of course not," he said definitively. "How else could I keep my head straight?"

"Oh."

"You can get lost in those games, man, really lost. You can become a pinball, getting kicked by the flippers, bouncing from bumper to bumper, totally out of control, and forget you're supposed to be the pinball player."

"I see," I said, but I wasn't sure that I did.

"Every year we go on vacation, somewhere where there's

a deserted beach or up in the mountains, and Priscilla and I drop. That clears the cobwebs out.''

"Oh. That sounds good.''

"Oh, yeah, it makes for an incredibly healthy relationship. You know, most couples, all modern couples maybe, talk about how honest their relationships are, but that is mostly bullshit and cheap emotional chic. I mean the women learn that that's the way it's supposed to be from *Cosmo*, *Redbook* and Donahue; the men get it from *Penthouse* and their wives. If you look at the sources, you realize what incredibly crossed signals are being sent out. They all say 'Honesty, honesty, honesty!' but they communicate 'hype,' 'con' and 'hype.' ''

"I don't know. Glenda, that's the woman I live with, swears by Donahue.''

"Don't they all. But anyway, unless you really get down, really get out there, where you can look back and see your bullshit and the fungus that grows in your mind, fear, insecurity, the deviousness of your own defenses, see the garbage as garbage, you can't be honest even if you want to.''

"And that works?''

"Oh yeah . . .'' he drawled as only a true space cadet can, ". . . it's beautiful.

"Priscilla,'' he called out after an interval of self-appreciation. She came downstairs and Mel made enthusiastic introductions. Then he asked what had happened with me.

It might have been the space cadet atmosphere that floated genially behind the gray flannel facade, or a tactical decision that honesty and openness beget more of the same; whatever it was, I told more truth than I expected to.

"You were going to law school,'' he prompted.

"I dropped out,'' I said.

"Why? Law school is a terrific game.'' He giggled at Priscilla who was in on whatever the joke was. He moved off the couch and sat down on the floor where he was obviously more comfortable. She moved over so she could run a stray finger through what was left of his curly reddish hair.

"My father died. It was during the summer after my first

year. I was doing one of those intern things at a Wall Street firm. I told myself at the time that I was . . . that I had a vision, in a way. But it was one that shut things down, it didn't open them up. They had all the hotshots, the cream of the ivy crop, and they used them as chickenshit assistants to the senile and venal. With more chickenshit subservience than the army. The army was a world of blind obedience and a soldier was expected to try to evade the rules. The law firm was voluntary subservience and the associates were expected to love it. In school the law was fun. In a law office, it was finding forms. That was the reason, the reason I gave myself then.''

I poured myself another drink and settled on the floor.

''But maybe that wasn't true. There was enough money, if I let my mother keep it all, for her. If she invested it and worked till she got social security, she could get by gracefully. Or I could have taken the bread, finished school. But then I would've owed her, I would have been responsible. Locked in. I would have had to finish, and finish high, and taken the big law firm job and locked myself into the money. Maybe that was what it was about.''

''Someday,'' Priscilla said, ''you might want to grow up.''

''Lots of days,'' I replied, unoffended, ''I consider it.''

''Wasn't there some other way to score the bread?'' Mel asked.

''Yeah, I had, have, an Uncle Vincent. But then I would have owed him.''

''What he needs,'' Mel said, looking at his Priscilla, ''is the love of a good woman. To show him the way.''

''True, but what I want, is the Edgar Wood story.''

''Poor Edgar,'' Priscilla said, ''he sounded like such a foolish man. . . . He took it all very seriously. Didn't he, Mel?''

''Yeah, no sense of it being a game. No sense of fun at all.''

''Must have been very depressing for you to work with him,'' I suggested, trying to get into the warp and woof of things.

"Edgar Wood," Mel said, "acted as if everything was real. He was very serious."

"Attica is very real." I argued out of reflex. "Prison has a way of intruding on your sense of humor."

"I think I understand what you're saying," Priscilla said. "You would have to have a very strong core, a very firm and steady sense of unreality to maintain your sense of humor in prison."

"Oh wow, prison," Mel said, as if the idea was palpitating him for the first time. He was getting drunk. "We were going to keep him out, you know."

"Were you?"

"Oh yeah, that's the way the game is played." He brightened. "Trading up is one of the basic formats of all gamesmanship. I mean especially in law enforcement."

"He gave you good stuff then, huh?"

"Honestly?" Mel asked. "Honestly and truthfully?"

"Yeah, why not?" I said.

"Trade up," he said.

"What?"

"Tony," Priscilla prompted me prettily, "what can you trade for information about Edgar Wood?"

"Yeah, trade up," Mel repeated, drunken and impish.

I tried the riff about the bereaved, grief-stricken daughter who could never rest easy until there was proof of why Daddy died. Maybe it was because I had a thing about her, but I gave a hell of a performance.

"Tony, that's very interesting. And it's really great that you're a fellow non-Harvard man. An alumni of old State U and City High. Just like me. And Priscilla probably thinks you're cute. . . ."

"Oh definitely," she said.

"But. But! As an attorney. A man of Honor. A Gentleman. I am bound and sworn not to reveal an iota, a jot, a comma, a semicolon of anything that our witness, the late Edgar Wood, has revealed to me. . . . Unless! You have something to trade for it."

"It's hard to know, Mel, what's worth trading when I don't know what I'm trading for."

"Work at it." Mel was enjoying his game.

"Look, Mel, this is murder. I don't give a flying fuck about Over & East, and games on the big board, and I'll even guarantee you that nothing goes back to them from me. I'm just looking for a motive for murder."

"You're missing the point, old chum," Mel said.

"I am not, I'm evading it."

"Tony, it's quid pro quo, tit for tat and all of that. Unless you just want to chat about old times, which I think is a terrific idea."

"You want something sleazy on Over & East?" I mumbled and he nodded. They, who had been investigating Over & East for almost twenty years, didn't have anything solid.

"I don't know, there might be something. There might be a cocaine connection."

The gamesman's eyes lit up and came back into focus, and, I'm willing to swear, one ear actually cocked, like a beagle's. He waited for more. I waited for him.

"What is it?"

"What's in the testimony?"

"Tell me what you know, and, if it's good, you can read the transcripts."

"I'm going to have to track it down, nail down some details," I said. "It's going to take some time and money and it's dangerous. But I'll do it. I'll do it for you. Let me look at the stuff, because I might spot a tie-in that you won't, and because it'll help me investigating who I have to investigate. Then I'll do it, and bring whatever I get back to you."

"Tony, I would love to trust you," Mel said sincerely.

"He would," Priscilla chimed in. "He loves to trust, but he never does. It's part of the game."

"So here's what I'll do, and only 'cause we go way back," Mel said, "You give me one single thing that I can make a case out of, or even that's important as a piece of building a case, and you can read the transcripts."

11

CAPPUCCINO

GENE TATTALIA HAD done his homework. The guy in the front seat who did the talking, who had all but shot my ear off, now had a name: Hencio deVega. He worked at the Colombian Board of Trade and had diplomatic status.

Gene's people had tailed him for two days. The first day he made them nervous. He kept turning around while he was driving. They thought he was aware of being tailed, or frightened of being tailed, but they had tagged the wrong cause onto the effect and finally realized that deVega was turning around every time he saw a blonde. Any blonde, honey to platinum to dirty.

To pry him open, Gene had an incredibly complicated scheme based on the Letelier investigation. Letelier, ex-ambassador from Chile, had been assassinated in downtown D.C. U.S. Justice Department investigators traced the bombers to Chile and managed to extradite them, even though the killers worked for the Chilean Secret Police. Along the way they brought about the downfall of the colonel who ran the secret police. As a result, the one person who could frighten a South American diplomat-criminal was a Justice

Department Investigator. The case, Gene assured me, was an absolute legend from the Rio Grande south.

"What this case needs," I said, "is a blonde and a slug from a .45. That's all these guys understand."

"What's wrong with this business," Gene bitched, "is no innovation, no elegance, no creativity. I bet you even want to use Franco Polatrano."

"Whatsamatta wid Franco?" I said.

"Wassamatta wid Franco is he talksalike dis. If Franco haddanuf taste to gedda silka suit, he could maybe qualify to be an extra ina *Gonfadder Tree*, ya unnerstan'?"

"That," I said, "is not necessarily a bad thing."

Gene got Whitney, five feet ten of ash-blonde refeened hooker—think D.A.R. with cleavage—at the bargain rate of $350 a night, based on the promise that she would only have to act. She normally made far more, but at the moment she had a minor infection and the dentist was doing some work on her gums, so promises were all that she could deliver in good conscience, which is something she had, and we were the only ones around willing to pay for just promises.

The .45 I already had.

The first night we followed deVega, he had company and stayed with them. The second night, he went out alone. When he went into a Georgetown restaurant, Gene and Whitney followed him in. A fair tip to the host got them a table close to Hencio's.

Gene is the kind of guy who does not waste. He waited until he had finished his entrée before he staged the quarrel.

"You've seen a lot of Anton lately," he said.

"Oh, Gene, don't be silly, you know there's nothing between us."

"There used to be," he muttered darkly.

"That was so, so long ago."

"You call six months a long time!"

"Nine months, darling, at least nine."

"You've been seeing him again. I can tell."

"Gene, I swear to you . . ."

"Whenever you see one of those dark Latin types, you

just have to spread your little white legs, don't you . . . don't you!''

"Stop it, Gene," she whispered. "People can hear you."

"Let 'em," Gene announced. "I'm not the slut."

"You really are a bastard, aren't you?" she said with her head down, hand twisting the napkin and a sniffle.

"That's us, baby, the bastard and the whore."

"Gene, take me home," she said with repressed sobs.

"What," was the reply, slow and vicious, "and get another dose of the clap?"

At that point, Whitney, with a ladylike little gasp, gave Gene a slap as realistic as the accusation. Gene slapped her back. DeVega rose on cue to defend the lady's honor.

"A man who hits a woman is no man at all!"

"Oh yeah!" Gene stood up and faced him. "I'll tell you what, you wan' her, you take her. Why not, everyone else has." Which was his exit line.

"Can I help you?" the horny deVega said to Whitney anxiously. "That was terrible. A disgrace."

"No, no," she sniffled, "just leave me alone."

The waiter had seen Gene storm out. As in many restaurants the waiter was responsible for the bill. He panicked, moderately and decorously. The check immediately appeared under Whitney's nose. On the verge of tears, she went to her purse, which, as planned, was empty. She began to search frantically. DeVega went up like a trout for a fly and snatched the bill.

"I will take this," he snapped at the waiter. "Can't you see the lady is upset? Get her a brandy."

Whitney's bottom swayed as she led deVega upstairs to the chic little Georgetown flat that Gene had sublet for a week. That easy roll shoved what was left of deVega's brains down behind his zipper. She opened the door. He stepped in. She stepped out and closed it with him inside.

Franco sat in an easy chair. Dark glasses, white silk tie, dark shirt, the flashiest silk suit we could find on short notice and a Colt Magnum. The gun had a silencer attached, making it look even bigger than Dirty Harry's.

Gene stepped out from the kitchen. He held a silenced .45. I followed. Compared to Franco, both my suit and gun were models of taste and restraint. Unfortunately the same could not be said about my tie.

"Is dissa de one?" Gene said through half a lip.

Gene did not like to stereotype Italians. But I had impressed upon him that stereotypes are easier for people to understand and that there is clarity in clichés.

I nodded and walked up to deVega. I hit him on the side of the head, hard, with the barrel of my .45. It was a cliché, but the point was not to confuse deVega with original thinking. Simple approaches elicit simple responses. Also, I enjoyed it.

"OK, kid," Gene said, "we'll take careit."

"Gino, I wanna piece a this mutha."

"Kid, ya uncle Vincen' saysa he don' wan you to do the deed, ya know, jus' leave ita us."

"What do you want?" deVega said.

I hit him with a cliché, in the solar plexus. He bent double, gasping for air. I gestured to Franco who rose with implacable and silent gravity. He crossed the room, silent and solid as death, until he stood in front of deVega.

"I have diplomatic status," deVega gasped. "My government . . ."

Franco's backhand came with no warning and smashed deVega to the floor. Franco smiled and straightened his silk cuff. He scared the hell out of me, and I was reasonably certain it was just an act.

I knelt down and put my gun to deVega's ear. Franco jabbed his silencer into deVega's balls.

"What the fuck is your interest in Edgar Wood?"

"I don't know who you are talking about."

"Hencio," I said, "you will be much happier if you do know." He didn't answer, so I explained. "Hencio, Franco is gonna shoot your balls off."

"You can't do this," he said.

Franco fired.

The bullet was a blank. But a blank contains powder and

some form of wadding, frequently wax, to hold the propellent in place. Even the wax, had it hit the genitalia directly, would, with that much force, have done serious damage. Franco was a careful man and it did not. But it did tear through deVega's clothes and rip some skin from his inner thigh, and the hot escaping gases from the gun barrel flowed like flame, searing the spot.

DeVega screamed. His urine rushed out and flowed on the floor. His hands grabbed for his crotch.

"Talk to me, Hencio," soft and weary.

"I di'n' hurt you, don' hurt me, please."

"Talk to me, tell me about Edgar Wood."

"I di'n' hurt you, I just' try to warn you."

I slapped his face.

"We were afraid he would talk."

"About what?"

"Who are you?" he pleaded.

"We're the people you don't fuck with, fuckface. Now, before I get bored and let Franco do what he came for."

"It's about what we did with Charles Goreman."

At last. There it was. "What?" I asked.

"It was a big deal, *mucho, mucho grande*, the biggest trading I have ever seen."

"Tell me about it, all of it."

"I could lose my job."

"Fuck your job, think about your life."

"If my government knew, I would not last ten minutes."

"Knew about what, you stupid fuck, stop stalling. What the fuck did you do?"

"We didn't do nothing . . . nothing. Goreman did it all. We just went along. I don't mean even went along, we didn't. We found out about it after, but we couldn't do nothing about it."

"You got a piece of the action, didn't you?"

"No, no, I swear," he said, but Franco jammed his gun into deVega's balls. "*Sí, sí*, yes, but not much."

"How much?"

"Just a hundred thousand. What is that? That is nothing on a thirty-eight-million-dollar deal."

"Tell me, Hencio, confession is good for the soul," I said. It was about the biggest coke deal I had ever heard of. And his numbers were wholesale, not the numbers D.A.s use, based on price per gram, after it has gone from ton, to kilo, to pound, to ounce, stepped on each step of the way.

"If I tell you, you will let me go? And you will not tell my government?"

"Hencio. You are an asshole. As long as you keep talking you are alive. If I like what you say, then you might stay alive. But if I hear one more fucking word of stalling from you, Franco is gonna shoot your dick off."

"OK, OK," he whined, "It was in '76. The summer of '76, and Charlie Goreman come to us, when the big freeze hit Brazil. You remember that, don't you?"

Of course I didn't.

"The price at that point was around eighty, sometimes seventy-nine, sometimes eighty-one, but no higher than eighty-two. And Charlie thinks, right away, that the price is gonna go up. Way up. Right through the rooftops he says. He wants to go long and thinks we should join him for the ride. That makes sense. So we put up ten million dollars and Charlie, I think, also puts up ten million, and away we go. He was right. Coffee takes off."

"Coffee."

"Sí. Coffee, what else."

I looked at Gene, which was a mistake. He was biting his lip and shaking with suppressed laughter. When our eyes caught, there was no holding it in and we cracked up.

Hencio was totally bewildered. Franco was Franco, stone-faced, implacable.

"Oh shit, go on, Hencio, tell us the rest," I said between giggles.

"Whatsammatta, whatsammatta, you laugh?"

"Just tell it," Franco said for me.

"OK. I'll go on. Coffee goes up over a dollar a pound, then one dollar and fifty cents. Then two dollars. Who would have conceived such a thing in '76? Nobody but Charles Goreman. At two dollars fifty, my government gets very nervous. It is crazy. The bottom has to fall out, they all say. Goreman says, 'No. It will keep rising.'

"But those stupid *maricones*," he said, still frustrated after all the years, "they don't believe Charles Goreman. They order me to order him to take us out. We started at eighty-two cents. At two dollars and fifty cents, splitting the profit, we have made eight point four million, net.

"Goreman says, 'OK, I will take you out.' But he is sure the market is going up. He stays in. With his money. And with our money. The market tops out at three dollars and forty cents. I think he got out, actually a little earlier, around three dollars and thirty-two cents. An extra profit of eight point two million. And just as if he had done what he was instructed, he credits us only with the first eight point four, and keeps the difference."

"Is that it?" I asked.

"No!" he said in outrage. "It happens all over again."

"On the way down," I guessed.

"*Sí*. Yes. He says the market will take the nose dive. I recommend very strongly that we listen to this man who has been so right and that we go short with everything, eighteen point four million."

"And Goreman," I said, catching on, "also went in with the eight million he didn't mention, plus his legit share."

"*Sí*. A total of about thirty-five million. It goes back down to two hundred cents, and my government, they get frightened and say to stop. Goreman says 'down, it's going down.' If he says it, I believe him, but I must obey orders. I tell him 'take us out.' He says 'OK,' but he keeps us in. It went all the way down to one hundred sixty cents. Once again I am guessing. Goreman rode it down to about one hundred sixty-eight cents, a penny less or more."

"So what happened?" I asked. "Did he pay?"

"Sure he paid. But only what it would have been if he had followed instructions. Twenty-one million eight hundred forty thousand dollars, that's the original ten plus half the profit. That is very good, eleven point eight million profit on ten million. But Mr. Goreman made thirty-two million three hundred thousand, net, on our ten million."

"How did you find out?"

"Commodities is a small community, like politics. I heard that Goreman's net was much, much higher than my figures."

"So you tried to shake him down," I said.

"I went to New York City to discuss the problem."

"Sure, what did you say?"

"I warned him that I would inform my government and the agencies of regulation in the United States. There would be an investigation and a lawsuit."

"What did Goreman say?"

"He said, 'I do not give a good goddamn what you do. I am closer to your government than you are.' He said that I would end up the scapegoat, I would end up barefoot, picking coffee beans and stepping in burro shit."

I laughed.

"Then I told him he must take this seriously. The Latin peoples are tired of being ripped off by Yankees and the *communistas* would make good propaganda from it."

"And?"

"He was not shaken. 'I do not care,' he said, 'if it brings down the whole damn country. And you know what, if it does you will still be the one walking barefoot in burro shit.' But then he smiles. He says, 'Hencio, you talked your government into this,' which is very true. 'And everyone did very well, except you. That is not right,' he said, and the next day he gave me one hundred thousand dollars in cash."

"You're lying," I told him. Franco cocked his gun.

"Yes, it was two hundred thousand dollars."

"Did Edgar Wood know about this?"

"I do not know."

"Is that why you were bugging his place?"

"*Sí*. Yes. That is why."

"Did he talk about this deal?"

"No."

"But you were afraid he would. And that's why you killed him."

"No. No."

"You killed him. Didn't you Hencio? So you wouldn't have to walk in burro shit."

"No. We did not," he whined.

"Tell the truth, you lying little fuck. If you hadn't done it, I would have had to. So if you did the job, you did me a favor and you can clean up and go home."

"I . . . I didn't do it. We were very surprised. This is the truth. *La verdad*."

"Sure," I shrugged. "He's yours," I said to Franco. "Give it fifteen minutes so I can make sure I'm seen somewhere else."

"*Señor*, mister, please. Please. I did nothing to harm you."

"You lied to me, Hencio."

"No. I told you it all, everything as it was."

"OK, get out of here."

"What?" Hencio said.

"Out, get the fuck out of here," I yelled at him. He was too out of it to move. Franco grabbed him by the collar and heaved him up. Gene held the door open. Franco threw him out.

"How are we gonna get the piss out of the carpet?" I asked Gene.

"Don't worry about it, I'll call a cleaning service."

"Right," I said. "Don't forget to mark up the bill."

"I won't," he reassured me.

"There's something else," I said. "Do you know any reporters who like to make fun of cops?"

"All of them," he said.

"I'm serious. I have this story about this crazy cop, out in Virginia, who's running all over the county looking for a lightning-struck tree by a babbling brook."

12

TRADING UP

WE FENCED FOR the better part of two hours, consuming the remains of the original bottle and cracking open a second one before Mel Brodsky and I came to an agreement to trade what I knew for what he had.

I had nothing to lose. He had two small children upstairs, who, without knowing it, were depending on Daddy to keep his job. So I asked him why he would do it at all.

"You know what they say, they say that when the SEC goes to court, it's amateur hour."

"That bothers you?" I asked.

"The thing is, they're right. So I want to get Over & East, show them a thing or two, and I'll do most anything to do it."

"And then what?"

He looked at me as if the point were obvious. "Why then, one of the pro scouts will notice me. They will pick up my contract and I will get to play in the majors, for Douglas, Cohen, or Choate, Winkler. I want to play pro law."

He had given his word that if I showed him mine, he would show me his, so I told him what Hencio deVega told me. My personal opinion was that what Goreman had done was more admirable than actionable, but I'm a law-school dropout, and while Mel was hardly ecstatic he thought he had something to chew on.

"Coffee is on," he told me. "I made a whole pot. If you get sleepy, the couch opens up."

"What are you mumbling about?"

"I said you could read the transcripts. I did not say you could take them out. You can make notes, but you can't make copies. You read them here."

"Oh shit," I said.

"You can stay every night, for as long as it takes," he offered generously.

"Oh shit," I said.

He and Priscilla went upstairs to bed. I poured a cup of coffee. It was good. Fresh ground, 100 percent Colombian. There was a pretty little porcelain pitcher and sugar bowl all laid out for me. The pitcher held real cream—100 percent Cow. It was good.

The testimony was not. It was in its raw form, rambling, angry, vindictive, steeped in envy.

It started in 1954. Charles Goreman was a hot young commodities trader, ex-shoe salesman, college dropout, ex-brokerage gofer, with his English still moving from broken to just heavily accented. Edgar Wood was already his attorney.

Samson Construction was a family-owned business in Suffolk County, the eastern end of Long Island. During the war they had grown fat on military contracts. In the postwar years the action shifted to the state and county levels, where their hooks were not as good. They did have one big contract, to refurbish and expand an army air force facility. They had invested heavily in the project, including buying the real estate around the base with the intent of selling part to the government for expansion and developing the rest as housing for the off-base personnel.

Congress cut the project out of the '55 appropriations, a victim of interservice rivalry. Samson was in big trouble.

Like one of the sharks that cruise off Montauk Point, Goreman scented blood. Samson was looking to sell before they went belly-up. They were asking $6 million. Goreman felt the true valuation was closer to $8 million if someone were willing to gut the company for its assets instead of running it. He offered $5 million.

Not that he had that kind of money, or anything remotely like it. He had about $200,000. Barely enough for attorney's fees, closing costs and the like.

He had what was then a radical idea. The collateral for the loan would be the company he was borrowing the money to buy.

It made sense if the new owner was willing to gut the company. The real estate alone was worth the asking price; if all the assets were sold, at least a minimum profit was assured. Goreman pointed out that while the current management might be willing to run the thing into bankruptcy, selling and mortgaging the assets bit by bit in an effort to keep afloat, he would, if necessary, quickly and cleanly bleed the company dry for the cash value of its assets. The banks that Samson was into liked the idea.

But the logic of bureaucracy is to not do anything new. And by and large banks would far prefer to make bad loans to established companies than good loans to an unknown. Particularly when the loan applicant has no background in construction, real estate or running any sort of company whatsoever.

The official version is that Charlie convinced them of his good intentions and converted them with dollars-and-cents arguments. The Edgar Wood version is that Goreman offered options on Samson property to two senior bank officers. The estimated value of the land under option was $50,000. The option price was $1,000 against a purchase of $25,000. Goreman, according to Wood, even advanced the $2,000.

Later, when the deal did go through, Samson Construction, now owned by Goreman, bought back the land at $50K. The only money that actually changed hands was $25K to each officer.

It was not yet Over & East. But Charles Goreman had his first company. The pattern was set. The saga of pillage and loot, raid, takeover and eat, had begun.

Goreman bought the abandoned army facility for another $400,000 from the government. He packaged it with the land around it and offered the whole thing to Bussman Aircraft, which was looking for a test field for its new generation of jet aircraft. Bussman paid $1,720,000 for the package. The net, after Samson's pre-Goreman costs were included, was about $300,000. But the gravy was the contract to do the expansion and building work for Bussman.

He sold off two major parcels elsewhere to competitors of Levitt who were building imitation Levittowns. But while those deals were being put in place, they were desperate for cash flow. The solution, according to Wood, was Wood's.

Instead of selling the inventory wholesale, they threw up a couple of brightly painted sheds, rented some colored flags and streamers, and went retail at discount prices. The move coincided with the second wave of the great postwar flight from the cities and the boom in home improvement. It was a cash machine. In the short run, it was cash flow; in the long run, it became Samson Home Improvements & Hardware, the number-three chain of its kind in the country.

By the time Samson Construction was renamed Over & East, it had two operating divisions, construction and retail sales, and $4 million in cash.

The cash was not going to stay around very long. It was as if Goreman hated the stuff, except as leverage. His theory was to borrow, borrow, borrow, that since inflation would outstrip interest—which it did through the seventies—the more you owed, the richer you were. It's an idea that apparently works only with sums over $10 million, not with real money. Also, since companies that kept cash around always were targets for him, he assumed that if he kept cash around, he would be a target for someone else.

It was, in a funny way, exciting reading. Like finding out how Napoleon got to be a general in the first place. But the crime, commercial bribery, was thirty years old, beyond proof, and beyond caring.

Mel urged Wood to get current. Wood replied, "Goreman was rotten from the start. Before I'm done it'll be a decaying fucking corpse, and everyone will see how rotten and reeking it is. I want you to see him for what he is. The American Dream, kiss my ass."

"Edgar," Mel said, and I imagined the patience in his voice, "the point is to get something I can prosecute with."

According to Wood, Goreman's relations with the banks continued to be improper. Certainly they supported him generously and completely all the way down the line. Also they made personal loans, below prime, to the inner circle of Over & East. Including Wood.

Mel kept pushing for names and dates and numbers. Wood came through with them, slowly. Still, Over & East was a good customer. They borrowed a lot, in huge chunks; they always paid, mostly on time. If a bank wanted to treat the officers right, the smell was no worse than fertilizer around roses. They were a better risk than Brazil, Poland or Cleveland.

Then the name Michele Sindona came up.

A name synonymous with corporate corruption, the banks, the government, the Church, the Mafia, all tied in one big sloppy web.

How rotten was he really? So rotten that when Maurice Stans was seeking cash contributions for C.R.E.E.P., he turned down a million dollars from Sindona. Even Richard Nixon did not want to be associated with him.

Famous as "The Vatican Banker," he came to the U.S. and bought the Franklin National just in time to oversee the biggest bank failure in U.S. history.

What probably killed the Franklin was a law, sponsored by Nelson Rockefeller, then governor of New York, that allowed big banks, like the Chase owned by his brother David, to expand geographically. Suddenly the neighborhood bank had a branch of a giant as a competitor, often across the street.

While it was true that the Franklin might have sunk with anyone at the helm, it is unlikely that many others would have embezzled $45 million and committed quite as many acts of bank fraud on the way down. Nor would most bank presidents have the imagination to kidnap themselves to avoid testifying.

Goreman had done business with Sindona. Even after the collapse of the Franklin, even after the indictments.

The strangest thing about the story that Wood told Brodsky was that it made Sindona—corrupter of governments, a man who conned popes, connected to both American and Sicilian crime organizations—look like a sucker. There was a very complicated swap. I had to re-read the testimony three times, backward and forward, before I got the sense of what happened.

Over & East owned Arco-Rich, a brokerage firm that was failing rapidly. It had cost $12 million. On the open market, at the time of the swap, it would have brought $5 million, tops. Goreman gave it to Sindona in return for shares in Società Generale Immobiliare worth $5.9 million at par and a Greek resort. It was no secret that Sindona's S.G.I., the largest real estate and construction company in Italy, was a gasp and a half from bankruptcy, and that market value was much lower than par. The Greek resort was also on the verge of bankruptcy. On the face of it it was trash for trash.

However, the Greek properties could be carried on the books at a valuation of $12 million. The actual worth was difficult to determine and impossible to verify. The Greek government, at that time under the Colonels, was in the midst of a drive for foreign investment. They were more than happy to overvalue the property and, in addition, offered Over & East various tax breaks. Over & East used the corporation formed to handle the Greek properties to sell its shares of S.G.I., which they did immediately. It was a tax-avoidance scheme; an overseas subsidiary selling overseas assets overseas. That was only necessary because what was an actual loss was disguised as a better than break-even operation by the inflated valuation of the Greek properties.

It was with pride that I realized I had figured that out at 5:08 in the morning. But it was hubris to stretch out on the couch to read the next segment, and I awoke to the vicious clatter of merry children. My head hurt, my feet stank and the homey smell of frying bacon brought acid from my stomach to my throat.

I begged Mel to let me take the transcripts and read them on a normal human's schedule. He was adamant, which was forgivable. He was cheerful about it, which was not.

At the motel, I showered and shaved. I called Detective Sergeant Bill Tillman to tell him what I had found and to see if he had come up with anything.

"Tony, we have trouble," he said as soon as he heard my voice. That sounded interesting, so I responded with a grunt of inquiry.

"That reporter you sent out here." Reporter? I sent? "I don't know if she's the right person for this. That psychic gave her a reading and told her she was gonna win the Pulitzer because her mind was more open than most and could see the value in things that most people rejected out of hand. I think she's falling for it."

While he spoke, my brain pretended to think. It came to me that I had spoken to Gene about it. He must have done something about it. Which meant he was going to bill me for it. And how was that going to go into the expense report: $250 (nothing Gene did ever seemed to cost less) to con reporter into doing story on psychic?

"Did you go up to the farmhouse, Bill?"

"Do you think she could be just acting like she's been conned so those nuts will be more open with her?"

"And the microphone, did you check it out?"

"Of course I did. Hey, you will not believe who it belongs to. Or belonged to, because they claim they lost it."

"OK, Bill, who?"

"The DEA!" he announced. It made sense. Why should the Colombians buy the equipment when there was so much of it around them from the Drug Enforcement Agency? With a gun pressed to his groin, Hencio deVega could probably

delineate the equipment transfer in detail. I explained all that
to Tillman.

"Thanks for telling me," he said. "How do you think I
should handle this reporter of yours?"

"Handling the media is a delicate thing, Bill."

"I know, Tony, I know."

"Just stick to the facts, dates, man-hours, manpower as-
signments, and hope for the best. Hang tough."

"I'm gonna do that. Thanks," he said.

I very much wanted to sleep. To trade day for night. I did
hated calisthenics and swam in the motel pool, but when I
lay down I kept mixing thoughts and dreams. Edgar Wood
in prison, and me there too, watching the rape of a young
boy. The boy tried to scream, but every time he did, they
punched his face and kept banging away from behind. Then
they came after Edgar. When they grabbed him and pulled
him down he turned to look at me. He cried for help. When
they tore his pants off his mask came off too, and it was
Christina.

I didn't want to dream that. I made myself awaken.

She was pretty, but if it was pretty I wanted all I had to do
was stand on the corner, Fifty-seventh and Fifth, or look in
on the aerobics class at the club, or go back to Clara Barton
High in Brooklyn and watch the Puerto Rican girls flash by.
I had too much to lose to trade it in on a tastier orgasm.

Lear jets were zipping down to the islands. Over & East
executives rode down with mistress-secretaries to hotels the
corporation owned. Everyone flying, eating, drinking,
screwing at company expense. Wood went on at length about
who did how much on Over & East money. The stockholders' money, he pointed out virtuously. And who they did it
with, and even specifically noted preferred sexual practices.
There was one vice-president who was convinced that anal
sex did not constitute infidelity. Later, apparently, his wife's
attorney invalidated that conceptual model.

Even skimming, it took another night to get the gist of that
hunk of gossip, and I resented the triviality of it all.

There was no scale to Wood's indignation and no perspective in his accusations. He sounded the same talking about sex in the office as he did when he spoke about political corruption, which he finally got to in his third week of testimony and my third night of reading.

The Over & East fleets, ground and air, had been put at the disposal of Stephen Caldwell, a big-time New Jersey contractor and, at the time Wood was speaking of, brother-in-law of the governor. Caldwell's use of the fleets coincided with campaign season.

Over & East also used Caldwell as their prime contractor in New Jersey. Several of the jobs, also coincidental with campaign season, were, according to Wood, overpriced to the tune of 300-400 percent, an estimated $5 million in overspending. Money that was intended, Wood said, to find its way to political figures throughout the state.

The results indicated that it had. Various municipalities, as well as the state, did Over & East some substantial favors. Zoning variances. Roads built and rail service improved when they led to O&E facilities. Jersey had a tax-abatement program designed to lure new industry. It was applied twice in favor of Over & East when they simply took over and reorganized existing companies. Exemptions were granted in dumping and clean-air ordinances.

It was a tale I read with mounting excitement. Hot stuff. Prison-sentence and vote-the-bastards-out-of-office stuff, even in New Jersey where four of the five mayoral candidates in the last Newark primary were under indictment even as they ran.

Mel confirmed my immediate reaction over the squall of breakfast children. It was indeed, he agreed, hot stuff.

So hot, Mel said, that Caldwell had already done time for it. As had several executives of the Over & East subsidiary, John's River Chemical and Refining, Inc.

Charles Goreman, speaking through his attorney, Edgar Wood, had expressed deep shock and dismay. Everyone in a position of authority at John's River had been dismissed or transferred. A special letter of apology and explanation was sent to every stockholder. At the next meeting the stockholders voted a special memo of appreciation to Charles Gore-man for responding so responsibly and promptly to the mess.

"What a load of crap," I said. "He sold you a bill of goods."

"We only had him for three weeks, dammit," Mel said. "Wood was at the center. He knew it all. He was spilling it, slowly, sure, but he was spilling it. We just lost him too soon."

"Brodsky, you know what occurs to me. What occurs to me is that Charles Goreman is a very smart man. Slick, tricky, sails close to the wind. And that is all. Edgar Wood was a very angry person who made a lot of threats, which were promises he couldn't keep. That happens when people get upset. For instance, there are people who have said they were going to blow me away, and here I am. And then, it occurs to me, a couple of dumbshit half-amateur car thieves got caught in the act, and they bopped Edgar Wood a little too hard. That all occurs to me."

13

A BODY OF WATER

I WENT FROM Brodsky, to National, to LaGuardia, to a pay phone and, when she said "come over," to Christina Wood's apartment.

"So far," I had to tell her, "there is nothing."

"I want you to, I need you to go on looking. Please."

"Of course I will, if you want me. . . . I want to go back over some things about your father. Now, you told me you weren't here at the trial. Were you here when he was arrested?"

"Can we take a walk? Or go out for a cup of coffee?"

We headed west. I got her to laugh by telling her about Mel Brodsky, acid king of the SEC. Crossing Sixth Avenue, she took my arm. The casual intersection of limbs seemed to curl through my whole body.

"Were you here when your father was arrested?" I asked again.

"Yes, yes, I was," she said like an admission of something.

"What did he say? How did he react?"

"He said, said it was nothing, nothing serious. He said

99

they couldn't prove anything and it would be over very quickly.''

"Is that all he said?" She let go of my arm. It left a void. Its absence filled me with desire.

"That's all he said to me and my . . . mother."

"Go on. You heard him say something to someone else."

"On the phone. I heard him on the phone. He was talking to one of his attorneys, I think. He was cursing a lot. Every other word was 'fucking,' and I'll try to remember what he said, but I'll leave that out."

"Sure, I can visualize it." It would have sounded like a great deal of the transcript.

"He said it was a personal and vindictive thing. That the other partners resented him because he was an upstart, he wasn't part of their little club. If, if it had been anyone else, he said—and that was the first time I realized he was guilty, that Daddy was a thief—they would have kept it very quiet and certainly they would have had the bare minimum of courtesy to come and talk to him first."

"Did you ever talk to him about it?"

She moved away from me. Then, after a long pause, moved back and answered, "I tried."

"What happened?"

" 'My dear daughter,' " she mimicked him, angry about it, " 'you don't have to concern yourself with this matter. It's just smoke, and where there is smoke there is not always fire,' and I knew that there was. But I didn't . . . he didn't let me talk to him."

"You called Charles Goreman 'Uncle Charlie.' You were close to him? He was close to the family?"

"At my sweet sixteen," and it was clearly a memory she was fond of, "Charlie gave me a fur coat. He was very sweet. He said, 'Now dat you are a grown-up woman you must have a grown-up woman's coat.' It was Russian sable. I was quite careful not to find out how much it cost. That way I could say to my girl friends, 'Of course I don't know how much it cost, it was a gift from a man.' "

"Your father seemed to have resented Goreman a lot, at least at the end. Did that have anything to do with it?"

"What?"

"Things like giving you a fur coat."

"No," she said nervously.

"Did he always resent Goreman?"

"In a way, thinking back, I guess he did," she said thoughtfully. "Daddy was very status conscious. There were clubs that invited Charlie in that wouldn't even speak to my father. Charlie spoke to presidents and kings. He made deals with entire countries and with the heads of companies that were bigger than some of those countries. And if Daddy got to speak to those people at all, they spoke to him like a . . . flunky. No, not that, but like a functionary."

We were at West Street, where the West Side Highway was until it fell down, six lanes of overanxious traffic. The sign said "Don't Walk," but there was a fragment of green left on the light. We looked at each other, grasped hands and ran for it.

Laughing and gasping, we beat the bestial charge of the cars and trucks and walked out onto the Morton Street pier.

Gay couples passed us hand in hand and with arms around each other. Single men sat, gazing at the wide, wide river, dreaming reams of sailors. A queen drifted past, looked me over, gazed at Christina with disdain and sniffed. We were the last heterosexuals.

"You don't have to do this out of guilt," I told her.

"Is that what you think?"

"I have no real way of knowing. I'm just telling you that you don't have to."

"Do you want to drop it? Is that what you're saying? Are you saying you want to give it up?"

"No. I just have to let you know the real status of things. It's your money, and you have to know how it's being spent."

"I don't care about the money, there's plenty," she said carelessly. "And if it turns out that he was killed by a car thief, as everyone thinks, I will accept that. I just want to know for sure. As long as it is proved and I know."

"I will do all I can," I promised.

We were at the end of the pier. The sun was riding down from its apex and clouds were coming up from the west to meet it. As they began to touch, color tinged the smog over New Jersey and it promised a lavish sunset.

"I don't know anything about you," she said. "You look like there's a woman in your life."

"Yes. Yeah, there is." I looked at the river and away from her. I did not want to see the way that she had been looking at me change when she had the facts.

"Tell me about it."

I turned toward her. Our eyes met, hers sea-green and looking up at me, and yes, it was all there. The poem in my head, the tension in her room, the look that I had seen the very first time and consigned to delusion—they were not projections of desire. They were manifestations of desire. It was all of whatever there is, and both of us knew it.

I stared into her eyes. My hand reached up and touched her cheek.

Passion lies sleeping like a dog in a kennel. Then there are fences, collars and leashes, so that even when the bitch wakes up she won't have her freedom. Later on, after the investigation, the accusations, the recriminations, still, no one knows who left the gate unlocked.

My voice was thin and hoarse when I spoke. "Does it matter?"

"I don't think so."

She turned her head so her lips nestled into my palm. They were moist, they were open and they kissed me. There was a sound unheard, a cry, and I lifted her mouth to mine. We came to each other so that every queen on the pier envied the royalty of our lust and the purity of my erection. We walked back to her apartment, to her bed, kissing on corners in full oblivion, gazing moonstruck, our bodies liquid and poured together, for all the honest world to see.

The door closed behind us. Breasts and buttocks, shoulders and thighs, eyes, thighs, penises, ankles, loins and finger joints are all day long such ordinary things, like fried eggs, shoes and doors. Then a moment comes when the days are torn off and the weight of a woman's breast, the fatness of the moon in autumn, the laugh of a fool, are as fresh and awe-inspiring as the moment you realized the bullet missed.

I wanted to recite poems. Once poets were dangerous men. Leading to war and insurrection, opening the seraglios of forbidden beds and unmentionable desire, taunting and arousing whatever gods their times had. Now the poets, it seems, are declawed and defanged, as good as gone.

But we still have rock 'n' roll.

The way was open. We both made sounds as I entered. We both reached down, deep into hunger, and yielded. We began the beginning of the end. It was a warm and liquid place, full of rhythms, we began to forget that it's only rock 'n' roll, and there was a ballad, ancient and tender, somewhere above the pounding Afro-percussion.

Fuck cannot be that good. Fuck can't be so full of wonder. When it's not bits and pieces of physiology, when your fingertips are as urgent as a cock, hands as clinging as a cunt, and your eyes seek each other as violently as your hips, then what is it? The word love floats in, but that just can't be.

When the first group of orgasms ebbed, I lifted the upper part of my body from hers and looked down into her eyes. We were wet and sweet with sweat; stray hairs clung to her moist forehead and I brushed them away.

"Can you stay the night?" she asked.

"Yes," I said. I had not called ahead to say home will be the sailor, and this one night could be lost in the slipstream of the shuttle.

Wordless, when the second group of orgasms ebbed, we clung to each other, still wordless. You can fuck on the first date, but you can't say "I love you," and each time I ambled through the catalog in my mind for a phrase, that was pretty much it. If glances were words, if touches were words, the style of giving and taking were words, and they are, then they pretty well covered it.

The clouds that had been forming in the west did not come in. The night was clear, and we stood at the window with a bright moon watching us. Close, light kisses hovered around the edge of sex. She slid to her knees looking at my body as if she thought it was the kind of miracle that I knew hers to be.

When I was young and first loving women, there was one moment that thrilled me above all. It was not a physical moment. Not when I would first touch the lips of a vulva and find them wet, or a clitoris and find it erectile responsive, or the ritual of making bodies naked for each other. It came earlier, fully dressed, most often with a close-held kiss. The moment of yielding. The moment when resistance was gone, the tension melted, and I would actually feel the girl's whole body become soft, her body letting her be mine. The moment when all her struggling "no" turned to "yes," to yielding.

It is a moment that has disappeared from my adult sexual experience. Possibly because times have changed and sex is no longer a contest of the male "yea" and female "nay." Yielding has been replaced by mutual agreement, by the consent between consenting adults, brittle and pallid.

Christina touched that adolescent place where sexual feeling is formed. The fantasyland inside met the reality before me as she found a way to give me that gift of her yielding. All of me pulsed with the heat of the blood that swelled me hard. The tools of sex are part of the body; sex itself is rooted in desire, and desire is a swelling of the mind.

The moonlight came. The hooks of her sexuality sunk into the heart of my desire. She looked up at me. Sea-green eyes soft with tenderness, her cheeks blushed with a faint hint of pink.

"I want you," she said, "to fuck my face."

14

HOME

THERE IS PREPARATION H, aspirin, Alka-Seltzer, Orajel, co-caine, Tylenol, Desenex, morphine, Valium, Brioschi, grass, grain alcohol, Ace bandages, stress-formula vitamins, and Ben-Gay for all the niggling pains that make the walk through life a trudge. Nothing beats infatuation as the all-in-one pain-killer, pick-me-up, body toner and stimulant. I went home with a spring in my step and a light in my eye.

I picked Wayne up from the after-school center early to give him his birthday present, a midget membership at my squash club, complete with an El Cheapo beginner's racket and a group of lessons.

The time would come soon, I thought, when he would also have to learn to fight. When I was growing up the Police Athletic League, the Catholic Youth Center and the YMCA all had boxing programs. I wondered if they still did. Every-thing was becoming karate and kung fu, which would do just as well. It's not the technique that matters. It's learning how to deal in fear, violence and pain, until you're cool enough to stay with your technique while the violence rains around you and rages inside you.

I'm not in love with violence, either way, coming or going. Nor did I want Wayne to be. But taking a blow and not returning it can be a pain far more insidious and long-lasting than a split lip or a cracked rib.

The second time my ribs were cracked was in a prison riot. They were busted by the rifle stock of a guard who was nominally on the same side. But he had reason to hate me and took his opportunity when it came his way. Ribs take a while to heal. So I had to wait for that, and then the opportunity. It took four months. Until the night we met outside his favorite bar, I felt a kind of shame and guilt.

It was something for Glenda and me to argue about, like the issue of public versus private school.

The first time on a squash court can be frustrating and downright bewildering. But Yogi, the tall, goodnatured Sri Lankan pro, made it fun for Wayne. I was grateful for that. After the lesson I got on the court with Yogi and he was merciless. Even though he's good at teaching midgets, playing down that far frustrates him. Then Wayne and I played.

On the subway home, Wayne got very serious.

"I'm not sure I like my name," he said.

"Oh, what's wrong with it?"

"I don' know . . . are people stuck with their names their whole lives, forever and ever?"

"They don't have to be," I said, "but I don't see anything wrong with Wayne."

"Wellll," he weaseled around.

"Come on, well what?"

"Welllll," he hemmed and hawed, "it's not real tough."

"What do you think would be tougher?"

"I don' know."

"Come on, kid, what do you have in mind?"

"I was thinking, maybe Rocco, but that might be too tough."

"Yeah, that's pretty tough. How about Angel? I know a lotta tough guys named Angel." I did. And Jesus.

"Awww, come on, you're making funna me."

"Maybe I'm teasing a little bit. Just a little. Now tell me what you have in mind."

"I'll tell you," he said, "but only if you're serious."

"OK, I'll be serious."

"Promise?"

"I promise. Cross my throat and hope to choke and all of those things," I said.

"Well, Rocco is too tough, you know, so I was thinking, maybe Anthony."

What do you do with that? Ruffle his hair? Give him a hug? Punch him lightly on the upper arm, yeah, that's the tough thing to do.

The Korean fruit stand on our block had a fine display of early summer flowers. I instinctively went to buy a bunch for Glenda, then wondered if I was doing it by way of secret apology. Worse, if she would see it that way. Then I thought, I would have done it anyway, and stopped mind-fucking myself and spent the whole $4.98 with a smile.

Just before we went to the door, Wayne said, "Don't tell Mom, about changing my name. I don't think she's ready for it."

Glenda greeted the returning squash players with hugs and kisses. Mine was a lot sexier, but Wayne didn't mind.

In spite of his workout, Wayne didn't want to finish his dinner; he wanted to rush up to his friend in 26D who had a new video game. He asked, as he did about every fourth day, if we could get a dog. Dogs, he explained, were always glad to finish leftover burgers. I would have liked one also. It was the sole positive association I had with marriage. But not in the city, and probably not until Wayne's intermittent sense of responsibility came in longer bursts. I was drifting into commitment. Irrevocable, householding, even suburban commitment. I wondered if I was afraid of it and if fear had led me down into the valley of heavenly thighs. Maybe I was just intermittent.

In any case, I said, "No."

"Why not?"

" 'Cause I only like big dogs. And a big dog might eat

you up. So we can't get one until you're big enough to fight him off.''

"How big?"

"Very, extremely huge.''

Glenda nodded emphatic agreement. She looked at me with an expression that said, ''That logic should hold him.'' Wayne said a thoughtful, ''Oh,'' as if it did.

"You have been gone a long time,'' Glenda nibbled on my lip when the door slammed behind Wayne. The dishes were going to wait and we waltzed to the bedroom. She ''ummmed'' as I lifted her sweater. She lifted her arms up and I pushed her back on the bed with her arms trapped over her head. She mixed giggles and yums when I nibbled her belly. I attacked her bra and her nipples popped up to say hello.

"It's been too long, I need my piece.''

I moved from her nipples to her lips. Between kisses I said, ''C'mon, you had your vibrator.''

"That's not the same,'' she blushed, ''as having you inside me.''

I knew what pleased her and the items that satisfied her. I did them. Something inside me was aware that I would rather have waited until dinner had settled in my stomach. Which is, I suppose, the difference between infatuation and a relationship.

Later, I went down to pick up milk and coffee for the morning. I called Christina from a pay phone. Our actual dialogue was hesitant and inane. Her voice enveloped and caressed me.

After Wayne went to bed, Glenda asked me about the case.

"I don't know,'' I said. ''It's not there, and it sort of is.''

"There's something going on inside your head. I can feel it,'' Glenda said. ''Do you have a thing for your client?''

"Oh, come on!''

"I suppose she's some hot young number. Wealthy, young, clothes-horsey,'' Glenda teased. And probed. The only reason I was not terrified by her intuition was that she had been equally paranoid when there was no cause.

"How is Sandy these days?"

"I don't know, I didn't see her this trip."

"How could you pass it up? I suppose her tits are as big and gorgeous as ever."

"I don't know," I protested. "The time I did see her I kept my eyes devoutly above her neck and ordered her to wear bulky sweaters."

"If you didn't have such sexy shoulders," Glenda said, "I would have thrown you out a long time ago and let all those evil women devour you."

"You just love me for my body, is that it?"

"Of course. Your character is nothing to boast of. And your manners, I certainly can't take you home to mater."

"You could take your husband home to mater."

"Mater adored my husband. But then, she never went to bed with him."

"Are you suggesting I take your mother to bed, just to create a good impression on your family?"

"She is not your type."

"What is?"

"Big bosomy things like Sandy. Or hot young numbers like Christina Wood."

"What," I said with mounting irritation, "is making you go on like this?"

"I wish I could trust you."

"I don't know what my next step is going to be," I said, offering up a different piece of meat for her to chew on. "I would love to talk to Charles Goreman. But I have to be patient with that. Everything I hear about him is that he's tough and smart, so if I hit on him before I have some kind of opening, he'll just blow me off."

"Couldn't the lawyer, what's his name, Haven, introduce you?"

"Over & East is about the biggest legal meal ticket in New York. So I better have a damn good reason before he will want me to go and upset them."

"You're really concerned about this, or are you just changing the subject?"

"I think maybe it offends me, that there is, I don't know, an upper circle, a rarefied sphere, where crime isn't crime . . . that sounds like something right out of my father's mouth . . . I don't even know if Wood was murdered, with malice aforethought, I mean. But if he was, the wall around it is going to be high and wide, and if I find out whodunit, there's gonna be a high wide wall to keep me from doing anything about it."

She stroked my hair. I stood up and paced, naked.

"Do you know Stew McCarthy?"

She looked blank.

"Judge Paul Stewart McCarthy, the judge who sentenced Wood. The judge who was on my Corrections Department investigation," I explained.

"You liked him," she remembered.

"Yeah, I'll tell you one thing. I understand why he wanted to send Wood up the river. All day long, he sits there. The stupid hopeless junkies, the petty slime, parade through the courtroom with their desperate nickel dime crimes. The law commands us to send them to hell. And make no mistake, Attica is hell. Then comes Edgar Wood. With his money and hotshot lawyers and connections, he is damn sure positive convinced that prison is not the price that he will pay. Prison is just for the slobs, the lumps, the dopes and dopers.

"And the judge," I went on, "who knows what he has been sending them away to, and in spite of everything, feels it. He feels it. He sees Edgar Wood and for the sake of the soul of Judge Paul Stewart McCarthy, McCarthy must send Wood away. Otherwise he is living a lie. Otherwise it's not justice, it's just . . . something else."

"Tony," my woman said, "it's all right."

I stood, silent, as she sat, also silent. Both of use were surprised by the depth of my feeling—the furious puritan I had tried to bury years ago, when I saw the harm and horror that it, like any passion, could cause. I had buried it, and with it guilt, knowing that I had been as guilty as anyone I had put away.

"Why don't you talk to McCarthy?" she said after a while.

"Why?"

"Well, when I was on jury duty, it seemed that a lot went on in court that didn't go into the record. Not just the intonation and the way people looked at other people, but things that were actually said."

"Smart lady," I said, and got back into bed. I snuggled beside her. She turned out the light. I was home and settled into a deep, quiet, dreamless sleep.

15

TAIL

"WHEN DID YOU get back?" Joey D' asked me.

"Yesterday afternoon," I claimed.

"That's not the way I figure it."

"Oh yeah?"

"Yeah. I was talking to Gino, and he thought you must be back, and then you checked out of your motel, day before yesterday. But that wouldn't make me suspicious, and it could all be explained. What nails you, kid, is that shit-eating grin on your face. That only comes from doing fresh stuff."

"Who the fuck do you think you are, my father?"

"Then I'm right," he said.

"Or maybe my mother."

"Tony, you are a stupid shit. I know you. You need some goddamn roots. You ain't no good when all you got to take care of is yourself. When you don't have a home, you go doing every stupid thing that a stupid man can find. I don't want to watch you snort stuff and pop pills, I don't want to go find you in gutters and bail you out."

"You're not my wife, you're not my mama, so fuck off," I yelled at him.

"OK, but I'm gonna say what gotta be said. I'll do it calm, no yelling. I helped you get straight once, or half a dozen times, depending on how you count it. Maybe 'cause your father and me, we were friends. Maybe 'cause I think that when you're not looking for oblivion you're a smart kid and a good partner. But I'm older now. I'm tired. I ain't got the patience to baby-sit no more. You're older now and you should know better."

"OK, I heard you. Now, let me ask you something. Why is it, I get laid, just once, it's supposed to be the end of the world? Since the world began, Joey, when was there a time when guys didn't want something on the side? Back in Sicily, where if you fucked around with a girl, her husband and father would kill you. If you fucked a guy's wife, he would kill everybody. In the Bible, they punished adultery by stoning people to death. So even with that kind of overreaction did you ever once hear of someplace where adultery became extinct? You know when a piece on the side will become extinct? When men and women are born without the parts to do it with," I said with an appropriate gesture.

He laughed. Thank God.

"It's just I like Glenda, and she's good for you, and I don't want you to blow it."

"You know what, I like Glenda too, and I agree with you, she's good for me. Now that group therapy is over, let's pretend this is an office again."

"Sure. By the way, I think you done good down in D.C.; at least you didn't embarrass me and they think you do a good Al Pacino."

I brought him up to date. The thing that pleased him most was the billings we were racking up, courtesy of the Wood estate. Then he asked me to cover a surveillance for him that night. A divorce thing, an easy tail.

"My grandchildren," he explained, "are visiting their grandmother. They're four and five now."

I said that was OK. I called the judge. He couldn't see me till the next day anyway. I called Christina. I talked to her machine. Then my mother called me. I told her I was alive, that Glenda was healthy, that Wayne was larger and learning to play squash. We made a dinner date. Christina called me back. I jumped in a cab.

She was on the phone when I got there. But it started without waiting anyway. When I began to stroke her hair, she arched against me catlike. I bent and kissed her forehead, her cheek, her ears. She put her hand over the phone and offered me the heat of her mouth. Ignition. She stood and leaned her back into me. My arms went around her, and my hands found the flesh of her waist and belly. She said a few strangled things into the phone, hung up and we went to bed.

There have been enough women in my life to have stopped the count sometime back. I've done most of the things that I've conceived while masturbating. And ever since the first, the worst I've had was good. But Christina's sexuality and mine were better custom-cut than her father's Savile Row suits.

In the sweating and sounds that weren't words, I heard a voice say, unexpected and unbidden, "I love you." It was my voice. She held me harder. Her arms clamped around me to force my body into the sink of hers.

Later, in the shower together, she said, "You shouldn't say things like that," with her eyes, her voice, her body contradicting the words. "I'm glad," she said, "that you have someone else. I don't want you to be my problem."

"Sure," I said, and kissed her beneath the spray.

When I left we shuddered like a fabric was being torn, the separation palpable.

Joey D' was waiting for me at Forty-ninth and Madison. He was too sharp not to notice my hair was still damp, but all he said was, "Thanks for covering me, kid," and went off to see his ex-wife, son, daughter-in-law and grandchildren.

Within ten minutes, by four-thirty, the hordes were starting to flow from the towers. I was looking for one rock in the slow rolling landslide, but my subject made it easy, trying to rush a half-pace harder than the rest of the herd. A typical adman type from Doyle, Dane: health-clubbed and tan, yet harried and drawn, with plenty of money that wasn't enough. At least not for what his wife wanted to do to him.

He turned north. He went only half a block and turned into what was once the Arch Diocese of New York and is now a hotel, through the cobbled courtyard, into the vaulted lobby and down the marble steps. He turned left into Harry's Bar. Diocesan wood and leaded glass separate Harry's from the lobby, so I didn't even have to enter to watch.

He sat at the bar, watching the door, watching his watch, trying to slow his drink but rushing it. Then she came in.

She was nothing special. Every head in the bar did not turn, dazzled by her length of leg, flaunt of bosom or swing of butt. But to him, she was the everything. He emerged from anxiety like a butterfly into the sun, and I could see the bar fade away, with it the rest of the world, as they shone for each other.

The shutter of my mini-camera opened and closed silently over the frames of ASA 1000 Kodak color negative, capturing another Kodak moment to remember in court.

He tossed a bill on the bar; they walked out; I followed. They only went as far as the elevators. I got right in with them. I exited after them. Their eyes were only for each other.

When they stopped and embraced in front of the hotel room door, I strolled on as if I had someplace to go. When I heard the door close behind me, I turned around. I found the service closet and stepped in. I opened my briefcase, took out the microphone and recorder. I buried the tape machine in some towels. The microphone, with its tiny suction cup, went on the upper-right-hand corner of the door. The transmitter went on the top of the doorframe, stuck with double-face tape. I went back to the closet, checked if it was all operational and left.

I killed forty-five minutes in Harry's, went up, flipped the cassette, then gave them another forty-five and collected everything. The early evening was warm; the sun slid a shaft onto the steps of St. Patrick's cathedral down the block. I sat on the broad steps of the church and spot-checked the tape.

If there was sufficient dirt, the job was done; if not, I would go back and roll another reel.

The Account Exec was thrilled. He got it up so quickly with her. And it was so nothing limp with his wife. . . . I fast-forwarded, and it turned to a high-pitched squeak in the earphones. . . . And so often! . . . She liked his tongue just there, just there! And slower, slower . . . whack! He liked his ass slapped while he put it to her. . . .

We had him. You gotta pay to play, that's what the wives say. When his wife had stripped him down to his toothbrush and jockey shorts, I wondered if he would lose his tootsie too. It often happens that way. Another job, successfully concluded.

16

JUDGE

His honor Judge Paul Stewart McCarthy let loose a non-judicial pealing laugh when I finished summing up, as coherently as I could, the SEC transcripts of Edgar Wood.

"The thing that's funny," he explained when he was able, "is that if that was all Wood had to show when he came back for resentencing, you know what I would have had to say? . . . Three to five, Attica."

"Did you expect him to come up with more than that?"

"Interesting question. Order us another round and let us cogitate." It was more Jameson's for him, beer for me.

"At the sentencing," he said when he had wet his dry, "the man was extremely upset. Shocked I would say, but then they were all shocked." He chuckled at the memory. "He promised he was going to blow the lid off. Expose the whole filthy crew."

"Do you remember exactly what he said? Exactly?"

He closed his eyes, flipping through the cellular file in his skull. The lids snapped open and he recited, in a monotone, "The whole fucking bunch is as bad as I am. The whole fucking barrel is rotten. Superwasp Choate Haven, that cocksucker Goreman, fuck Culligan, Scott and Shaw . . ." He blinked and paused. "I'm not sure that last trio is right, but I think it is. They're all at Choate, Winkler, Higgiston, etcetera, I think."

"Yeah, they are," I said.

"You know what it is that's a real pity," he said, swallowing more of the Irish. "Today's cursing is of a very low order. It's all simple fucking and cocksucking. Back when I was a lad they would have said Choate Haven, that smug and superior son of Satan, sittin' and sniggerin' in his super clubs, is a low-life, lickspittle scum of an informer who would sell his own dear mother to the Black and Tans for the price of a used roll of asswipe. The decline of the language, even if it is English, is a sad and piteous thing."

"When," I asked, "did you get so Irish?"

"I think maybe I'm trying to escape the reality; it's wearing on me, truly it is."

"What else did Wood actually say?"

"To business. To the point," he complained. "But without the asides, this life would be a desperately dreary thing. . . . Let's see now, did he mention any other names. . . . No. But there were two or three fellows there from Over & East. Klughorn was one. I remember because he testified. And . . . Silly? Sally? Diller, it was. Wood pointed at them and said, 'You fucks are going down with the ship. You won't fuck me up the ass and get away with it.' "

"How did they react?"

"All very 'tsk, tsk,' and proper they were. As if Edgar should have taken it like a man. It never does surprise me when they break down. It always surprises me when they don't. Anyway, it used to surprise me."

"Did you have any reaction at the time? Did Wood say anything that sounded like he had something special on someone? Did anyone react to his threats like they were scared?"

"At the time . . . I thought it could turn into quite the event. Scandal of the year. Particularly with that bunch from

Choate, etcetera. Such a bastion of respectability they are, so lily-pure and snowy-white. What a shame, I thought at the time, that it probably wasn't the lawyers he would tell his tales on, but the corporation. I wasn't so much looking forward to that. You expect scandalous doings from a thing like Over & East. That makes less of a scandal, do you see?"

"That doesn't give me a whole lot to go on," I sighed.

"The lad wants a lead."

"Frankly, Stewart, it is going to be very difficult to investigate them without one. The only thing to do is look for paper, and they've had legions, with warrants, doing that for years. If the IRS with unlimited everything, including desire, can't nail them, how can I?"

"Tony, boyo, I'll say something that will make it even worse. It occurred to me at the time of the trial that if our Mr. Wood really had anything so tremendously hot, he would have used it long before it got so far as sentencing. He would have bought himself a deal with the D.A."

"Shit," I said.

"You know what your problem is?"

"Your Honor, as much as I like and respect you, and you're the only judge in New York I would trust with subway fare, I am sick and tired of people telling me what my problem is."

"You get to taking it personal." He went on as if I hadn't spoken. "And it's not, of course. If you want to find out who did the deed, that's your business, but it's not your life."

"I saw that movie. 'It's not personal, it's just business.' "

"The thing of it is, boyo, that it is. You don't understand that. It's what made you a good cop, and it's what ruined you as a cop. Hell, my boy, I would imagine that you probably fall in love every time you get laid. That is a woman's thinking."

"What is it about me, Your Honor, that makes everyone feel so astute?"

17

PASTA FAZOOL

ONCE UPON A time my father's older brother, Vincent, was my favorite uncle. The one who always drove the new car and came with big presents.

I don't entirely know what happened. My father was a construction worker. Before the war he had been a union organizer; after, a union official. In the fifties the government and the racketeers joined forces to purge the union of leftists. They let my father keep his card, they let him work, but they eliminated him from union politics. More to take up time and save himself from bitterness than to make extra money, my father became a part-time contractor.

Getting together with his brother was a natural. Vincent had the money. He had the contacts. He was doing big business over in Jersey. They went partners in Brooklyn.

Then they quarreled. I don't know what the quarrel was about. I was only eight at the time. Later on, my father would never be explicit about the details. The next time I saw my uncle was at my father's funeral, fifteen years later.

Our next meeting was only one week afterward. I came in with an attitude. My father had wanted nothing to do with

Vincent. They had not spoken from the time of the quarrel to the day my father died, leaving me to assume that Vincent represented all that my father fought, the things he despised.

Then this stranger—and by then he was a stranger to me—assaulted me with emotion over veal picata as if I were the prodigal son and it was I who was returning. He offered to pay for my education. To introduce me to the people who could help me. To guide me through life, now that I was an orphan and had no father to help me. That lunch was the last time, deliberately, that I saw him.

So when I walked into the restaurant with Glenda and Wayne and saw Vincent sitting beside my mother, I was pissed. I was also trapped.

Uncle Vincent rose graciously for the introductions. Taking my hand he said, for me alone, "I hope this doesn't embarrass you."

I shrugged and moved to sit down. He held on.

"I'm getting old, very old, Tony. I wanted to see you."

"OK," I said.

"It's all so long ago. I never meant to quarrel with my brother. You gotta understand that."

"It doesn't matter," I said. "Let's sit down and get it over with."

I kissed my mother—she is entitled to her trespasses—and sat on one side of her. Vincent was too quick for me. He held out a chair for Glenda, an offer she couldn't refuse, which left him sitting beside me.

Wayne whispered to Glenda over the antipasto about how old Vincent looked. Glenda shushed him. That sort of thing affected her sense of propriety the way the sound of a dentist's drill hits my nervous system.

"That's OK," Vincent said. "That's OK. I am an old, old man. Just like you are a young one. Neither one is something to be ashamed of. Right, Tony?"

"How old?" Wayne naturally asked. Glenda was scandalized.

"I'm eighty-three. Pretty good, huh?"

"Wowww!" Wayne was impressed. It took him a while to digest a number that awesome. "Were you before TV?"

"Yes. And before lotsa other things."

"Like what?"

"Video games. Pictures with sound. Computers. Air conditioning. Dishwashers."

"We don't have a dishwasher," Wayne said. "I have to do them."

"A modest exaggeration," Glenda said.

"Did they have baseball? Did they have the Brooklyn Dodgers? Tony saw the Brooklyn Dodgers lots of times," Wayne went on.

"Sure, they had baseball. I remember the very first time I came here, it was 1919; that was the year the World Series was fixed."

"It was broken?" Wayne asked.

"No," the old man said seriously. "The gamblers paid the players on the better team to lose."

"Awhhh, baseball players wouldn't do that," Wayne said, faced with a reality even more cynical than I usually presented.

"Things was tougher back then, Wayne. A lot tougher. That's something even Tony doesn't know, how tough it was. Sports athletes did not make so much money like they do now. Listen to this—you too, Tony, you might learn something. It took me three years, working seven days a week, to get enough money to bring my brother, Tony's father, from Sicily to over here."

When we were on dessert, Uncle Vincent leaned over to me and said, "Tony, look, I know you are not gonna take anything from me. I tried before and you said no. So I don't want to upset you. But I bought a little something for the boy. I would like to give it to him, if I have your permission. Only with your permission."

If there was a way to say no, I couldn't think of it. Could he get Wayne less than the most expensive? A custom-strung Head Graphite. The $120 was pocket change for Vincent. So was the dinner, which I found out was prepaid, so I couldn't even argue about it.

Outside, he grabbed me for a private word again.

"Listen to me, Tony. If there is anything, ever you need, you call me. No strings attached to it, no nothing. You could send me a postcard, you don' even have to speak to me you don' want to. You need help, I help." His hand dug into my shoulder. He kissed me on the cheek. His breath smelled like death sautéed in garlic butter.

Then it was my mother's turn for a last word.

"Listen to me, Tony," she said. "Vincent, he's an old man. He is your family. This thing, you don't talk to him, that's wrong."

"Pop was wrong?"

"I don't say that. I never said that. . . . Tony, are you angry with me?"

"No, Mom, I love you." I gave her a hug and a kiss. Vincent gave her a ride home in his Cadillac.

18

REOPEN

DETECTIVE SERGEANT BILL Tillman called me the next morning.

"I was just thinking of you," I said.

"Don't say things like that, please, now that she's finally gone back to Nutley."

"I'm sorry," I said. "How did that story work out?"

"How did the story work out?" Tillman said. "Let me say this about that. I had the story of the psychic and the policeman mounted, covered in clear acrylic and framed. It is now hanging on my wall. Let me quote something for you; the first sentence reads: 'If you ever want to see a slick con, see the Psychic who promises Pulitzers to reporters, promotions to Police Captains.' . . . So, my friend, I owe you one, and it is now my pleasure and privilege to pay. We got a break in the case."

"I'm on my way."

"What it is, we busted a busboy from the restaurant where Wood ate his last meal. It turns out that two guys came into the place two nights before Wood was killed, asking about him. Now the other thing I'm trying to work on is that DEA,

Colombian thing. That is a bitch. They are both claiming diplomatic immunity.''

"Forget about them. How's tomorrow?"

"Fine," he said. I made flight reservations, then called Christina.

I said "hello," and she said, "I don't think I want to see you anymore."

"What's wrong?"

"It's fine for you. You come over and have a nice time, then you go home to your—to Glenda. And I'm alone. I was doing just fine without you."

The dream of falling, I'm told, is a very common dream. I have it sometimes. I'm standing on the edge of a cliff, or a bridge, or, most often, on the ledge of a roof. Suddenly, what is beneath me is gone. A dream voice tries to scream, but its vocal chords are paralyzed.

"Christina, we are so good together."

"That's what's wrong. You take me up so high. Then I go down so low. If it wasn't so wonderful, it wouldn't matter. It's fine for you, you go home. You belong to someone else, and if I were her, I wouldn't like it."

There was no way I was going to tackle all of that on the telephone.

"Listen to me a second," I said.

"No. I've made up my mind."

"It's about your father; it's about the case."

"What? What is it?"

"I'd rather tell you in person."

"All right. But don't expect me to feel any different when I see you."

Sure I didn't, and ran from the cab up her stairs. She held herself stiffly, untouchable, unkissable. She led me into the living room and offered me a chair that fit only one. She sat so that the table was between us. The chess game she was playing didn't matter at all. I was happy just to be in the same room with her.

"The Virginia police," I explained flatly, "have come across some indication that your father was deliberately murdered. It's thin, but I'm going down to see if we can make something out of it.''

Her eyes grew moist. She leaned forward. I told her the few details I had.

"Tony, Tony," she said, and her hands reached out.

I moved around the table and her arms went around me. Her head buried itself in my waist and her tears moistened both of us.

"I hate them. Whoever they are, I hate them. Are they going to get away with it? Are they?''

I looked down on her moist eyes and wet cheeks. "I'm going to find whoever killed him, and I will do what can be done about it.'' As I spoke I realized I had made a promise that perhaps I should not have made. Because I would live up to it. Like a kid who takes a dare, I hold the dumbest promises the most sacred. I think that was how I ended up married. I said it. Since I said it, I did it.

Silence framed the promise. Perhaps she understood what I had just done. Perhaps not.

I took her hands in mine and lifted her gently. She came up and into my arms. Our lips touched, her pain and anger became lust and hunger, and the afterburners kicked in.

"You're back, you're back,'' she cried, as if she had thought me gone forever. Or dead. There was no time to find a bed. We were on the couch and half our clothes still on us. Her legs opened and wrapped around my hips as if that was the only place in the world for me to be. It was. I entered her, desperate and helpless as the search for truth.

"I love you,'' I said, just before the orgasm took me. It was roaring and full of darkness. "I love you, I love you,'' I heard her say through the storm.

And when it's open, when you've got it, when it's all yours,
When nobody else in all the world is where you are,
When your arms have really gone around something,
When your thighs know all the answers to all the questions,
Why is there always one bead of sweat that doesn't come from
        either of your faces?

A great well of laughter started deep down below my bowels and came bubbling up as we lay tangled in clothes and limbs. Part of it, sheer joy. I was high as a cocaine kite in love with the woman in my arms, and I had a happy and contented home with a woman as good as any it has been my privilege to know.

It was a conflict so old that the jokes about it precede the written word. Twenty thousand years, from clubs to computers, and the only intelligent commentary that I had ever heard about this situation came from Tommy Moe Raft, a burlesque comic who stood five feet four, with jowls that hung to his chin and basset-hound eyes. "Please, please, puleeeese," he begged Enid, the blonde he did his routines with. She, six feet one without her heels, Death Valley cleavage and legs that came up almost to his jowls, whined, "What about your wife, Tommy?" Tommy reassured Enid, "We can start without her."

Then we did it again. She didn't understand my laughter, but she knew how to touch me clear through.

19

PIGEONS

"WHAT HAVE YOU got?"

"Walter LeRoy Johnson," Bill Tillman said, pulling out the file, "a.k.a. LeRoy Johns, John Walters, John Waterson, Walter LeRoy, Roy Walters and LeRoy Watson, has been married under each of those names. He is prolific, but not imaginative." He looked up and said, "That's not in the file, that was a comment," then continued to read. "Male, black, sixty-seven, hair black, eyes brown. A record going back over forty years for nonsupport and bigamy. His latest warrant, the one we picked him up on, is from Seminole, Texas, on a complaint from a Mrs. Althea Johns. There are outstanding warrants from Alabama, Arizona and two from next door in West Virginia."

"Do you see him," I said to prick at his cool, "as an unfortunate caricature?"

"Yes, I do," he replied, forever unruffled, "not of the so-called shif'less kneegro, but of the cultural deficiencies of po' southe'n trash of any color. A vanishing breed as economic and educational standards rise."

We exchanged bland smiles.

"If I may continue with something pertinent . . ."

"Please," I said.

"Apparently," he said, shuffling through the file, "no, not apparently; in fact, I have a sworn affidavit here to prove it. A Mr. and Mrs. Clayton Delaney of Seminole, the employers of Mrs. Althea Johns, were visiting relations in Casanova, just over the line in Farquier County. They stopped for dinner at Scotch 'n' Sirloin, Mr. Johnson's place of employment, and while he was collecting their dishes, recognized him as the man who had run out on their domestic employee, Mrs. Johns. They said nothing to the suspect, but upon returning to their place of residence, they duly informed the said Althea Johns. Mrs. Delaney apparently felt it was her duty."

He turned a page. "Mrs. Delaney was so sympathetic . . . that's not in the report, that's from a conversation . . . to the plight of abandoned wives in general that she retained an attorney for the complainant, who sent a subpoena, etc. etc. You can see it if you want."

"Thanks, I've seen them."

"Well, they called to follow up," he said, closing the file. "Both the attorney and the employer. So we dug the subpoena out of the bottom of the file, where it was rightly buried below lots more urgent business, and went to pick up Walter Johnson. Of course, once we picked him up, we did an automatic check.

"I don't know whether you know it, but we've recently gone statewide on the computer, with a federal hookup to boot. I got it in an anticrime grant a few years back. Sometimes it works real well. With D's, M's, W's and P's it works particularly well. On the other hand, if your name starts with F or B your record will never catch up with you. Unfortunately for Walter LeRoy, he used all those W names, and the computer loved that.

"The arresting officer, Samuel D. Culpepper, who is, off the record, a regular old-time red-neck cracker, gets the printout and goes and does an almost authentic imitation of a southern sheriff. 'You in a heap o' trouble, boy.' . . . Has anyone ever considered forbidding peace officers watching TV? . . . According to Culpepper, the prisoner began to plead, making biblical references to the weakness of the flesh. The suspect offered to trade 'important information' for his release. Culpepper doubted that someone so old and ignorant could know anything useful and expressed those doubts forcefully. At which point Johnson says, 'How 'bout that rich ol' white man done got his head turned to grits and gravy?' Even Culpepper seemed to be aware that this is an important case. 'Stay right there,' he instructed Johnson, redundant to a man in a cell, and ran to Deltchev. Deltchev, much to Culpepper's discomfort, sent him to me. I had to compliment him on excellent police work.

"Apparently Mrs. Althea Johns is not only an extremely moral and churchgoing woman, but a physically powerful one as well. Johnson would rather do time than be sent back. We went back and forth a bit, and he finally told me that he had been approached by two men, two days before the murder. They had a photo of Wood and asked Johnson if he had ever seen the man.

"Johnson claims that at first he denied any knowledge, but they pressed him physically, and he felt that he had no choice but to identify Wood for them."

"You sound," I said, "like you don't entirely believe Mr. Johnson."

"No. Not entirely. Maybe they did threaten him, but I know that ten dollars would have done the job. I don't think he was reluctant at all."

"Any names?"

"Afraid not," he said.

"Description?"

"Some, but I don't know how accurate. Johnson started with a simple black, big and young. 'How big?' was my first question. He started with big enough for the Redskins' offensive line. After some coaxing we got down to one six-footer, one a couple of inches taller. The six-footer is a little heavyset. The taller one is thinner, has a big scar on his right cheek, or maybe his left. They're both brown, right down the middle between African blue-black and octoroon. Age, out of their teens, early thirties at the top end. In Johnson's words, 'young but not childrens.' Hair, medium short and natural, except the shorter one might have had corn rows or something. . . . Johnson is not a wonderful witness. Oh yeah, the skinny one, he seemed a little high.''

"On what?" I asked.

"Johnson couldn't say, just a little high."

"Hyped up, finger-poppin' high, stoned out, spaced out? What flavor high?"

"Just high was all I could get from him."

"Is that all of it, Bill?"

"I was under the impression I was giving you a detailed report. In fact, I was afraid you would complain I was too loquacious."

"How can I complain about something I can't spell?"

"Why not? We got officers here, can't spell larceny, perpetrator, even homicide."

"How is the war on dumb going?" I asked.

"Deltchev will have his twenty in about eighteen months. He could try to stay on for twenty-five or even thirty, but it's looking good for twenty. There is also talk afoot that if he stays, the Chief will find him something very administrative. Astral file work or something." A trace of a smile appeared on Tillman's bland face.

"Where is Johnson now?" I asked.

"Isn't it slick how you reminded me of the favor that you did me, then slipped in the key question, like I wouldn't notice it," Tillman said, his face returning to his unflappable look. I think I actually blushed. He gave me time to do it, then continued blandly, "We let him go and told Texas he skipped. Right now, I need him more than they do. Mrs. Althea Johns can have him when I'm done, but I did not explain that to him."

"Are you or are you not going to tell me?"

"Or course I am. And you will approach him without Miranda, which is OK because you don't have to make a case that the courts will buy. I am certain you will even be rude to him. And you may be able to get something from him that I couldn't. All I ask is that you do not commit any chargeable offense. These southern cops can get ugly.''

"Thank you,'' was appropriate.

Johnson's place of residence was a trailer, resting slightly askew on concrete blocks just off a country road with an RD address. There was a patch of black-eyed Susans out front; sunflowers, pole beans and tomatoes grew on the side.

He worked late, toting plates and bearing abuse. So Franco and I arrived at dawn. I had made Franco resurrect the silk suit and the Dirty Harry cannon for the visit.

There was a rosy glow over the hills, promising a lovely day, as we kicked the door in.

Johnson rolled over on his narrow bunk and looked at us with gummy eyes. His teeth were in a glass on a table afflicted with rickets. There was a gooseneck lamp on the same surface. I flipped it on and pointed it at his face. Franco pointed the gun.

"LeRoy,'' I said, "you have been fucking with the wrong people.''

He rolled his eyes and shook his head.

"In March you fingered a dude called Wood, down the restaurant where you work.''

"No suh, no suh, I don' know what you talking 'bout.''

"LeRoy, don't do that ignorant-darkie routine with me. I don't buy it.''

"I would tell you, sho nuff, but I don' know nuffin.''

"LeRoy, that's not true. You even spoke to the police. You spoke to po-liceman Culpepper, and to Detective Tillman.''

"Then you knows what I said.''

"There's more, tell me.''

"Let me put in my teef . . .''

Franco slashed out with his gun and smashed glass and teeth to the floor. Then he grabbed the thin mattress and yanked it. The old man tumbled to the floor of the trailer; the mattress was flung to the opposite wall.

"How much did they pay you to finger Wood? How much?'' I screamed at him.

"Nuffin, nuffin, they done scairt me."

I took my .45 out, cocked it, put it to his head. "Pray, LeRoy, pray. 'Cause you gonna die now."

"Onny twenny dollars, tha's all."

"They paid you twenty, just because you said the man in the picture ate at your restaurant."

"Tha's right, tha's right," he said immediately and emphatically. Truth is so complicated; lies are simple.

"No. That's wrong. Do you really want to die, you stupid motherfucker?"

"Tha's all I done. Tha's all. Please don' shoot this po' o' man."

"Last chance to live, po' o' man. Where did you call them?"

"How d'you know I calls them, how d'you know?"

"Where did you call them?" I pulled a hundred-dollar bill from my pocket and dangled it in front of his eyes. "When you tell me where you called them, this is yours. When I get tired of waiting, you're a dead man."

"I disremember the number," he said, close to tears.

I fired a shot through the wall.

"I think mebbe it's in my wallet," he answered.

"Take a look, Franco, take a look."

Franco found the wallet in the shiny pants hanging over the back of the one chair. He dumped the contents out on the floor. LeRoy had all of three dollars, a driver's license and various scraps of paper. Franco scanned the scraps and came up with a torn piece of napkin with numbers on it.

"Tha's the one," LeRoy cried with revivalist fervor. "That do be the one. The Lord is with me. He done saved the number that done saved my life."

"Names, I want names," I said.

"God's honest truff, I don' know. If I done knowed I would tell you."

"Mr. Johnson," I said, dropping the one hundred dollars on the floor, "it's been a pleasure doing business with you."

Back in my rental car, Franco said, "You ain't bad for a kid. How'd you know the old man called them?"

"He answered too simple, too easy. But mostly, there was something missing. How did the perps know to be in that lot at that time? Did they wait there three, four days? I don't think they had that kind of patience. So someone had to finger Wood.

"You know what else," I said, feeling sick about abusing senior citizens, even one who was a grandfather forty or fifty times over, "I'm an asshole. Likewise Tillman, you, Deltchev. We're all assholes."

"Howzzat?"

I held out a scrap of paper. He looked away from the road and glanced at it. He shrugged, not seeing anything in it.

"It's a two-oh-two number."

"So?"

"So it's a long-distance call. There's a record, probably from the pay phone, maybe from the restaurant phone, but I'll bet on the pay phone. A traceable record made during the one or two hours before Wood died. The police could have had that way back in March. I could have had it my first trip down; all anybody had to do was think, fucking think, instead of terrorizing an old man."

"Old don't mean good. He fingered a guy for murder, for twenty bucks. As far as I'm concerned," Franco said, "he's part of the slime."

"You have phone company contacts?"

"I got department contacts. I'll get you a name and address to go with the number."

"Thanks."

"No sweat," he said, then added grudgingly, "You must've been a pretty good cop."

"I wasn't a cop. Corrections, I was with the corrections department."

"Oh," he said in recognition, and unease. "That Tony Cassella."

"Yeah, that Tony Cassella."

"There must be a lotta people don't like you."

"That's OK," I said. "Fuck 'em if they can't take a joke."

"That was no joke. That was a pretty tough thing you did. . . . If you ask me . . ."

"I didn't."

"You did the right thing. You had your job. You did it. That's the way the game is played. If somebody gets hurt, that's their problem. They didn't have to play."

"Thanks," I said.

"That's just the way of it. . . . You know. I should never have retired. I'm only fifty-six, two years off the force and going nuts. You get your thirty and that pension, you figure with the pension and a job you make half again as much as what you were making, without the aggravation and dealing with a better class of people. That's what you gotta figure, but I shoulda stayed a cop."

I checked out of the Colonel Culpepper Holiday Inn and called the Watergate, but they were full. The Best Western on U.S. 1 in D.C. had a vacancy sign up. I let Franco go to check with his P.D. contacts while I admired my room.

I called Glenda. She told me to be careful. I heard the inaudible bite of her lip while she held in whatever comment her insecurity and lurking jealousy wanted to prompt.

I called Choate Haven. I let him know I had a serious lead, the phone number of the probable perp.

I called Christina. She called me "Angel." The woman was clearly besotted. That made two of us.

Franco came in with his satchel and a thick old leather-covered notepad, the kind that cops carry, stuck in an over-size back pocket.

"The phone is registered to James Carlton Alexander, Jr.; he's on Franklin, just off New Jersey . . . according to Motor Vehicle, he drives an '83 Pontiac Firebird, black, license, R,U,S,H, One—Rush 1."

"Well done," I said. "I'm gonna call Tillman."

"You think you should do that?"

"Yeah," I said, dialing. "In the first place, he's playing straight with me; he gave me Johnson, remember. In the second place, let's say I do something on my own . . ." the phone was answered. I asked for Tillman. He wasn't in. I left a message. ". . . I am now on record as having tried to contact the authorities."

"What were you thinking of doing?" he asked.

"The problem is, let's say the cops haul him in. They put him in a lineup. If LeRoy has the balls to ID him, then I'm not a devout heterosexual. On the other hand, I don't know that I want to brace him myself, at least until I know more about him."

"That is very intelligent, 'cause—" he flipped open to another page "—Mr. Alexander, Jr., is not your sweetheart type. Priors include a conviction—'77, armed robbery. Plus four arrests, no convictions: narcotics '78, assault '78, assault with a deadly weapon '82, and a possession of stolen property. He's twenty-seven."

"I'm gonna go take a cautious look at the man."

"See, that won't work. Soon's you go into that neighborhood, they're gonna make you. The thing to do is make that work for you. We run a two-man stakeout. You let him see the first guy, and you hope he cuts and runs. Then you do a tag-team tail. You let the suspect lose the first tail, then when he thinks he's clean, the second man picks him up."

"That only works with some technology. . . ."

With infinite smugness, Franco reached into his bag and pulled a couple of walkie-talkies out of his satchel. I grimaced.

"I know what you're thinking," he said. "Walkie-talkies are mostly more trouble than they're worth, more show than talk . . . but these are pretty good. And . . ." he tossed another item on the bed ". . . a beeper, magnet keeps it on the suspect's car, and here's the directional finder goes with it." Things kept coming out of the bag like clowns from a midget car. "And finally, I got Rabbi Begin with me, and some spare clips."

"All right," I said, feeling armed and dangerous.

I followed him down Rhode Island, left on New Jersey, then a couple of blocks down to Franklin. Franco was right about the neighborhood. My white face was a full moon in a midnight sky.

RUSH 1, freshly polished and gleaming black, sat in the middle of the block, two doors down from Alexander's address. Franco rolled on past. I pulled up next to the Firebird and got out of my rental Dodge. Together the two cars looked like beauty and the basset hound. I looked the Firebird over, with no attempt to be inconspicuous, twirling my own keys in my hand. The keys slipped. When I bent down to pick them up, I slapped the little transmitter up inside the back bumper.

There was an open space, four cars back, and I rolled into it.

Every person who passed gave me a lookover. It ran the gamut from the ill-disguised corner of the eye squint to the confrontational strut. I could feel eyes in the windows as well. The topper was a cute-as-a-button six-year-old on a chopped bike with a bright blue-and-red-striped banana seat, who circled me twice, popped a wheelie, came down at my open window and said, "I know who you is, man."

Several citizens entered Alexander's building and came right back out. They were either quick-stop shopping or dropping in to mention that "the man" was on the block. Or both. I saw a face at what I thought was his window.

When he came out, he came out in a rush. To my surprise, LeRoy's description was reasonably accurate. He was six two, light brown, about 170, with a scar that slashed the right side of his face from his yellow eye to his heavy upper lip.

He banged his rear bumper backing up, cursed, slammed the automatic into drive, crunched the accelerator and burned rubber out.

He tore right on Fifth and up to Florida as the light was changing. I almost lost my rear bumper but stayed with him, not wanting him to lose me too easily. I called Franco and, to my surprise, got through.

"Don't worry, kid, the directional is working, we ain't gonna lose him."

I stayed with the Firebird, heading north on Georgia. He cut left across traffic onto Farragut, gaining a beat. I thought

I saw his taillights making another quick left onto Arkansas, but when I got there he was gone.

"He just made a circle," Franco said. "I got him. North on Georgia."

I got back on the avenue, trying to catch up. I caught a glimpse of him bearing right onto Piney Branch, but it was just evasive tactics. He made about six turns just to get back onto Georgia, but when I got there, heading north again, I didn't see him. Franco's directional had him heading southwest and away.

I headed in that general direction until Franco said he had stopped moving. "Stay put while I find him," he said. I did.

"Come on up to Kalmia and Myrtle," he told me. It took a couple of minutes to find on my map. When I saw Franco I parked behind him, got out of my car and into his. It was a beautiful area, bordering Rock Creek Park, hilly, full-grown trees, lots of landscaping with big, expensive, one-of-a-kind homes. Very expensive.

"Well, well, well," Franco said with immense satisfaction, "pigeons coming home to roost. . . . See that house, last one you can see on the curve?" It was two stories, twelve rooms, stone, set back deep, with a large garage set off to the side.

"I don't see the car," I said.

"I got it figured for the garage. . . . You ever hear of Mark Wellby?" I shrugged in reply and he continued, "He is to the District what Nicky Barnes or Ricky Sams used to be in New York. He is the heavyweight. They call him the Doctor."

"I remember something about him, the name from somewhere," I said, "something very odd."

"He wanted to put a statue in one of the parks, but the city wouldn't let him," Franco said.

"That's it," and I remembered that it had been a memorial for Rashaan Roland Kirk. Wellby had commissioned a design—with Kirk possessed by jazz, tenor sax in one side of his mouth, clarinet in the other—was ready to have it cast, offered to pay for installation in any public place and for its maintenance in perpetuity. Nobody seemed upset when he was turned down, but I for one thought it was a great idea. I had seen Roland Kirk play.

THE LATE SHOW

"When you shake the tree, the fruit falls down," Franco mumbled to himself. "I'll be a son of a bitch. Doc Wellby.

"This is what we're gonna do," Detective Polatrano instructed. "My guess is that the Doctor is right now telling the pigeon to fly away. Probably on the next flight out of Dulles to nowhere. If he heads for the airport, we pick him up. If he does something else, we follow and find out what. You lead, I back up. If he panics, that's OK. If he comes back here, I get on the horn with some friends in the department, and they get to visit Doctor Wellby with a warrant. They will like that very, very much."

It sounded reasonable. It was his town. I agreed with it.

About forty-five minutes later the garage door opened. A full-sized black Buick came out. Franco and I ducked as it went past. I had enough of a glimpse of the men inside to know that Alexander Jr. was not one of them.

Twenty minutes later, the garage opened again. This time it was the pigeon and the Firebird.

He took it easy, as if the Doctor had instructed him not to do something dumb, like get picked up for speeding. We followed a roundabout route, with me fairly far back. I lost him once, but Franco, behind me, figured it out from the beeper. We started north, then back south, and Alexander led me into Rock Creek Park. It was a beautiful night, aromatic with trees, flower scents I didn't recognize and the smell of fresh-cut grass.

We went down Beach Drive, through the center of the park, east on Military Road, then south on Ridge Road. It was hilly and twisty, and suddenly he floored the Pontiac. I put the pedal to the metal, I juiced the goose. But we just didn't have it. I was losing him.

Which was the way it was supposed to go. I called Franco to tell him that the suspect had made his move, but there was no answer. I tried a second time. As I did, I caught some movement off to my right.

A large black shape was roaring at me and I knew we were headed for a collision. I tried to avoid it. That took me up on the shoulder. It wasn't until my wheels were skidding on the grass that I realized it was deliberate and they were going to keep on coming.

Their car was heavier than mine. Worse, I was already going in the direction they wanted me to, over the edge.

I was bashing against saplings and shrubs when they leaned into me. I tried the brakes. It was right about then that the left side wheels tried to ride on air.

The car tumbled in slow motion. I had the leisure to see the leaves caught in the turning patterns of my headlights. I had time to think about seat belts. About why I wasn't wearing mine. As I clutched the wheel to keep my head from bashing on the roof beneath me, I could not think of a single valid reason not to wear a seat belt.

During the next roll, the walkie-talkie came by. I grabbed it in passing and yelled, "Mayday, mayday!" I released it when my head hit the side window. But on the next half-roll the walkie-talkie came back by itself and hit me dead center in the crotch. I very much hoped Franco was on his way.

The car kept rolling until the front end hit a large tree. That stopped the tumble, which was nice even if it stopped wheels up. We kept moving, in a kind of spin and slide, riding on the roof, banging from tree to tree.

When it finally stopped I was sort of hanging upside down, severely hunched, with the weight of my body on my neck and my chin attempting to penetrate my breastbone. I twisted over sideways, untangled my legs from the steering wheel and came down with a thump on the roof.

I felt panic, the kind you feel underwater without enough breath left. The driver's side door was stuck. I tried the passenger side. The handle worked and the door cracked open. Unfortunately there was a tree just outside.

I wriggled over to the driver's side. I told myself to suppress fear, to be calm, to be rational, to be professional. It was then that I decided to pull up (down?) the dumb little lever that keeps the door locked. When I did that, I could open it.

The tree on that side was farther away, but not farther enough.

Finally I had a stroke of genius. At another time it might have been a perfectly average thought, but at the time a comic-strip light bulb went on over my head: windows!

I could roll down (up?) the window. The conflict between phraseology and reality plagued me. Which way was up? Why did I care? The conflict had to be resolved. And it was. I decided to roll the window to "the open position." That is how the mind of a pro operates under stress.

I slithered out. It wasn't graceful, but it was out.

There was blood in my eyes, salty, stinging and obscuring my vision. I wiped it away. Then I started checking for injuries. Then I heard the noises. I looked up the hill and saw two men coming. They had guns, and neither one was Franco.

They saw me at the same time I saw them. One kept coming; the other raised his weapon. I dived; he fired. He missed. I did an imitation of a snake, writhing with my head and body as close to the ground as they could get.

I moved behind a boulder, an excellent defensive position.

With one hand I reached up to clear the debris from my eyes; with my other I reached for my gun. It wasn't there.

It had fallen, I assumed, when the car was tumbling.

I was alone, at night, in the woods. Two large people with guns were chasing me. My own gun was lost and they were between it and me. It was the stuff that dreams are made of, and I did exactly what I would have done in a nightmare—panicked and ran.

"I hears him," I heard, and I dove for the ground. Whatever type of shooter he was using, it went off like thunder, the sound rolling down the slope, across the bottom and up the other side. I imagined the bullet going where my body had just been. It may have.

I started crawling again, trying again to believe what I had heard about Indians, that it was possible to move without cracking a twig. Once again, myth shattered on the rock of reality. Fortunately they made more noise than me.

The gun boomed again. Using the sound for cover, I dashed a few yards and dived.

"Did you see something to shoot at?"

"Mebbe I did, yeah," the shooter said.

"That fucking cannon, too fucking loud. Ain't you got a silencer?"

"No."

"Then don' use it less you got a good shot, you gonna bring someone down on us."

"Where the fuck he gone to?" the other one mumbled.

What a reassuring inquiry, I thought, wondering the same about Franco.

"You head that way, I go this. . . ." said the one with the silencer.

Now that they were split, I thought I might have a chance of jumping one. I didn't actually want to, but it was possible that I was going to run out of choices. As I went along on all fours, I found all sorts of fallen branches, all waterlogged, soft and moldy, and not of weapon caliber.

I heard the crashing coming closer.

My knee hit something hard. It turned out to be a piece of

pipe. Normally I would have been upset to find it there. I think trashing public parks is the worst sort of antisocial behavior, and I never liked James Watt. But context is everything, and I fell in love with that piece of iron. It was just a bit over two feet long, like a squash racket.

I went creeping through a new set of bushes. They had thorns and I didn't enjoy it. Finally I came out the other side, kind of rolling over and looking up. There he was: a mountain with muscles and a gun.

I gathered my feet under me. He heard the movement and began to turn. As he did, I stepped in and swung, aiming my racket at the gun. One thing I am good at is keeping my eye on the ball. Otherwise you swing where you think the ball is going to be, rather than where it actually is.

I connected. The gun flew.

It was far from over. He had size on me. I'm sure he was often embarrassed when people mistook him for a wall. He was also very fast. He started swinging before I was even ready for a second shot. His fist, with his weight behind it, caught me low in the ribs and I went over backward.

He came swarming, playing sack the quarterback. I rolled. He kicked. It caught me on the ribs again. He brought his foot back for another shot. I saw the boot coming at my head and lifted my shoulder up and in the way. He connected and lifted me off the ground. I flipped over again.

I continued the roll and somehow came up on my feet out of his immediate reach. When he charged, I went sideways and back, my shoulder hitting a tree. I rolled around the trunk and started running. He shifted direction and came after me.

I stopped abruptly, planted my foot, dropped low. As he came in, I swung a perfect backhand pipe to his knee.

It went with an audible crunch. An immensely gratifying sound. He went over tumbling. He shrieked. It felt very good to know he was crippled, I hoped, for life.

His partner was still armed and dangerous. The scream would bring him fast enough. I ran like a rabbit. The cannon fired. And again. I dodged trees and hopped ground-flung branches. Just before the third shot, I took a dive. Something tore across my arm and helped throw me down.

I grabbed the spot reflexively. The arm was there, but it was wet. All that was missing was a little skin off the top, like a circumcision.

The crip was still screaming, and the one with the cannon yelled back. "Where you at? Where you at?"

Figuring the shooter was going the other way, I was up and running. Suddenly I was out of the woods and onto cut grass. Ahead of me was a road, then more grass, then woods again. It was a no-man's land, a free-fire zone. Praying that the cripple was occupying the gunman's time, I went for it.

When I hit the woods on the other side, I collapsed. I crawled into the bushes and lay there panting. The shock and adrenaline were beginning to wear off. Breathing hurt. It grew worse, and I realized my ribs were broken.

I tore a piece of my shirt off. Using one hand and my teeth, I tied the rag around the wound in the arm. The only thing to do for the ribs, rest them, was not an available option.

When you've gone a certain distance by car and later back by foot, it's amazing how much farther it is. Maybe getting kicked around exaggerates the sense of time and distance the same way cannabis does, but in a less pleasant way. I don't know how long it took, clambering up rocks, sliding down loose earth into gullies, stumbling through branches, but it was the longest day of my life as well as a distinctly nonurban experience.

I found that I couldn't think about progress, about getting to the top of the next hill or through the gully. All I could do was take one step at a time. There was a lesson in that, that I looked forward to forgetting.

Then I was at a road. I could see the park entrance not fifteen feet away.

I was scared.

It meant going out in the open, where if they found me I would be helpless. I lay in the dirt, to wait for a moment when no one was around. When the moment did come, I rose, got dizzy and blacked out.

I don't think I was out long. When I came back, I dragged myself to a tree and crawled up the trunk. Things started going black again, but even in the darkness, I could feel the rough bark. When the dizziness passed, I was still standing.

I called myself a self-pitying wimp. I told myself that there was no need to descend into pseudo-delirium. I gathered up my self-respect and stumbled out into the city. I was not so whacked out that I didn't understand why cabs wouldn't stop. I was bloody, dirty, with my hair uncombed.

A patrol car cruised by. I waved to them. They waved back and rolled on.

There was something vaguely familiar about where I was. It was somewhere near Sandy. She had a phone. And water. I knew she had water. I wanted water very much.

The closer I got, the harder it was to keep going. My body was overeager to give up. Not that I blamed it. But I knew that once down, I was staying down. Even when I entered her building and buzzed her intercom I knew better than to sit down. I leaned against the door. I heard her voice, electronically mangled, and croaked mine back. Falling through the door snapped me awake. I had to grab at it to keep from crashing. That pulled the muscles across my ribs. It reminded me to move very carefully. I think I was crying.

In the elevator I couldn't remember the floor. Eight sounded right, but there was no eight, so I pushed three because it looks like it.

Nor did I know which three it was, just that there were a lot of them. I was pleased to see she knew I didn't know and was standing with her door open to show me which it was.

"Do you know it's after one in the morning?" she said.

I shook my head no and kept on coming.

"Tony," she said.

"Where the fuck was Franco?" I asked her.

"What happened to you?" she asked me.

"Who the hell is this?" her husband inquired generally.

"Call a doctor," she said. I smiled. It was the most sensible idea I had heard all day.

"I doubt," the husband said, "that his name is 'call-a-doctor.' It's more likely 'anotha-luvva.' "

"This is not the time for this," Sandy said sensibly. I nodded in agreement.

"When a strange man arrives in the middle of the night in disreputable condition, and the two of you clearly know each other, I think I'm entitled to know who he is."

"Please call a doctor," she said.

"Police," I said, but it came out "P'lease," and she came to me.

"I'm sure that's not his name," the husband said again. It was a tasteless moment to be facetious.

"His goddamn name is Tony," she snapped at him, "now call a doctor."

"I'm going to have a brandy," he said and walked away.

Sandy started to help me toward the couch. I rested my bad arm on her shoulder. It burned and ached and I felt the scabbing break, but it was far too much trouble to change sides.

"Once I'm down," I explained, "I can't get up."

"That's all right," she said and helped me to sit. When the ribs are gone, the hardest moves in the world are the sequences from vertical to prone and back up again. Each move needs the muscles that pull across the ribs.

"Need help," I said, and she let me use her as a brace.

The couch felt wonderful. The husband walked back in with his brandy. The brandy looked wonderful. We had not been formally introduced, so I felt uncomfortable asking him for some.

Sandy was calling a doctor. "It's an emergency," I heard her say. Then very patiently, "Will you please call him and have him call me?" Then she slammed the phone down. "Damn answering services."

The husband swirled his brandy. He spoke to her although he was looking down his nose at me. "Is that the way you like them? A little rough around the edges, a slight touch of the gutter?''

"Oh shut up," she said. "That son of a bitch Bernstein has his home phone forwarded to the answering service." She dialed again. The service must have picked up because she slammed the phone down again.

"Perhaps the emergency room would be more apropos," her husband said, "unless there is some reason you would like to keep him here."

"Where the fuck was Franco?" I asked.

The phone rang. Sandy answered. "Allan," she said, "I need you here. . . . Someone's hurt . . . Allan, I don't even know if he should be moved. . . . There's blood and he has trouble moving. . . . Yes, Allan . . . thank you . . . I know you don't . . . I know you need your sleep, but at least I didn't interrupt your Tai Chi practice; now get your butt over here, please.''

She hung up and said, "Doctors!" It was an expletive. She came to my side and said, "Is there anything I can do?"

"A drink," I suggested.

"All right," she said and started to rush away. I grabbed her hand. "It's not that bad," I told her, "I'm gonna live." Realizing that, I began to enjoy the drama of the situation.

She came back from the kitchen with a glass of brandy. Just like the one her husband liked to swirl. He noticed that too. I could tell by the way he looked at her that I was getting the private stock, not the stuff at the front of the liquor shelf for unwelcome guests.

I couldn't drink in the position I was in and I couldn't sit up. She put her arm under my head; she lifted me tenderly and put a cushion under my back to support me.

"What happened?" she asked. I took the glass from her. The alcohol cleared the clogs from my throat. I thought about it. What had happened? I had been overambitious. I had taken on something by myself that needed the police. I had been careless. I had not had the best of backups. In sum, I had not been quite bright.

"If you want to be an asshole," I explained, "you have to pay the price."

She laughed. I laughed. Laughing hurt; it made the muscles across the ribs jump. Each "ha" was a jab. Her husband understood that laughing hurts. So he didn't.

"I better get you a little cleaned up," she said.

"That is sweet," her husband said. I agreed.

She ignored him. She went into the kitchen and came back with a bowl of warm water and some towels. He glowered. I winced as she began to wipe my face. Our arms tangled as I tried to drink more brandy.

"Are you going to tell me what happened to you?" Sandy asked.

"Are you going to tell me who this is?" her husband asked.

"Would you believe," I said to Sandy, "that I ran into a jealous husband?"

"Again?" she teased.

Sandy and I laughed again. It hurt again. It hurt her husband more. I held my side where the ribs were twanging. She rinsed the towel.

"I insist that you tell me who this person is and what he is doing here."

"Tony was a friend, is a friend, from some years back. I suspect he's here now because he's hurt."

"My own place was too far to go," I said. He was building himself up to something, and I was helping too much, so I added, "I'm sorry if I intruded; it was the only place I could think of."

The intercom buzzed and Sandy said, "Would you get that, please?"

"Come here often?" her husband said to me.

Sandy got up to answer the intercom.

"I don't know what it is," he said to her, examining me, "but I have the distinct impression that this is one of your lovers."

"Please stop it," she said. "Dr. Bernstein is on his way up."

"I thought he was Allan to you."

"Only," she said, "when I'm irritated."

"Tell me you haven't been to bed with him."

"Who him? Dr. Bernstein? Tony? The grocery boy? What are you going on about?"

"Let's start with the swarthy one bleeding on the four-thousand-eight-hundred-dollar couch."

"I'll stop," I said, hearing the price.

"Please don't do this to me now," she said.

"Tell me you haven't been to bed with him," he insisted.

Sandy paused, stuck on her weak point, her inability to tell a direct lie. She knew how to be polite, euphemistic and evasive, but she had her limitations.

She was saved by the bell.

"Would you get that, please?" she said.

"I would really rather not," he said, sipping. "This whole thing is pretty much entirely your problem. I would rather keep it that way."

She went to the door. Dr. Bernstein came in looking like Mark Spitz. Does everyone work out these days? And diet? What happened to the kindly old flabby-looking doctors of yore? The husband shared the glare, that had been all mine, with the doctor.

"Hiya, Sandy," he said, kissing her on the cheek. "Howdy, Paul," he said with a wave at the husband, "what's the crisis?"

"Me," I croaked.

Bernstein strolled cheerfully to the couch. Only the tousled hair and the T-shirt on inside out indicated that he had just been awakened.

"Do you want to tell me about it?" Bernstein asked me.

"Are you going to tell me about it?" Paul asked Sandy.

"I'm pretty sure this rib is broken; everything else is just scratches," I said.

"Tell you what?" Sandy sighed.

"That looks like an awful lot of bleeding just for scratches," the doctor said.

"Go on, tell me you haven't been to bed with him," Paul said.

"Yeah, I guess so," I said, looking over and realizing blood was caked from just below the shoulder to the elbow, "but I think it's just a flesh wound."

He started to poke at it and it hurt.

"With who?" Sandy said.

"Do you remember knock-knock jokes, Doc?" I said, to distract myself.

"Sure, I do," the doctor replied, starting to untie the rag.

"Knock, knock," I said.

"Who's there?"

"Our surprise guest, the dirty one," Paul said, "or the doctor from down the block."

"Owhhh," I said, as he started pulling it off.

"Owhhh who?" the doctor replied.

"There has been no one since we got married," Sandy said. "Since we met, in fact. You know that."

"You're being evasive," Paul pointed out.

"Not 'Owhhh who,' " I said, and winced again.

"I think I better soak it a little before I pull anymore. Why not 'Owhhh who'? That's the way I remember the game."

"Sorry, my fault, the owh was a real owhh, not part of the game. I should have said 'fuck,' " I said, wincing again. The scabs were breaking up and blood was flowing.

"What possible difference does it make?" Sandy said.

"To you? Probably none," Paul said.

"You prefer to say 'fuck' when you're in pain?" the doctor asked me.

"No, no, in the joke," I explained.

"Please, can't we stop this?" Sandy pleaded.

"There. It's coming off," the doc said. "OK. Fuck who?"

"No. Fuck whom," I said.

"That's not a very good joke," the doctor said, "even for a knock-knock joke. Do you know any grape jokes or elephant jokes?"

"No. It can't stop. Not when you bring your filth into our

home," Paul said. There were tears in Sandy's eyes. "Have you been to bed with that man?"

"A long time ago," she said, beaten. "Before I even knew you."

"Now I get it," the doctor said. "Not funny, but pungent indeed."

"Fuck," I yelled as he yanked the cloth from the wound.

"Not again," the doc said.

Paul stared at Sandy. He spoke slowly, deliberately, and mean. "This is the apartment we moved into together. This is not where you lived before you knew me. How did your lover know to come here?"

"I must admit you're right," Bernstein said to me, "it's just a flesh wound, didn't even touch much muscle."

"You really want to pick a fight," Sandy said, losing.

"I guess I better look at the rib," the doc said. "You get kicked around a lot, do you?"

"I hardly need to pick one," Paul declaimed. Very deliberately he threw the remainder of his brandy in her face.

"Ouuarrghhh," I said when Bernstein's fingers felt for the break.

Sandy slapped Paul across the face. Paul marched out of the room.

"Yup. It's broken."

He felt around some more. I winced and bit my tongue. Sandy stood stockstill, dripping in the middle of the room. Paul came marching back. He had exchanged slippers for shoes. He carried his suit in one hand, his briefcase and socks in the other. He gave us all, and the room, one last imperious gaze and marched out.

"Some Demerol and tape, X rays in the morning," I said.

"That's a pretty fair diagnosis and prescription. I hate to agree with my patients, but that's what I would have said," Bernstein said.

While he rummaged through his bag for a needle and the pain sweetener, Sandy wandered over to the couch. It was something to watch instead of the door that had just closed.

"Do you get beat up a lot?" Bernstein asked.

"Not as often as I would like," I said fluttering my lashes in an imitation of Alan Alda imitating Groucho Marx.

"From the way you diagnose," the doctor explained, "you seem to know your pain very well."

"We all know our pain well," I said as sententiously as possible.

"You bastard," Sandy said.

"What?"

"You just had to make your grand entrance. The big dramatic gesture. And bleed all over my couch." Then she hiccuped and said, "Oh God," starting to laugh with the tears. I started laughing too. Of course that hurt like hell, and I clutched my ribs to hold the pain in place.

"Good," Sandy said, "I hope every 'ha' hurts like hell."

"We have to turn you over," the doctor said.

"OK, if you help," I said. I opened my pants before the turn.

In midroll the pain shot through my stomach and washed up and down, but when I flattened out, it backed off. Once I was over on my side, he yanked my pants down.

"Usually I let my nurse do this. She gets off on it," he said, jabbing the needle in my ass. I was only a few moments away from lovely and I knew it. "I love you, Doc."

"Are you sure you want to say that to a man who just pulled your pants down?"

The pains were beginning to recede as I drifted into the Demerol. I rolled over onto my back. All by myself!

"You want a shot too?" Bernstein said to Sandy.

"No, thank you, Allan, I think I'll just do inner resources."

"Sandy, do you think he's gone for good?" he asked.

"Who knows?"

"Well, you know, I mean, what I'm trying to say," Allan tried to say, "is that you know how I've always felt about you . . . and in this time of loneliness and loss, I would like to take advantage of your weakness."

"Allan, it would be unethical."

"The doctor-patient relationship is sacred," I put in, wanting to discourage this.

"That's not the problem," Allan said, "she's not my patient."

"That's right," Sandy said, "I'm his therapist."

"Sandy," Allan swore, "I swear it would be all right with me. I would not feel victimized."

"Allan, don't you think we should deal with your dysfunction first?"

"A sexual dysfunction?" I asked.

"No," he replied, "medical."

I went out at that point, drifting away from Sandy and the doctor with the medical dysfunction, wondering where Franco had gone.

When my eyes opened, Bernstein was gone; I was alone with Sandy. She was sitting on the couch beside me. I was thirsty as hell and took a sip of the drink she was holding.

"I'm sorry I busted things up."

"No. He was just looking for an excuse."

"Do you have many lovers?"

"It is a common thing to project your own faults and guilts on other people. He does that."

"I'm sorry," I said again. She leaned over and kissed me. Soft, clean and cool. I slid my good arm around her and held her to it. It was a kiss that went with Demerol the way strawberries go with cream, soda goes with whiskey, bicycles go with spring.

"Do you want to do this in your condition?" she said when it stopped.

"I'll manage," I bragged, "but only if you're gentle with me."

"You don't have to brag," she said. "Everyone knows you'd have to die before you admitted you couldn't fuck. I was asking about your emotional condition."

"My emotional condition?"

"The last time I saw you, you were very serious about maintaining a relationship. I'm reminding you, just in case that hasn't changed."

"Well, the truth is, I'm in love."

"Oh," she said.

"With another woman; actually, with both of them."

"You are a bastard," she said pleasantly, "and I'm glad you're not my problem."

"It's a real problem," I said defensively. "It's a conflict."

"You can tell me about it during office hours. I'm off duty now."

"Well, then," I said, "can I nibble your lower lip? I always had a thing for that lip." She came close and let me do it. It became one of those strawberry, whiskey-soda, spring-day kisses. And her breasts felt ripe against my chest.

"So you're not worried about infidelity anymore," she murmured in my ear.

"I don't know. I mean since I already am, does this make it twice as bad, or half as bad, or is it a geometric progression?" She giggled. "Besides, I can always say I was stoned. And out-of-town. Out-of-town doesn't count, does it?"

I was stoned. I was grateful to be alive. Sandy had just gone through a confrontation and a trauma. She was an abandoned woman. And I was out-of-town. None of those things were excuses. They were the spices. It was a scene right out of *The Late Show*. It was heaven.

21

THE TODAY SHOW

THE ONLY NICE thing about the morning after was that there was no blood in my urine.

Sandy helped me get up. She loaned me a toothbrush. She found some of her husband's clothes and helped me into them. She called a cab and guided me into the backseat.

"How about some Demerol?" I said to Dr. Bernstein.

Just as cheery and bright as the night before, Bernstein said, "Let's do the examination first."

He X-rayed the ribs. He pulled the bandage off the wound, inspected it, antisepticed it, rebandaged it. I gave him a urine sample. He stared at it with apparent satisfaction.

"Now are we ready for the Demerol?" I said.

"How about some Tylenol? Or aspirin?"

"Don't be cruel," I whimpered. "I'm in pain. I can't sit by myself. I can't stand my myself. I need help."

"I'm sure you would enjoy the Demerol," he said. "But you don't need it. The pain is not that severe, nor is there shock, as there was last night. I hate to disappoint you, but I believe doctors should be ultra-conservative in prescribing substances open to abuse."

"Look, Doc . . ."

"No. No. Which will it be? Aspirin or Tylenol?"

"Aspirin," I said. He gave me a free sample of generic aspirin. It must have been worth all of $00.000015.

"Look, Doc, I'm sure you get people hustling you for the fun drugs all the time, but just gimme a listen. You're right. The pain is bearable, or would be bearable, if I did not have to move. I'm in the middle . . ."

"Look, I'd like to help . . ."

"Just hear me out," I said. "Number one, I was following a guy, a killer, before this happened. I have to find out if he's still around."

"I wouldn't recommend that," Bernstein said. "The job he already did on you seems quite adequate to me."

"Number two, there was a guy who was supposed to be backing me up. When I got in trouble he wasn't there. Maybe something happened to him, maybe not. But I gotta find that out too. Number three, I do have to talk to the police, the D.C. police, about what happened last night, and the Virginia police about the man who got away. He's the perp in a killing in Culpeper County. Number four, I got to try to explain to Avis why their car is upside down on a cliff in Rock Creek Park. . . ."

"Didn't you get the extra collision coverage? You should always get the extra collision."

"I did. I did, but . . ."

"So you have nothing to worry about then."

"Goddammit, Allan, you're not listening to me. It's not the fucking car. It's not the pain. I gotta get things done. . . ."

"I would like to oblige. But not as a doctor."

"Allan, if I have to get down on my knees and beg, I promise you that you are going to have to help me back up."

"All I'm trying to say, Tony, is that I do understand. I will do what I can to help. How about some coke? Will that do it?"

"What?" I said.

"Some coke."

"Sure, that should do it."

"The thing is, it has to be between you and me personally. Not you and me as doctor and patient. And please don't tell Sandy. As my therapist she'll be very angry with me."

"I understand," I said, thinking I might figure it out at some later date.

"It's a buck seventy-five a gram, and I can let you have one."

"Hey, hey, hey, Doc. I know this is D.C. and I'm from out of town, but that is a little steep."

"Hardly. This is pharmaceutical."

"Sure," I said. Pharmaceutical is one of those things one hears about but never sees. Like water into wine, levitation or a good garage mechanic.

"Really," he said with pride and sincerity. "We have an optometrist in our little medical group here."

"Sounds good," I said. He went to his desk, opened a locked drawer and brought out a premeasured bottle. I gave him money, he gave me coke. I laid out four lines and we each snorted two. The blood that had been trudging so sluggishly through my veins began to surge for my arteries. The acceleration was smooth.

"I take my role as a doctor," the doctor said, "very seriously. I will not overprescribe. I will not be a drugstore. As a private person," he giggled, "of course, my situation is a lot looser."

"What I will do," I said, "is continue to be irritated at Dr. Bernstein because he wouldn't give me the Demerol, but be grateful to my friend, Allan, for helping me out with a little of this pharmaceutical, but nonprescription, pick-me-up painkiller."

"That," he said seriously, "is precisely the thing."

I called Franco's home. I was very eager to find out precisely what he had been doing with himself while I was being shot at and used as a football at field-goal practice. If he didn't have a darn good excuse, I intended to say several offensive things to him.

He was not home. I called Gene, in the hopes that he might know Franco's whereabouts. Gene wasn't in either.

But his secretary had a message for me. If I called, she was instructed to ask me to meet him at St. Agnes, Mother of Mercy Hospital, in or around room 510. I asked if there was something wrong. She said no, he was there on some sort of business.

The cabbie the cab company sent was a polite little cracker who moonlighted as an alcoholic on his off years. It had taken a lot of his strength away. When I clung to him to climb into the back of the cab, he fell against my ribs.

After the color returned to my face and I was able to shut off the flow of apologies, I told him I would get in the front seat by myself. Thank you.

I spotted Gene in the fifth-floor corridor. I called to him, and he turned and headed toward me.

"Tony, where the hell have you been?"

"Where the hell have I been? The real question is where the fuck was Franco?"

"Jeez, Tony, you look like hell. What happened to you?" He reached out, with concern, and grabbed my upper arm on the bullet wound.

"You stupid fuck, get your hands off me."

"Whatsamatta? Whatsamatta?"

"That's where I was shot, you stupid fuck."

"Jesus, I'm sorry, I didn't know you were shot."

"Is thatta him? Is thatta him?" another voice cried from down the hall. I turned to see a woman of about sixty-five, short, squat and mean-looking, rolling at me like a tank. By the time I realized who she was talking about, it was too late to run.

She came at me, spinning her pocketbook like a Russian hammer thrower angry about not going to Los Angeles. She was screaming in a mixture of Italian, English and a Sicilian dialect.

Roughly what she was saying was, "You bastard, you bastard, you did this to my Franco. I'm gonna kill you. I'm gonna make your blood flow till your veins run dry. I'm gonna wring your neck like a scrawny chicken."

First I gaped in astonishment, then I grunted in pain and shock as the pocketbook connected with my ribs.

She wound up for another shot. But I was too smart for her. I doubled over and sank quickly to the floor. The pocketbook whistled over my head and caught Gene, who was stupidly trying to step between us.

Disappointed at hitting only a secondary target, she drew back her foot to kick at me. Screeching in her mangle of languages she said, I think, "I'm gonna tear off your little balls and put them in a garlic press. I'm going to remove your tiny masculine tool and sell it to the sausage factory where they will grind it up into small Neapolitan salamis." Sicilians generally have a low opinion both of Neapolitans and their salamis.

At that point a tall young man reached us. He put his arms around her, and as I watched from shoe level, he dragged the screaming Eumenidie away.

Gene squatted down beside me.

"Are you OK?" he asked.

"No."

"Listen," he said urgently, "you gotta act like what happened to Franco is your fault. It's real important."

"What the fuck are you talking about?" I inquired.

"You know, act like what happened to Franco was your fault."

"Who was that woman? Have they removed her for good?"

"That's Mrs. Polatrano. She's upset."

"No shit."

"So will you do what I asked?" he asked.

"Gene, you better explain what you're talking about. What did happen to Franco?"

"You don't know what happened to Franco?"

"How the hell should I know what happened to Franco? In fact, it better be something fairly horrible to excuse him for not being there."

"Being where?" Gene asked.

"What are we, Jews? Every question gets answered with

a question. Be Italian. Make statements. Use your hands for emphasis. But don't touch me.''

''You didn't know that Franco had a heart attack?''

''No more questions. I'll do questions, you do answers. Later, if you're good, we can switch.''

''Sure, Tony, sure.''

''Franco had a heart attack. You want me to say it was my fault. Why?''

''Isn't it?''

''Stop that. Just do answers.''

''Yes, I want you to say it's your fault.''

''I think that's very dangerous. I assume the killer bag lady is his wife. I could die. Besides, it's not my fault.''

''It doesn't matter, Tony. I mean you can go back to New York. Franco has no escape.''

''Then he probably wants to die. Have you thought of that?''

''Yeah, but the poor bastard is gonna live.''

''How is he?''

''Oh, the doctors say he's gonna live. He can live a normal life except for this, that and the other thing.''

''Good.''

''Will you do it?''

''Do what?'' I asked.

''Tell Mrs. Polatrano that it was your fault and you talked him into whatever he was doing. You know, take the weight off him.''

''Yeah, I'll do it. By telegram. I'm not going within pocketbook distance of that woman. Help me up.''

''You know, Tony, you don't look that good.''

''No shit, Gino. The old bitch clobbered me right in the ribs. The ribs were busted last night, and I have a doctor who thinks aspirin is top of the line in painkillers.''

''Jeez, maybe I can get you some percodan.''

''Please do that, Gene,'' I said, and my sweet brown angel eyes pleaded.

''Trade you,'' the blackmailing bastard said, ''you do the routine for the wife, I'll get you the percodan.''

"Done. But I get the percs first. I'm not going back in the ring without 'em."

He helped me up off the floor, then went off to find my pacifier. I went into the john to take a little toot. I carefully scanned the hall before I re-emerged. She was nowhere in sight.

I went in to see Franco.

"Hey, paisan," I said, "you look like hell."

"Yeah," he grunted. "Didja get him?"

"No. He got away."

"Damn. You'll get him, Tony, I'm counting on you."

"Sure, Franco."

"It's gonna be one damn big case, kid, the biggest."

"Sure, Franco."

The nurse came in. "It's time for our rest now," she bustled. "Can't get too tired now, can we."

"Jesus, you really do talk like that," I said to her.

"What!" she bristled. "You. You don't belong here."

"Hey, Franco," I said, "I'll see you around."

"See you around, Tony," he said sadly.

When Gene got back with the percs, we went to a visitors' lounge made entirely from torn green vinyl. First things first. I made him give me the percs. He offered to get me water, but one was down my throat by then. I dug through my wallet. The note was dirty and worn, but the name that Gerald Yaskowitz had given me, way back when it all began, was still legible. I gave it to Gene.

"I need some assistance," I told him. "Would you call this guy? Then let's find a relatively friendly cop who's not going to bust my chops too much while I explain how I fucked up a murder investigation. Then let's all three of us, the cop, the attorney and me, meet up at the same time and place. Can you do that?"

He read the name and appeared to recognize it. "Did you kill someone last night, Tony?" he asked with concern.

"What has happened to you, Gene? Why are you answering questions with questions?"

"Aren't you doing the same thing?"

"Gene, snap out of it."

"Yeah. Sure. I'm upset about Franco. Also, if you told me what was going on, it would be easier for me to help. I mean I'm kind of in the dark here."

"Yeah, well, you come along and you'll hear everything. I don't mind you knowing, but I'm too damn tired to repeat it anymore than I have to."

"I'm telling you it'll be easier to help if I know what's going on."

"Goddamn it, Gene," I flared. "I'm paying the bills. I got two busted ribs and a shot-up arm. I'm tired and I have a Demerol hangover. Now do what I tell you."

His body tensed like he was ready to start swinging. Then he took hold of himself, gave me a look that said he didn't beat up crips and marched off down the hall to a pay phone.

Seymour Whitaker had iron-gray hair swept back from his high forehead and spilling down over his collar. His sideburns were almost muttonchops. He slouched into interrogation with his hands thrust into the pockets of his chino pants so that his arms held his chino jacket back and open over a belly that lunged over his belt. Everyone called him Cy and he wanted cash up front, $300, against $150 an hour. He knew his way around the precincts and, I guessed, D.C. criminal court better than the cops, which is the way I wanted it, and I gladly paid his fee.

He kept a detective named Moynihan civil and pleasant while I summarized. The first thing Moynihan did was put out an all-points on Alexander Jr.. Then he called the D.A. for warrants to search his domicile.

When I described my assailant it seemed to ring a bell. There aren't that many people who look like Dave Butz, except they're black, like to use a silencer and work for Doc Wellby. I picked out George Roland "Peanut Butter" Bernard from the mug shots. He had once been a thirteenth-round draft pick for Buffalo but had been cut after two weeks in camp because of an attitude problem. He apparently liked collection work better than the offensive line, as any rational person would, since in one job he traded pain, in the other he only dished it out.

"I'm surprised," Moynihan said with a certain grudging respect, "that you got past him."

I was flattered. But I was also in pain. I went to the men's room, swallowed a perc and snorted a couple of lines.

When I returned, the mood in the room had turned sour. I soon found out why. We all packed up, the four of us, and went to the morgue. There, I ID'd the remains of James Carlton Alexander, Jr.

Whoever took him out, got up close behind him with a shotgun. A large portion of the back of his head and some of the side was missing, but most of his features were still intact. Unlovely in life, he looked worse dead.

"This punk could have led us to Wellby," Moynihan said across the corpse.

"Maybe," I said.

"And he was 'it' on your Edgar Wood thing. You crapped up that case too."

"Could be," I admitted.

"I could keep you around and make life extremely difficult for you. . . ."

"But you won't," Cy cut in.

"But I won't," Moynihan said. "The hell with it. There's plenty of harm done. What can be cleaned up, I'll clean up. Your attorney assures me that you'll be available to testify against Bernard . . ."

"I do," Cy said.

". . . and about anything else that comes out of this load of crap. You got a good lawyer, so I know it's a waste of time to do a number on you. You wanna know why I would?"

"No," I said.

"Cause you think I'm so stupid you can snort cocaine in my men's room and I won't know it. . . . Get the fuck out of here," he said and punched me on the arm. The wound opened under the bandage and began to bleed.

22

LIAR

I *WENT FROM* the morgue to National, from National to LaGuardia. Snortin' and swallowing percs, thinking savagely lewd thoughts about two out of four stewardesses. Slipping back to my same old used-to-be. From LaGuardia to the office. When I arrived, Glenda was there.

"I did something foolish," she said.

"Oh? You too?"

"Well, you have to understand, when I didn't hear from you, I began to worry. You didn't call or anything."

"Go on," I said.

"I called Joey, and he hadn't heard anything more than I had, so I came here."

"Then what?" I asked, watching the tension in her slender body crying out.

"Then I noticed your answering machine. It's none of my business, but I was worried, I thought you might have called and left a message for Joey. So I played your messages."

"You played my messages?"

"Yes," she said, biting her lip.

"OK, what was on there?"

"You don't know?"

"No. I don't know. Why don't you play it, then we'll both know."

"I've heard it about twenty times," she said.

Making no attempt to hide the effort it cost to cross the room, I shuffled over and switched the machine to play.

"Oh Tony," Christina's voice, all yearning and soft, came off the tape, "please, call me, please, as soon as you get in. I need to talk to you. To see you." It wasn't something to go to court on, but it was enough to shipwreck a relationship. My insides went hollow, but I played it poker-faced. She had played her card, I hadn't. It was a game that I needed to win, and could, because she also needed me to win.

"So?" I said, looking square at her.

"What's going on between you and . . . her?"

"Don't be ridiculous, that's a client."

"Don't lie to me. I can stand anything, but not lying."

"Oh, you can stand me being unfaithful?"

"I never said you had to be. I never said you had to be anything. I don't tell you what to do. You make your own choices."

"So what if I said yes, yes, I'm screwing her?"

"Then go right ahead!" she yelled. "Go right ahead, pack your bags, get out of the house and screw your little prick off!"

"I'm sorry," I said, shuffling toward her. "Forgive me, I'm irritable, mean and nasty. I've got two busted ribs and a bullet hole in my arm." Thank God. "In fact, if you'll help me, I want to change this shirt. I'm bleeding through again."

I started unbuttoning the shirt so she could see the contusions around the ribs. She looked at them in shock, then noticed the redness oozing from my upper arm.

"Are you all right?"

"I was just pissed. I'm sorry, I shouldn't've said that. You know how I get sometimes. Ms. Wood, as far as I'm concerned, is just a client. She is a very anxious little JAP. She has a tendency to hysteria. She hates her mother. She feels guilty about her father. She doesn't trust her lawyer. She feels she has no one in the world to turn to except me. Sometimes she even says I'm an angel. But I can't help that. It's still a job. It pays very good bucks; we're talking triple what I get from some people, which I deserve if people are going to shoot at me, and as far as I'm concerned that's it.''

I got dizzy and let it happen and clutched on to her. A brief black swirl passed me by and her face was there, swallowing and blinking back tears, when it was gone. ''Baby, I need you,'' I said. That, at least, seemed true.

Glenda helped me get my shirt off.

''She's the pretty one, isn't she?''

''I'll tell you a story about Ms. Wood,'' I said. ''I went to see her to give her an update. While I was there, her mother called and wanted to meet her for lunch. Christina got very upset, started yelling at the woman and said she had plans. She really got upset that her mother had the presumption to call at the last minute. I figured her plans must be something really important, so I asked her what they were. She says, very seriously, 'I was going to Bloomingdale's to buy bathing suits.' ''

''I bet,'' Glenda said, ''she wears the kind I don't dare.''

''That was not the point of the story.''

''I'm sorry, I shouldn't have listened to your machine,'' Glenda said, full of false contrition and real regret.

It struck me funny. I started to laugh. It hurt, of course, and I had to hold my ribs still against the laugh heaves.

''What?'' she demanded to know, ''are you laughing at?''

''Listening to other people's machines,'' I tried to explain. ''As in 'I'm worried about Harry, have you heard his machine lately,' or 'She looks like butter wouldn't melt in her mouth, but you should hear her machine.' '' The laughter loosened fear's clutch, and I wanted to feel warm and affectionate. ''Why don't you,'' I said, ''come here and give me a kiss.''

''Why should I?''

''Because I'm glad to be home, and with the woman I live with and love.''

''Are you sure?''

"Sure, I'm sure," I said, and she came into my arms, carefully. "Will you help me get on a shirt and get home?"

"Yes," she said.

"And hold me, don't let me slip away back to my same old used-to-be."

"What happened to you?" she asked.

"Wait 'til we get home, and I'll tell you and Wayne at the same time."

"Why?"

"It's great stuff, full of thrills, chills, car chases and stuff."

"Better than *The A-Team*?" she asked, knowing Wayne's point of reference.

"It would be," I said, "if it weren't real."

But Wayne seemed to think it was just as good. Except that I hadn't caught the bad guys in the end.

"We have not arrived at the end yet," I explained; "this is one of those shows with episodes; you have to wait 'til next week or the week after."

"Like a miniseries."

"Yeah."

"Then are you gonna catch 'em?"

"That's a good question."

"When you say that," Wayne said knowingly, "it means you don't know."

"Right."

"But you'll catch 'em. You're Tough Tony."

"You better go to bed now."

"Can I see your bandages again first? Just one more look? Huh? Huh? Can I?"

After having his way with my battered body, he went to bed.

"Truth, Tony. Is there anything between you two? Don't lie, you know that's the one thing I can't stand."

"There is nothing going on," I said immediately, before I had a chance to say something dumb, and I looked her squarely and honestly in the eye as I said it.

I was exhausted. My shoes felt like they were far, far away. Farther than effort could reach. The cocaine in my pocket would have picked me up. But I was home now and I didn't need that shit. With Glenda's help I undressed. She lay down beside me and, as we were talking, I drowsed off.

Christina was there. She said, "Arise and save what is beautiful," so I followed the sway of her hips, downward, down the stairs. Her mouth caressed me there. On the flight north, a stewardess named Laurie had helped me in and out of my seat, served me drinks, declined my offer to share a cab to the city, but left me her phone number. She walked into the dream. She lifted her uniform skirt to the top of long naked legs. The pubic hair was thick, curly and warm-colored. "You won't mind," I said to Christina as Laurie moved closer. "I'll always, always hate you," she replied, "and so will Glenda," but her mouth grew bigger and took more of my body. There were shapes moving in from the walls. Big men muttering, "Who's the heroine," or "Where's the heroin," I didn't know which, but wanted to find out. As they started jabbing the needles into my arm, I heard Sandy laughing and laughing. "You're such a bastard," she said. Then the sirens began.

They were real, coming up from the street through the open window. Glenda was real. She was stroking my erection.

"You really could do it in your sleep," she said wryly.

"Yeah, but you better climb aboard if we're gonna make the station."

"All right," she said and straddled over me. She moistened the tip and eased on down. Once she was in place she gallantly raised her hand, mimed the pulling of a train whistle and said, "Whoo awhooo."

"Chuga chug, chuga chug," I replied, and we were off and rolling on the giggle track. It can be found in *Even More Joy of Sex* in the index under funny fuck.

"I keep thinking about you and her," she said afterward.

"Don't," I said, and passed out.

23

LOVE IN PAIN

THE RINGING PHONE that woke me at 11 A.M. was as vicious as a kick in the ribs. I had had the experience to make the comparison and it was not an exaggeration.

"You get your messages?" Joey D' asked me.

"No, what?"

"The lovebird and the lawyer."

"Ahh, my clients."

"Clients, my ass."

"What did they say?"

"They both appear eager for your presence. The lovebird breathes a little harder about it."

"Are they both on the machine or did you take 'em?"

"Both on the Panasonic, kiddo."

"Do me a favor?"

"Sure," he said, "I'll erase 'em."

"Thanks."

"Do yourself a favor, kiddo."

"What?" I asked.

"Tell the lovebird to be a little more discreet."

"Joey D', how do you know about these things?"

"I'm a detective, ain't I?"

"Joseph, it is time for a serious answer."

"I got a call from the girl friend this morning. The live-in, not the lovebird. Apparently your explanations of last evening were not totally satisfactory."

"So?"

"So I covered for you, asshole. Which is more than you deserve. I explained that victims often become fixated on investigating officers. Irrespective of that officer's conduct. That, in point of fact, the response is so normal that it is covered in the 'Conduct and Relations with the Public' course at the academy. Even in the ancient days when I attended and they were not so hip about psycho-evaluation as they are in these modern days."

"What did she say?"

"She said, 'Tanks, Joey, I feels better for talking to you'!"

"Tanks, Joey," I said sincerely.

Getting out of bed, getting to the bathroom, brushing my teeth, keeping my eyes open to watch my urine for blood were all major productions. So I swallowed a perc and two aspirins, then snorted four lines. Small ones.

Dear, dear Glenda had left coffee on the stove and it only needed warming, thank you. I sat slumped over it and called Mr. Haven.

"How soon can you be here to give me an update?" he asked.

I wanted to say at least a week, but I croaked, "How about tomorrow?"

"I will be out of town tomorrow," letting me know in his quietly imperial way that he meant now and was paying for it. I got two hours' grace.

I actually searched the apartment before I dared call Christina. Even then, I sat so I could see the door, in case the knob should turn. I told her about Glenda and the tape.

"There's no place I can call you," she said. "I don't like leaving messages with your partner; he sounds like he resents me. I know I can't call you at home; now I can't even leave a message on your machine."

I asked her if I could see her after my meeting.

"I have some things scheduled, but I'll try. Tony, I don't like rearranging my life around your . . . convenience. I'll try, but I'm not promising anything." She hung up.

Something chilly and tight moved through me. Some close kin of fear. The thought of losing her squeezed moisture from the pores on my back, arms and neck.

I had no more compunction about snorting up in the men's room of a law office than I did in a police station, so when I saw Choate Haven I didn't mind the pain too much and was able to give him a coherent rundown of events.

"Your extraction of what is significant from these events is actually quite adequate," he said. I wondered if he had learned the manner from John Houseman or if Houseman had learned it from him. "However, your suppositions appear to me to be merely that, suppositions."

He leaned back and made himself look both thoughtful and astute before continuing.

"Your inference that Alexander acted on behalf of this Marcus Wellby, alleged heroin dealer, is not necessarily supported by fact. He did not know the thrust of your investigation. Your associate had previously been employed as a police officer, and it is reasonable to assume that Alexander perceived your approach as, for example, another narcotics investigation. That would explain the facts as well, or better, than your theory.

"You are obviously aware of the weakness of your other major supposition, that Wellby was a mere conduit. The lack of apparent motivation and the lack of an obvious connection do not mean that both do not exist.

"In law, as in science, the obvious inference, the clearest and simplest explanation, is to be preferred over the more complex, insofar as they both account for all the facts. The principle is called Occam's Razor, as I'm sure you are aware.

"The lack of apparent motivation and connection between Wellby and Wood is a lack common to Wood and to everyone else. It is therefore not a reason to dismiss Wellby as the prime mover. . . . Unless I've missed something.''

"No, Mr. Haven, in fact I find your analysis very much to the point, clear and lucid. The direction of my continued investigation should and will use your perceptions as a basis.''

"Excellent," he said, "what will that be?''

"There are, in a sense, two investigations. One is a physical trail, in D.C.: looking for Alexander's partner; finding 'Peanut Butter' Bernard; trying to get a lead on Alexander's executioner. Right now, the police are better equipped to handle that than me. If they should, excuse the expression, 'crap out,' then I'll stick my two cents in. The other investigation is the paper chase. If Wood and Wellby had a connection it'll be in phone records, or a file or his diary.''

"That makes sense." But before I could heave a sigh of relief, he went on, "There are, however, inherent problems in the procedure. Any client associated with Wood is protected by the attorney-client privilege. I cannot permit you to root blindly through the papers of Edgar Wood. They contain the affairs of our clients. Unless, of course, you were able to obtain evidence of a quality to show cause, to search for some specific item or items.''

"If there is any trace at all, it has to be in his papers," I said. I needed access to them.

"This may be a frustrating discovery for you, Mr. Cassella, but this is a society of rules and laws. The police find that frustrating. Prosecutors find that frustrating. Even I, at times, am irritated by it. But it is something we must live with if we are to survive as a social organism, and I for one am glad and grateful for that fact.''

I rose to go.

"Mr. Cassella," he said, "bring me due cause, or the equivalent thereof, and I will speak with the other senior partners, and we will make available as much as we can to you.''

When I left, my stomach was in knots. I expected the worst when I saw her. I expected her to say she couldn't deal with it anymore. The thought filled me with fear and I forgot that it should have been me saying "this can't be," just plain forgot.

When I came through the door, she was standing in the middle of the room, looking distraught and distracted. When my arms went around her, hers went around me. When my mouth opened on hers, hers opened in welcome. Her softness leaned into me, and my body, battered parts and all, sang with joy. Love, opiate and analgesic.

Her shirt lifted up and off her, leaving her breasts and belly bare to my mouth. She made sounds in her throat. Her skirt unlatched easily and floated down her long legs. The small bikini pants followed and so did I. Her warm moisture tasted just fine. Her fingers trembled when they touched my head and her knees lost their strength. She slid down so that we knelt face to face and she tasted herself on my lips.

"Angel, my angel," she said.

When the time came to try to get up off the floor, I got dizzy and had to cling to her. Pain thudded through my middle in a double mismatched beat, one for my blood and one for my breath.

"My angel, you're hurt. Why didn't you . . ."

"It's just a disguise," I said.

"Are you all right?"

"Yeah," I hoped. "Just help me up."

She helped me get to bed and helped me undress. The magic pick-me-up was in my pants pocket and I asked for it. The snort woke me up. It felt good, so I did another round and suddenly grew afraid.

"Do you want some?" I asked.

She nodded yes. I gave her the bottle. After she snorted I asked if that was enough. She said yes.

"Then flush what's left," I said. "Now. Do it now."

I waited. When I heard the water running I yearned for it not be happening; somewhere down in the drains I could snatch it back.

When she returned, I summarized again. I downplayed the violence, trauma and death, just like John Wayne would have. She reacted perfectly, concern on her face, a tear in one corner of her eye, her cheek laid gently on my wounds. It would have ruined the moment to tell her how perfectly Sandy's kiss went with Demerol, so I left that out.

"Don't go on. I don't want you hurt. My angel, I don't want to lose you." The cynical side, the son of a bitch that hides in back but never leaves, said that her lines were right on cue. But even he loved her for saying them so damn well.

"This is gonna sound melodramatic," I said. "A lot of evil things have been said about vendetta. In fact, I've never heard anything good about it. And all the bad things are probably true, but there is a deep satisfaction in knowing that any blow against me and mine will be returned. Avenged, if you like."

"Are you doing this for me or for you?" she asked.

"I don't know. All I know is that there is too much pain and shame living with an unavenged wrong. Like rape, it's the victim that feels dirty."

"Yes," she admitted, "it is."

The tears gathered in the corners of her eyes.

"I can't let you live the rest of your life like that," I explained.

Another kind of dam broke; she clung to me, sobbing hard.

24

THE MAN HIMSELF

WHEN CHOATE, WINKLER, Higgiston, Hahn & Moore informed Over & East of the charges against Edgar Wood, a whole set of procedures was set in motion. Over & East's in-house legal department took care of things like seizing Wood's papers and sealing his office. They informed the banks that Wood was no longer authorized to sign checks or transact business for any part of the vast empire. They instituted the actions required to remove Wood from the board of directors and from the boards of various subsidiaries. Personnel and administration also took part in shifting what had been the domain of Edgar Wood into other hands.

But certain things Charles Goreman did personally.

Immediately after the meeting, he went to the basement of the Over & East building and found the head of night maintenance. Together they went to the lobby. The maintenance man opened the glass doors of the building directory. Goreman reached in with his hands and removed the name of Edgar Wood.

Wood had his name in bronze letters on his solid-mahogany office door. Goreman pointed out to the maintenance man that even if the letters were pried out, the name would remain engraved. Though it was well after business hours, the entire door was removed, and another one, blank, replaced it within 120 minutes. Goreman stayed until it was done.

Goreman was hounded by the press for comment. The only thing he ever said, publicly or privately, was that Wood's activities were hardly of a size to do substantial damage to Over & East, and that the interests of the stockholders were, as always, secure.

I told Christina that I had to talk to Goreman. Yet I had no leverage, no angle, no introduction. I had tried calling. I spoke to the assistant executive secretary, who wanted to know my business, which I didn't tell her, but I did leave a name and number. The call was not returned.

"Oh, I'm sure Charlie will see you if I ask. He'll see us together if you like," Christina said. I expressed some surprise.

"I told you . . . Charlie was always sweet to us, to me. He was a real dear to the family, even after . . . He's still cordial to Mother, even though I don't think he ever really liked her. He still invites her to the sort of social events she dotes on. Are we planning to sneak up on him and pop the questions? How should I arrange this?"

"Tell him that I want to see him because I'm investigating the murder of your father. . . . Yeah, tell him that straight up. And I need to talk to all the top people at Over & East and at Choate, Winkler. You can even say it's because that's where the dead man's hand points. But you don't have to tell him he's number one on the list; he knows that."

"If, if it turns out to be Uncle Charlie, I won't believe it," she said, and I looked at her with my questions. She cuddled closer to me, her strong young woman's body somehow very soft, perhaps with the moment's contentment. "Right now, it all seems, far away . . . when you're here, sometimes when we're not talking about it, I forget that it happened, and that there are people who kill people. And even when we do talk about it, I don't feel the anger as much. I feel, safe, I guess."

"I'm so in love with you," I said, feeling so close to making her mine.

"Don't love me," she said so softly I almost didn't hear, and I didn't say anything back.

The weekend after next, Goreman told Christina the next day, would be perfect. The two of us were invited to be his guests from Friday night to Sunday at his house in the Hamptons. When she told me about it she was as happy as a schoolgirl on holiday. She had accepted for both of us.

Selling the lost weekend at home was not easy. I kept telling Glenda how hard I was maneuvering to see Goreman. Lying and legend creating are tools of my trade, but they're on the outside, they're a game. Home is supposed to be, and had been, a refuge from all of that. Bringing them inside was a violation. Two days before the weekend, I announced that Goreman had at last agreed to see me and told her that I would be at his Hamptons' house for the weekend.

"I assume Miss Bikini is going with you," she said.

"Gimme a break."

"Well, is she? A cute little weekend by the shore. It sounds perfect for Miss Bikini."

"Look, this isn't personal. This is my job. As far as I know, she won't be there. I have to do what I have to do to make a living. If you start fucking around with me about that, I don't know how to deal with it. . . ." And on and on it went, until I left and spent the night in the office. I didn't tell Christina because I would have ended up at her place and not been in when Glenda called at 6:15 A.M., not having slept and ready to make up. Which she did and we did.

Not that the Other Woman was content and pleased with me that week either.

"How can you love me and not see me?" was one of the things she said. "I've talked to my friends and they all tell me the same thing. That I'm crazy to hang around with you. That I'm just a toy for you to play with on the side."

"When women talk among women," I said, "and I've taped enough of them to know, no man is ever good enough. . . . Christina, listen to me. I didn't want this to happen, neither did you, but it happened. You complicate my life, but I can't stop, I can't let go. Something inside me thanks God you exist.''

"It does not make me feel good about myself. It makes me feel used.''

"What if I were free?'' I said. It was an offer, and I was stupid enough to follow through on it.

"Don't do that. You'll regret it. This—thing—we have. Infatuation, hot sex, is going to wear out. And when you need me, I won't be there. That's the way it is. If you leave her, I swear, I will never see you again.''

Which I didn't believe either.

And when we got on the seaplane that Charles Goreman sent for us, it was all different again. Sort of.

"I've been behaving like a neurotic idiot, haven't I?'' she said.

I agreed.

"I'm sorry,'' she said. "I have been wondering, day-dreaming, what we would be like if we had more than eight hours together. Do you think it will all fall apart?''

"We are about to find out.''

"A whole weekend with you. I am so excited. You have no idea how I've been looking forward to it. Do you know what you do? You make love to me the way I make fantasies about it when I do it by myself.''

"It's the 'us' that makes it happen,'' I said with several different parts of me feeling overwhelmed.

"How can you go home at night then?''

"Because, I guess, it is home. It would be different if I could say, 'My wife doesn't understand me,' but I can't. She's not my wife and she does understand me. And there's Wayne. I'm trying to be honest with you. But there isn't the magic there that there is here.''

"I'm sorry. Let's not talk about it. I promised myself that I wouldn't ruin the weekend by thinking like that. Our first weekend, and maybe our last.''

We landed on the calm of Shinnecock Bay and there was a Mercedes waiting for us. The mansion was built in an age

that predated income tax and presupposed an affordable ser-
vant class, in the style favored by old-line WASPs so that
they could call twenty-two rooms a cottage.

The housekeeper, an elderly but vigorous example of that
rare breed, the native Hamptonian, was at the door to meet
us. Her mouth was prim, her iron-gray hair was cut in austere
battle lines and her name was Agnes. She greeted Christina
fondly, calling her Miss Christina, and declined to snub me
only because she saw the way Miss Christina looked at me.

Goreman did not appear at dinner. He sent his apologies
from whatever end of the vastness he occupied.

Obscure signals passed between Agnes and Christina, and
after dinner our separate rooms became a single room on a
corner of the second floor overlooking the sea. The sound of
breakers rolled in and joined our own joyful noises.

We came down to breakfast in a glow of inexhaustible and
wholesome carnality. Agnes even smiled at me. Goreman
was there, avuncular when he wasn't preoccupied with
Forbes, Friday's *Journal*, the *Times* and his notes. I was preparing to broach the topics that had ostensibly brought us
here when what I guessed was a male secretary came in to
announce an overseas call.

"You will excuse me," Goreman said, "but sometimes
what is supposed to be a vacation cottage becomes just an
office over and east of Manhattan." Everyone, including him,
smiled politely at the weak humor, and he disappeared.

I didn't give a damn. I had her.

When we got back from the beach, late in the afternoon,
I attempted to find the area he used for an office.

Agnes intercepted me.

"Excuse me, Mr. Cassella, but Mr. Goreman is not to be
disturbed. Might I suggest you try our tennis courts?"

"Agnes," I said, trying to look down the broken ridge of
my crooked Roman nose, "I am a Squash Player. I never hit
a ball without a wall."

"That must be terribly limiting," she replied politely, "By
the by, do you have a jacket and tie?"

"In my entire wardrobe?"

"With you, Mr. Cassella."

"No."

"Then we shall have to find you one for this evening."

"Is it required?"

"Of course not, but you will blend in rather better that way, and that should help you with your investigations."

"You're quite right, Agnes. Please do find me something." She turned to go. "Agnes, wait. Why are you concerned?"

"Miss Christina has been one of ours for many, many years. Since she was quite a little girl. We're all fond of her. And though, if I may speak for the rest of the staff, we're all quite shocked by Mr. Wood's conduct, we're all quite sympathetic to Miss Christina's loss."

For a moment she made it seem that some lost and lovely world had drifted out of *Masterpiece Theatre* into reality.

"May I ask you an impertinent question?" I said.

"Nothing you could say would be impertinent," she lied.

"Is he really busy or evading me?"

"Oh, do be sensible, Mr. Cassella," she clucked. "If he wanted to evade you, do you think he would have gone through all that folderol with the seaplane? Would he even have invited you? Therefore you might deduce . . . is that the proper detective term? . . . that he actually is tied up."

"Thank you."

"There is one other thing, actually two, that I have to say to you, Mr. Cassella, if I may."

"Please."

"Don't do anything to hurt Miss Christina. She seems terribly vulnerable right now."

"That's one," I said.

"That's not a reply."

"I don't want to do anything to hurt her. I will try not to do anything to hurt her."

"Oh dear," she sighed, "that means that you will. . . . I'm certainly glad that I am past the age where a pair of dark brown eyes will start a fever in my blood."

"No, you're not," I said.

"I certainly am, young man, but I appreciate the flattery."

"What I meant was that you are not glad of it."

"I stand corrected," she said severely, but her eyes smiled. "The second thing I wanted to tell you was this. I have read enough Agatha Christie to know that character is always the key.

"Look for the overachiever," she echoed Sandra. "Rather like the late Mr. Wood was. Someone who achieves more than his natural gifts would normally lead to. That's the sort who breaks the rules. Someone like Mr. Goreman, who is really quite gifted, does not have to do that. You see, he is clever enough to play within the rules, or find the legitimate loopholes or create new rules. He does not have to break them."

"I see," I said solemnly.

"If you don't, you're probably a terrible detective. I'll find you a tie and jacket now. A tweed for you, I think."

"I'm sorry," I said, "no one told me we were to dress for dinner."

"Dinner is come as you are. The jacket is for the party tonight."

It was a major Hamptons bash. There were items on the buffet that I could not afford as an appetizer for one, let alone as a meal for 250. The catering budget, calculated by federal guidelines, would have fed a family of four through generations yet unborn. The futures market in scotch whiskey nudged up another quarter point. The rock 'n' roll was subdued, the dancing discreet and everyone asked if Woody Allen was really going to show up.

I was looking for the lord of the manor. I finally spotted him, moving through the party, performing his chores as host graciously but perfunctorily. I cut through the whiskey sippers, contact makers and hustlers. He greeted me as graciously as he did any of the other guests.

"I do have to talk to you," I said.

"Indeed you do," he said, taking me by the elbow and guiding my path, "and indeed you shall." We moved through the crowd. I thought the moment had come, but he stopped to introduce me: "This is Andrew Klughorn, our wonderful comptroller, and much, much more. This is Tony Cassella. Tony is the detective investigating the murder of Edgar Wood."

"How interesting," Klughorn said coldly. By then, Goreman had moved on.

"It's gotten to be."

"Oh," he replied, as if it weren't.

"You know that it was a contract, that Wood was hit to shut him up."

"I had heard something, but it seemed to me to be merely a rumor."

"Not at all. A pro took him out. Then he was hit to tie up the loose ends. But it won't work," I said.

"You'll excuse me, Mr. Uhh . . ."

"I won't, and it's Cassella."

"I beg your pardon?"

"When Wood was sentenced, he made threats. Threats to expose other people who were supposed to have done as much as he did, or worse. Comptroller and director of financial operations. A good position to be in, if you have sticky fingers."

"That is the most ridiculous thing I've ever heard," he said and began to turn away. I put my hand on his arm to stop him.

"There's a dead hand from the past. It's pointing, and one of the people it's pointing at is you. You're gonna have to face that. You're gonna have to deal with that, Andy."

"Please take your hand off my jacket."

"Did Wood have something on you?" I asked, not letting go.

"Absolutely not."

"There are a lot of people hot for this thing now. The Virginia cops, the D.C. cops. And Wood was a federal witness. The FBI hates it when a federal witness gets bumped. They're gonna come looking at Over & East, and one of the people they are gonna come after is you. You do see that, don't you?"

"On a purely theoretical basis, perhaps. In reality, un-likely."

"OK, they're looking at Over & East. Who should they be looking at, if not you?"

"I cannot imagine anyone . . ."

"Did you imagine that Wood was a thief?"

"No."

"Can you imagine that there is someone else with another dirty secret? Why not? And whoever it is, if it's not you, is willing to kill to save his reputation, his money. To stay out of Attica. You better imagine it, 'cause it's true."

I let go of his arm. It didn't matter. I had his attention.

"It's an interesting theory. Forgive me if I'm somewhat skeptical."

"Think. Think about what I said. Think about who it could be. And think about the news stories. *Forbes* might make it a cover story. 'FBI Goes Over Over & East,' across the top, then a kicker across the bottom: 'And the Charge Is Murder!' Call me, Mr. Klughorn, if you think of something."

I went looking for Goreman again. He was affable and guided me to Stephen Marlowe, head of acquisitions.

Marlowe was in resort attire, powder-blue jacket and red pants. Ghastly. I started running the same game on him. If Klughorn was put out, Marlowe was insulted.

"I think," he said, "I'm going to ask Charlie to throw you out."

"What the fuck do you think 'Charlie' brought me here for?" I replied. " 'Charlie' doesn't want a six-month federal investigation into the top brass of Over & East with daily leaks to the *Times* and CBS. Charlie would like it solved nice, quiet and in-house."

"Do you actually suspect me?"

"There are only four logical suspects. Klughorn, Diller, you and Goreman."

All of them had gone eyeball to eyeball with the SEC, with foreign governments, with congressional investigations. I did not expect to see anyone twitch. No one would break down and confess. But they would start looking at each other, looking for what I wanted to find. And the guilty party might get nervous enough to jump.

Lawrence Choate Haven was also at the party. He was far more surprised to see me than I was him. He asked what I was doing there.

"Charlie," I said, "wants me to clear this mess up before it gets more out of hand."

"You spoke to Mr. Goreman without consulting me first?"

"No."

"Then how is it I am unaware of your contact with my client?"

"He heard about me from a third party and was so impressed that he felt he had to have me for his soirée."

"Mr. Cassella . . ."

"Pardon my sarcasm, sir," I said. "But he did call me. The thing is that there are so many loose ends, with two killings and all, that it has to unravel. The feds are going to think the same thing I do, because it's what Wood said to think, that there are two places to look: Over & East and your outfit. It would be better all around if I got to whoever it is before they come in and tear everything up."

And I wondered, even as I said it, what Goreman's real game was. I didn't particularly believe in the motives I was ascribing so easily to him.

"The investigation was initiated by my office. I am, therefore, not at all happy with steps taken without consultation. Under these circumstances, I'm not sure that all parties would not be more satisfied with a more reputable agency handling the matter."

That was something I had to deal with, and Christina was the key to it.

"Look," I told her, "I'm going to need you to stand behind me. To fight for me. I'm making a lot of enemies tonight, including the people who control your trust fund and your estate, which is what pays for this investigation. They may try to stop me."

"Tell me what to do," she said.

"Do you care enough to pay the bills yourself until you can get your money?"

"That could be a lot of money. I'm not sure I have it."

"Just the fact that you're willing is probably enough. But you can't run the bluff unless you're willing to get called. Now what's it gonna be?"

"Whatever you tell me to do, Angel."

I found Goreman again. He asked me if he had introduced me to Diller yet.

"Do I have to go through the whole circle before I get to you?"

"That is a most reasonable approach," he smiled. "Also, I have my duties as host, which must occupy me for another hour at least. Then we will have a good chat."

Midnight came. I saw him, looking tired, retreat to his den. "I guess it is time," he sighed when he saw me.

25

HUNGARY

"NOT HERE," HE said, "let's walk."

"It's very good of you," I said on the south lawn, "to gather all the suspects together here in one place."

"Did you shake anything loose?"

"No."

"Good. Anybody on my team should know how to hang tough," he said with pride.

"What did Wood have on you that was so hot?"

"Nothing."

Shrubs and trees bordered the lawn, helping to hold down the dunes. The moon was bright enough to illuminate the path through them to the beach. It was bright enough to cast shadows.

As we walked along, I made out the shape of two figures rustling behind the foliage. From the shape of the shadows and the tenor of the sound, it seemed that one man was having his cock sucked by the other.

"If there was nothing there," I asked him when we got to the beach, "how come you hired Douglas, Cohen to handle it?"

"Well, Choate, Winkler was compromised. We needed an outsider, and Douglas, Cohen, in my opinion, is the best."

"They tried awfully hard to get Wood's testimony. They were up to, what?—Federal Appeals Court?—before Wood got it."

"They were simply doing their job."

"Off the record, strictly off the record, because I could not care less, what could Wood have told the SEC?"

Goreman sat down on a piece of driftwood. He untied his shoes, took off his socks and rolled up his pants. I did the same.

"He was privy to everything you and your company have ever done. He was your personal attorney in addition to everything else. He must have known a lot."

Goreman tied his shoes together, stuffed the socks inside and put them over his shoulder. "He didn't know everything," he replied as he walked toward where the sand was hard and wet. I followed, down toward the crashing breakers.

"Do you know how blessed we are to be here? In America? Between these two oceans?"

"Maybe."

"I could kneel down and kiss the ground here."

He had done so. I knew that. In 1968, after a trip to the Soviet Union, when the Aeroflot landed at JFK, Goreman had gone down on his knees on the oil-soaked tarmac. Staining a five-hundred-dollar suit, he bent down and kissed the pavement. There was dirt on his mouth when he stood up.

Some people thought it was all phony. I didn't think so. Some people laughed at it. My father wouldn't have. Then again, neither would Uncle Vincent.

"From penniless refugee to multimillionaire. Of course you should kiss the ground," is what I said. "Kiss ass, kiss anything for a deal like that. Shake hands with the devil, do a deal with a heroin peddler and kill Edgar Wood, for a deal like that."

"I presume that you are being deliberately rude to provoke me."

"Isn't that what we're here for? To discuss why you killed Edgar Wood?"

"Do you expect me to break down and confess? Here and now? To you?"

"Why don't you, Charles? Confession helps. The sins eat at our souls. The burden grows heavy. There is no one here but the seagulls and the surf, and they don't care. Me, I don't care about punishing, just knowing."

He bent down and picked up a broken piece of shell. He studied it, then tossed it in an arc toward the water. A wheeling gull saw it, turned and dived for the splash it made.

"OK, Tony, you want a confession, I'll give you a confession. I am a killer. I have killed, more than once. Not hired anyone. No Doc Wellby for me. With my own hands I have killed. What else should I confess to? Stealing? I have stolen. Money, food, even shoes. Bribery, forgery . . . all those things I have done."

"Anything else?" I asked.

"Well," he paused and thought a moment, "Charles Goreman is not my real name."

"Who did you kill?"

"My real talent, I think, my special ability, Tony, is to be able to assess value. The whole thing, Over & East, is built on that single ability. I see a company. It is not making money. Perhaps it is badly run, it doesn't matter what the reason. What matters is that it is only trading for twenty million, and the assets can be sold for twenty-two million. So I go to the bank, borrow the twenty and know that I will come out ahead. That's the whole thing, and it's that simple."

"Where are we going?"

"How is your history? Do you now anything about Hungary?"

"Mostly about the revolution. When was it? '56?"

"We have such a narrow view here, it is peculiar. . . . I have asked many Americans about Hungary. College students, professors, politicians, educated, aware people. How many of them know that Hungary was the first fascist country? In 1932, when Adolf Hitler was just applying for German citizenship, Horthy and Gombos brought fascism to Hungary. They killed the Reds, persecuted the Jews and shot anyone who argued. They needed no urging to join the Axis. In 1941 they declared war on the Soviet Union and on the United States. I know. I was there. . . . The Hungarians deserve the Russians.''

''Is there a point to this?''

''Maybe, maybe not. You told me confession is good. So I am telling you, and the seagulls, and the surf, what I am made of. Then maybe you can figure out if I killed my old friend Edgar Wood. . . .''

Our feet splashed through the water that rushed up on the beach.

''But the Hungarians had two redeeming qualities. Yes. They did not believe in the final solution. And they could be bought. With money. With money there were false papers; for money the police would ignore false papers; money would even keep you out of the army. Money meant survival. Life and death were measured in cash. Do you understand that?''

I grunted. I probably didn't, not the way he had lived it.

''Where was I to get money, Tony? I will explain. The Horthy government was confiscating Jewish property, moving area by area. So I would go to a Jew, I would say, 'You are going to lose your home. You can let ''them'' take it, or sell it to one of these goyim, vultures, who will pay you only one-tenth what it is worth.' They would moan and cry then. 'There is a third way,' I would tell them. 'Here, I have Hungarian papers,' and I would show them the papers. 'Sell it to me.' The first time I did this, I was fifteen. . . .

''Then he might say, 'How much?' I had no money. Instead I would tell him that I would sell the house for him, maybe to the second wave of vultures. Instead of one-tenth, I would get half. Then we would split that and we would both be better off. You see how I learned this thing of value?''

''Yes,'' I said. ''And then the next time you could pay cash up front and buy for less, make more.''

''No. It was not that easy. I would have to pay for the

papers. Pay for the bribes. The clerks at the registrar, they knew. Even they would have to be paid, to record the transaction. Usually the, the . . . there is no word for it in English . . . the people who did the confiscating, they had to be paid, government people. Also, I had a family then. Parents, two sisters. Also, education. I wanted education and Jews could not go to school, so I paid for tutors for myself and my sisters.''

"And the killing?"

"That came later. In 1944 the Soviet Army was at the Carpathians, and Horthy tried to negotiate terms before they came through the passes. The Germans would not permit that, and German troops occupied the country. Immediately, the first priority was a special rail line from Budapest to Auschwitz. Two, three hundred thousand people were murdered in six months. For them, the extermination of the Jews was more important than winning the war. They were mad.''

"You mean they couldn't even be bribed?"

"Oh, they would take Jewish money. They loved to extort the money first and then put you on the special train after.

"I paid one, to save my sisters. He took the money and then he tried to arrest them, on the spot, right before me. He was the first man I killed. He was *Geheime Staatspolizei*, Gestapo.

"I used his papers to escape. Also his clothes. I went west to Austria, because once, as a boy, we had gone to the mountains. Then I was almost caught because the murder became known and the papers were no good anymore. It was almost December and the mountains were getting cold. I was growing ill from hunger and exposure.

"That is how I came to kill my second man. He caught me in his home, stealing his food and an overcoat and socks. He was an old man. Over fifty anyway.''

"Why did you kill him then?"

"He came for me with an ax. Can you imagine that, here in America, killing a man for a loaf of pumpernickel and an old overcoat?''

"Yeah, actually, I can.''

"Maybe you are right," he said, and the idea disturbed him. "That is a very sad thing."

We walked some more, until he spied a large hunk of driftwood and we went and sat on it. He took out a cigarette, a Gitane, and offered me one. It was formal and ceremonial, so I took it.

"Is that all of them?" I asked.

"All of what?"

"Of your dead. Of your sins."

"There is one more. A German. He tried to stop me when I was trying to get to the American lines."

"And Edgar Wood?"

"I better tell you how I met Edgar," he said. Then he explained how he had been classified as a DP, displaced person, and how, normally, he would have been sent to one of the DP camps, or to Hungary, but for a young American. A lieutenant who took pity on him and showed him how to get papers.

"Did you bribe him?" I asked.

"No," he said, still with wonder more than a quarter of a century later.

"But you made it up to him later."

"Yes, but who could know that?" We sat on the smooth, bleached wood, smoking. It was making me dizzy and a little high. "My name. I made it up when I got to the American lines. Gore man, it is a pun."

We smiled at each other, there in the moonlight, enjoying a good pun.

"What was your real name?" I asked.

"What does it matter? I had many. Once I was even Horthy. For two or three weeks, I think."

"And Edgar Wood knew all this. That's why he had to die?"

Goreman laughed aloud. "No, no, Tony. You don't understand what I'm trying to tell you."

"No?"

"Edgar knew none of this. He knew nothing of who I was

before I became Charles Goreman. There were many things he did not know.''

"There are two things I don't know and wanted to ask you about.''

"Who killed Edgar Wood and why,'' he replied.

"That wasn't it, but if you want to tell me, I'll listen.''

"I don't know either, so if you want to ask your other questions I'll try those.''

"I know that Wood was your attorney when you started. At that time he was a partner in a firm called Springstein, Saperstein, Cohen, and Wood. After you took over LTI, the attorneys for LTI, Choate, Winkler, et al, became the attorneys of record for Over & East. Why?''

"I felt that they were a key factor in creating a smooth transition. It was my way of saying 'thank you.' ''

"Gimme a break,'' I said.

"You doubt me?''

"I think it could be radically rephrased. You did a deal before the takeover attempt even started. LTI was bigger than you. They could have fought you off. So I figure you had a pipeline into LTI, that you knew every move they were going to make before they made it. Then your pipeline turned around and told LTI, 'Well, it looks like Charlie Goreman has us outmaneuvered. Maybe the best thing to do is let Over & East take you over.' ''

We looked at each other for a moment. He lit a second Gitane.

"You could phrase it that way,'' he said at last.

"Who was the pipeline?''

"Is that your second question?''

"No,'' I said, "it's part of the first.''

"I don't mind answering questions about myself, but I hesitate to speak about other people,'' he said.

"Was it Lawrence Choate Haven?''

"Yes,'' Goreman said, and realized where I would go with the idea. "However, Edgar did not know that. He was led to believe my source was at LTI.''

"He could have found out.''

"I doubt it. Lawrence and I were the only ones who knew."

"OK. My second question."

"Go ahead, Tony."

"How did you get started?"

"I thought you had investigated me. At least gone to the library. The story of Samson Construction is there. . . ." He sounded disappointed in me, while eager to sing the Saga of Charles Goreman and Over & East.

"I know about it. But what I don't know is where the first two hundred or three hundred thousand dollars came from. You were in commodities, you had a couple of jobs, but that's a big chunk of change."

"It was my patrimony. In '38 my father started sending money out of Hungary, to here, the United States. We were supposed to follow. We paid the Hungarians, they were willing, but the United States would not take us, not then. Suddenly we were there, and our money was here. If we had tried to bring it back, the government would have stolen it. So here it stayed."

"You got here in '47," I pointed out; "you didn't make your move until '54. How come?"

"I had a great deal of trouble getting the money. The man who sent the money to the United States bore the name Itzhak Oberetstock. I claimed to be his sole surviving heir, but my name was Charles Goreman. There were no papers, nothing to show who I was."

He sighed heavily. "It goes to show how much trouble you can make for yourself, making puns. I don't do it any longer."

"It took seven years for you to get the money?"

"No, no, only five. I got the money in '52. Actually it was only eighty thousand dollars. A lot in those days. Inside of a year I doubled it on the commodities market. By '54 I increased that amount by fifty percent. Then I spent six months looking for something like Samson Construction. . . . It is getting chilly. I am going back to the house."

He stood up and I followed him through the sand.

"How did you finally prove who you were?"

"I found some witnesses. People who knew me in the old country. It was not difficult. But it was time-consuming and expensive, in relation to the resources I had at that time."

"I would have been pissed."

"It was better than being in Hungary with the Arrow Cross Fascists or the Reds."

"So you're not angry about it."

"I cannot say that," he admitted. "I was angry. But anger, resentment, these are not functional emotions. Those are things that get in the way. I am a businessman. I deal only in the value of things."

"Who held your inheritance for you?"

"One of those big Wall Street law firms."

"Which one?"

"What matter, they are all alike. Big offices in a big building, with a lot of very American names."

"Like Choate, Winkler, Higgiston, Hahn & Moore. And the trustee was someone like Lawrence Choate Haven."

"Very much like that," he said.

"Did you feel like he was trying to defraud you?"

"Feel? I felt many things. But did I have grounds for suspicion? There were complications in establishing the facts. That is all that I know."

"Yeah, but what did you feel? What did you think?"

Goreman shrugged.

"When you started Over & East you had to choose an attorney. Here was a lawyer who was well connected; he knew the banks, he knew everyone on Wall Street. He was tied into all the powers. You didn't choose him. Why not?"

"I did not like the man."

26

LOVE IN VAIN

THE SEAPLANE TOOK us back to Manhattan early Sunday afternoon.

"I have done a lot of thinking," Christina told me. "I think I've come to terms with 'us.' I know that in the long run it would never work out. We're just too different. And there's the money problem. Traveling is very important to me, and living in a certain . . . style."

"What are you talking about?"

"When this is all over, I would like to go to Greece, or maybe Ibiza. For the winter. Can you afford that, Tony? Or would you go with me on my money? Could you handle that? I don't know if I could. Eventually I'm going to get married, and I have to marry someone who . . . who has more money than you do. Otherwise it wouldn't work out. Now that I understand that, I can relax and enjoy us. Just be good friends who happen to have the world's hottest sex. I can handle it on that level."

If only it were on that level, I thought, then I wouldn't have to have it at all. Life would re-stablize.

I spent the rest of the afternoon with Wayne, bike riding and squash playing.

On Monday, I called a shyster named Carmine DeSalvo, one of the nastiest people I know, specializing in those aspects of the law that verge on blackmail. Tuesday, I took Christina to see him, to represent her interest in the estate, charging Choate, Winkler's trust department with conflict of interest. I didn't need him to win, just to keep them off balance enough that they would be afraid to shut me down. Since I had once seen Carmine make a perfectly inoffensive nun, wearing her habit on the stand, appear to be a sleaze-monger, I was reasonably confident that he could do the job.

After the meeting, I offered to escort Christina home, my mind full of lust-tinted pictures of romance, or vice versa.

"Go home to Glenda and Wayne. That's the best thing you can do for all of us."

"Christina . . ."

"Don't say anything. Don't even look at me. You have honey on your tongue and the eyes of an angel. This weekend was all I thought it was going to be. It was heaven and you were my angel. I cried Sunday night. I woke up Monday morning so lonely I cried again. I didn't eat all day and I cried myself to sleep. This morning I woke up, and all I wanted to do was cry, because . . . I refuse to keep hurting myself this way."

"I love you," I said.

"I believe you. That's what's wrong. If you just wanted to fuck me I could live with that. Or maybe I couldn't. But I could throw you out and make it stick. I wouldn't keep coming back for more misery."

"What do you want me to do?" I said stupidly.

"Go home. Stay out of my life. Stay out of my bed. Don't even call me unless it's . . . don't talk to me at all unless it's to say who killed Daddy."

"I'm going to have to talk to you."

"Have that partner of yours do it. The one who doesn't approve of me." There were tears in her eyes. She whirled away from me toward the curb and waved for a cab. A dent exhibition slewed to a stop on uneven brakes and she jumped in. She sat there and dug a tissue out of her purse. "Where we going?" the driver asked. She wiped her eyes. Then she leaned out the open window.

"There's one, one other thing you can call me to say. You can call me to say, 'Meet me at the airport, let's go on the flight to Rio.' "

The cab drove off.

I trudged back to the office. The whole thing could only end in court, with Carmine DeSalvo pioneering the revolutionary legal concept of emotional whiplash. Christina could countersue on the same basis.

When the phone rang I was sure it was her, but it was a muffled male voice asking for me.

"Mr. Cassella," the voice said, "we met at a party. . . ."

"OK. And you are?"

"If there was anyone that Wood could blow the whistle on, my bet would be Marlowe," the voice told me.

"Oh. And why is that, Mr. . . . ?"

"Head of acquisitions. He knows where things are going to go, and when, long before anyone else. Smarter men than he are going to prison for insider trading these days."

"That is real nonspecific."

"Perhaps it is, but if someone were to add up his houses, his alimonies, his cars plus the boat, plus that woman's apartment at Sixty-fifth and Park, plus the money he drops at Tahoe, someone might come up with an outgo that exceeds reported income."

"That could be said of a lot of people, maybe most people in his position."

"You're supposed to be the bloodhound. All I can do is show you where the trail starts. Good luck, Cassella." He hung up.

It sounded like Diller. I wondered how long it would take for Marlowe to finger Klughorn, then for Klughorn to complete the daisy chain.

I called Chip and made a squash date. I was still stiff and sore, far from at my best. Still, I enjoyed beating up a little black ball that hardly ever hit back. I lost, and Chip was excessively pleased with himself.

"Angry at something?" he asked in the steamroom.

"Women trouble," I muttered.

"If you have to have trouble, that, I'm told, is the best kind."

"You're told? Never had any yourself?"

"Never."

"Why is that?"

"My approach to sex is rather clinical and cold," he said. "What surprises me is that it is successful. More and more women seem to like it that way. I think my style might be the coming thing."

My reply was a grunt.

"You, on the other hand, are probably very passionate, all that Mediterranean blood. Just the way you played squash today, and see where it got you."

"Chip, I have a favor to ask you."

"Sure. You want me to cover for you?"

"No. Listen. Feel free to say no, but I want your word that whether you say yes or no, you're not going to tell anyone about it. Anyone at all."

"My word is my bond. Or, if you prefer, my debenture."

"I'm serious," I said sternly.

"OK, OK, seriously. What is it?"

"Absolute secrecy. What I want to do is wait 'til we get out of here, then I'll give you a hundred bucks and consult you as an attorney. Then you're bound by the attorney-client privilege. OK?"

"Fine by me, buddy. I'm always glad to pick up a hundred, but it's not necessary."

We found a coffee shop. I gave him the hundred and made him write out a receipt. Then I told him what I wanted.

I wanted the records of Choate, Winkler, Higgiston, Hahn & Moore relating to the takeover of LTI by Over & East. I also wanted the records of any refugee funds that the firm had handled from 1936 to 1952, most specifically a file on Itzhak Oberetstock.

"You are kidding, of course," Chip said.

"No. There's something rotten, and I want to find it. . . . What if I told you that Lawrence Choate Haven sold out LTI to Charles Goreman?"

"Tony, you shouldn't even say things like that. Even here, even to me. You're wide open to a slander suit. You can't fool with guys like that."

"I have it on good authority."

"Yeah, well, maybe you do. Let them say it and let them take the rap. I think somebody is lying to you."

"During the war, old W.W. II, some people ran a racket. They handled refugee funds. A couple of senior partners up there, Shaw and Haven to name two, were on various refugee committees. Let's say they were sincere, why not?"

"How do you know that?"

"I spent Monday afternoon in the New York Public Library. It's in the *Times*, mostly in the Society pages. So-and-so throws a ball, proceeds to charity, to help refugees, on the committee are, and then there's a list. Simple."

"So they were good guys."

"But let's imagine what could have happened," I went on. "They not only helped people, they helped money escape from Europe. Sometimes the people didn't follow the money. It's 1945 and the American armies stumble over the death camps. Suddenly we discover millions of people died. Entire families, parents, children, cousins, uncles, aunts, the lot. Every possible heir. And you are holding the funds. . . . Then what happens? Tempting, isn't it?"

"Tony. I don't want to hear any more. I don't know where you got the nerve to come to me with, with, allegations like this. . . ."

"Wait, Chip, there's more."

By then he was standing and headed for the door. I threw a five on the table to cover the $1.25 tab and ran after him. I caught him trying to catch a cab.

"You've used up your retainer. Also our friendship. Don't say anything more."

"Just one thing more. You do work for Ricky Sams. Who

in your office is connected with a Washington dope dealer named Doc Wellby?''

A cab stopped. He jumped for the door and hauled it open.

''Because that's who had Edgar Wood murdered,'' I said through the window as he rolled it up.

I had his solemn word that he would not tell anyone what I told him. I was protected by the attorney-client privilege, with a signed receipt to prove it.

As the cab disappeared I wondered if he was going straight back to the office to bring my allegations to Choate Haven. Or would he wait until morning?

27

BLAST FROM THE PAST

I *WAS JUST* shaking the tree to make the nuts fall out. I used Ol' Chip, ol' squash buddy, to give it one shake. Mel could give it another one for me.

I told Mel that he should look into the LTI takeover, in particular the role that was played by the attorneys for LTI. I passed along the tip on Marlowe, which Mel appreciated, since insider trading was the offense that the SEC had the most success in prosecuting.

"All I want in return," I said when he thanked me, "is some instant noise."

"How instant?" he asked.

"Today."

"Gimme a break, Tony, what do you expect me to do today?"

"Mel, you're a bright guy. You'll think of something. Maybe you could just call up Over & East and say, 'Hi, Over & East, get your paperwork in order 'cause I'm gonna start prosecuting.' "

"What are you up to, Tony?"

"Think of it this way, Mel. If you can scare them enough, they just might try to buy you off with a decent job."

"I'll do what I can," he said.

I called Marlowe. It took him a day to get back to me. When he did, I explained that someone was pointing a finger at him. I didn't see him as the killer, I claimed. But if it wasn't him, who was it? He said he had no idea. I told him he better think about it.

Klughorn was next. I asked him how come he had missed Wood's embezzlement for all those years. He got huffy. I suggested that if another problem turned up, and if he, as comptroller, had missed that too, Over & East might start looking for replacement parts.

I checked in with Diller, with Scott, Culligan and Shaw. No one was particularly eager to speak to me, or even pleased to hear from me.

I was wondering whether or not to call Goreman when he called me.

"Young man," he said, "you are shaking people up."

"Do you have a problem with that?"

"If it goes on too long, I will. In the short run, it's interesting."

"You set this game up with your party, your introductions, your stories and confessions. What is your game?"

"I won't know until you play it out." Then he said, "Good-bye," and hung up.

When I had Christina, it somehow made things work better at home. I was happy and dealt with Glenda and Wayne from that happiness. Without her, I grew restless and hungry. Glenda and I began to fight. Maybe the waiting for something to happen was part of it also. I'm not good at waiting. An argument over the profound matter of who did more shopping found its way down the spiral of every irritation we had ever felt. It ended with me storming out and sleeping in the office for two nights. I avoided Glenda's calls as Christina avoided mine.

Finally I called her back. She was ready to make peace.

She never did quarrel for the sake of fighting. She was a fair and generous fighter. She never held a grudge.

Friday morning I left home early, just to get out. I went to the office. Joey D' was there, but there was nothing shaking. I went over to the courts, played badly and didn't enjoy it. I worked on the machines for a while. It hurt. I took a long steam bath and a long shower. I went out, ate, drank a lot of coffee, did the crossword. When I left the restaurant it was drizzling with gusting winds. I decided to walk the forty blocks to the office with the windy rain slapping my face, the cabs splashing me and the umbrella wielders trying to put my eyes out.

I shoved some people. Subtly and not too hard. But still I managed to provoke some antisocial behavior. One umbrella warrior got me in the ear. I reached out and knocked the thing away. When it tilted, the wind grabbed it and pulled it from his hand. It shot happily down the street, then died a messy but mercifully quick death under the wheels of a *Daily News* truck.

The umbrella man turned on me. He was bigger than me and probably younger. He cursed. I just stared back, letting him know that I felt meaner than he did, that I was perfectly willing to let him come at me.

"Asshole," he said. That sounded right, so I said, "Yeah." He hurried off, down into the subway.

Joey was waiting when I got back to the office. He suggested we go out for a drink together.

"Why?" I asked.

" 'Cause you're being some kind of asshole," he explained. There was a consensus forming.

I dried myself with brown paper towels, the worst kind, and got into some drier clothes. We walked silent and solemn up the West Side. The hookers huddled in doorways, dashing out occasionally to ask if someone wanted a date. I thought of Christina.

Come back when the policeman is in another street
And Beatrice will let you see her thin soul under the paint.

We went to Kevin Murphy's place on Ninth, off Fifty-third
Street. Kevin is long dead. They say his wake was something
to remember. The new owner is a Puerto Rican named Angel. When he first took over, he tried to spruce the place up
and attract the pimp trade. But the cops kept hanging out and
people who have money don't want to associate with police-
men. Eventually the photos of ballplayers from mythical
teams like the Brooklyn Dodgers and the New York Giants,
the signed photo of Cardinal Cooke, and signs that said things
like "The Lord created whiskey to keep the Irish from ruling
the world" went back up on the walls. Kevin Murphy's was
born a cops' bar, and as a cops' bar it lives. We walked in
among them.

They were all right, the lot of them, it wasn't up to them
And they knew it; if somebody had come along and said,
I've got a spot for a two-legged animal in the world I'm working
            on,
They wouldn't have made anything like they had been made.

We sat in a booth and the waitress came over. Joey ordered
scotch. I said make it two, and make it Johnny Black.
   "What's bugging you?"
   "It's just the waiting."
   "It's the broad. You've let yourself go bats over a broad."
   "When that guy came after me in D.C., I busted up his
kneecap so he'll never walk right again. It bothers me how
good I feel about that."
   "Johnny Walker Black," the waitress announced.
   "That's self-defense," Joey said.
   "I know what you mean," the waitress said. "If I drink
that bar scotch I wake up with a mean hangover. I mean
mean."
   "If it turns out that it was Charles Goreman that hit Wood,
I'm not gonna like it. I like the man."
   "Wallowing in ambiguity is like wallowing in self-pity,"
Joey said. "It's dumb, and you like doing it. You have a good

mind, you're a smart guy. You're supposed to use that to help yourself, not punish yourself."

"There's a real problem with this case. You know what it is? There isn't gonna be any smoking gun. Down in D.C. the trail will just dry up when it gets to Wellby. If Wellby has to have the second man, whoever he is, hit, he will. Then there's the gap between Wellby and the guy who asked for the hit. There's only one person who can close that gap: Wellby. And there's only one circumstance in which he would close that gap: to buy himself out of the chair. So if I find out whodunnit, whaddam I gonna do about it?"

"Maybe that's not your job."

"What? . . . Oh yeah, that's true," I said, "but who is going to do something about it? I'm going to sit there and know, and watch nothing happen about it?"

"That comes with the territory," Joey said.

"Well, well, if it ain't the world's prize fuck, Tony Cassella," another voice said.

I looked up. Jack Whelan was standing over me, drunk and sneering. I shrugged and looked away.

"Wazzamatta, cocksucker, don' wanna talk to me? . . . Well, I don' care, I wanna talk to you, fuckface."

"Go home," Joey said to him.

"Fuck off, old man," Whelan told him. "This is the little cocksucker who stuck a knife in my back. I just want to tell him that I'm looking forward to pissing on his grave."

"Get the fuck out of here, Whelan. You ain't gonna do anything to me and you know it. Stop the noise and get out of here," I told him and went back to my scotch.

The Corrections Department does not attract the highest caliber of recruits, mostly Jack Whelans. I knew how to read, write and pass tests. By their standards, a shining star. So they made me an investigator.

The Corrections Department takes the Whelans and gives them inadequate training, inadequate supervision and inadequate motivation. The corruption comes easy. I became aware of it very quickly and wrote memos. Nothing was done.

Then one day an inmate, flying on coke and infirmary morphine, went on a rampage and killed three other inmates before he was stopped. One was a nineteen-year-old, serving a year and a day for a barroom brawl, who was due to get out in two days. The family made noise. It came out in the investigation that the killer had gotten the drugs from a guard. That made the *New York Times*. The commissioner decided to mount an internal investigation before the outside world handed him his own Knapp Commission. My memos were remembered. I went in undercover. Whelan was one of the people I put away.

When it started I was clean and righteous. It seemed simple. But I was putting people away who had been my friends, some of them. And I was learning about them. For Whelan, who I never liked, the extra money he made doing favors for inmates was the difference between public school and parochial school for his daughters. When he was indicted, his wife filed for divorce and he lost the kids as well.

I saw how easy it was for me to keep my nose clean. I didn't have the financial responsibilities of a family. I had only applied for the Corrections job because there was a hiring freeze in the Police Department. When the P.D. started hiring again, my name figured to be high on the list. I was not stuck as a prison guard for life. My righteousness began to feel like a cheat.

I thought that the drinking helped. Fighting seemed to help too, when I was doing it. In the morning I began to realize that it was called assault and disturbing the peace. Some of the people I went drinking with, and some of the women I was sleeping with, liked a little cocaine. So did I once I tasted it. Simple possession was a felony.

Sometimes, when I was hurting and hungover, I'd use some coke to get me through the day. When a day costs an extra fifty or hundred dollars, a salary doesn't stretch the way it used to. One way to deal with that is to deal enough to cover costs.

Gradually I built a string of felonies as good as Jack Whelan's. The only difference left was that he had one arrest and one conviction. That wasn't different enough for me to live with putting him in a cage. If we had been that different to start with. I lost perspective on that question.

The center couldn't hold, and the pieces of me began to scatter farther and farther apart. I didn't have any trouble understanding why Whelan hated Cassella. At the time, it was something we could agree on.

"Maybe I will do something about it," Whelan said.

"You won't," Joey replied, "if for no other reason than you'd be scared to have an old man like me after you."

Whelan looked at Joey, then spit in Joey's drink.

I backhanded him across the table. Glad of the excuse to do it. It was a good shot. It sent him stumbling a half-step back. He slipped and sat down on his ass on the floor. It gave me time to get out of the booth. He was on his feet by the time I was out, but still off balance.

If he had backed off, I would have let it go. He came at me in a clumsy rush. I watched his move with pleasure, stepped in and hit him in the gut. My right hand sank deep in the soft belly. He began to fold, but I put two more in the same spot.

By then the room had responded. Five cops were around to break us up. I just stepped aside and let Whelan sink slowly to the floor, vomiting on himself.

Joey came out from the booth. He knew a couple of the cops and told them it was all right and it was all over. They backed off, and Joey said, "Let's get out of here."

"Sure," I said, shaking with anger and the adrenaline rush. "I shouldn't have done that."

"He requested it," Joey shrugged.

Somebody was helping Whelan up. He shook them off and started toward me.

"Don't," I said, raising my fists.

"I don't have to, fuckface," he said backing up, "there's a big fat fucking contract on you, fuckface. And somebody is gonna collect. When they do, I'm gonna shake their hand and go and piss on your fucking grave."

28

FAMILY

ANGEL CAME OUT of nowhere and stepped between us with his baseball bat.

I wanted to go for him, but Joey was pulling me back, Whelan's friends were pulling him back and half the cops from Midtown North were on their feet ready to play peace officer.

"I gotta find out what he's talking about."

"We'll find out," Joey told me. "Go take care of Glenda. Make sure she and the kid stay in the house."

He was right about what was important. The phone in the bar was busted again. I went outside. The phone on the corner was occupied, a hooker phoning home. She was smaller than me but looked meaner, so I moved up the block to find another phone. It was on the far side of the avenue. I ran through the rain, dodging cars, cabs, trucks and one mad bike messenger. I still found it unbelievably aggravating that they had gone up 150 percent to a quarter, but it was an emergency, and I paid.

The first thing I wanted to know was whether Wayne was home. I was relieved to hear that he was.

"What's going on, Anthony?"

"I'll explain when I get home. Don't open the door for anyone but me. In fact, come to think of it, don't open the door for anyone. I have my keys."

"I'm glad you didn't lose your keys. That's very reassuring. Are you all right?"

"Yeah. Yeah. Sit tight. I'll be there soon."

I tried to find a cab, surrendered and went underground, but the subway wasn't in a hurry either. It took forever to get home, and almost the minute I walked in the door the intercom rang. I jumped. It was Joey.

He was bursting to say whatever he had to say but didn't want speak in front of Glenda, so he just stood there and twitched like a man trying to shut the valve on his bladder after it's started to leak.

"We will not," I explained to him, "somehow succeed in sending Glenda out of the room so we can discuss this in private."

"That is correct," she said.

"Yeah, well, all right then. What we did was, we took Whelan out back. Nobody's interested in filing charges or makin' a case or nothing like that, so we did not discuss Miranda or anything of that other legal procedure. This is me, Chic—that's Tommy Ciccollini—and his partner, you saw them in the bar.

"Whelan's story is that he got into a conversation at a Blarney Stone down in the thirties, his regular hangout, with a guy named Bruno. Whelan doesn't know if that's his real name, never having met him before. But this so-called Bruno knew Whelan and asked him about you. Your habits, hangouts and such. Whelan wanted to know why. Bruno, who apparently knew that Whelan was somewhat hostile about you, says something to the effect of 'someone is looking for Cassella, cause they wanna bid him a fond farewell.' Whelan was, as we know, happy to hear that, so he pressed Bruno for confirmation 'in a discreet manner,' that the phraseology had been interpreted correctly. Whelan thinks he got that confirmation. That was last night, and we are lucky we ran into him when we did.

"It's a little thin," Joey concluded, "but maybe we should treat it like it's serious. Taking precautions and such. Chic is gonna hit the streets and talk to some informants and such. I assure you that we have obtained all the information from Whelan that could be obtained."

"I think, tonight, Joey should stay here with us," I said to Glenda, "mostly to make him feel better about things, because it is not really necessary."

"Yeah, indulge an old man."

"Now what might be a good idea is, tomorrow, if you want to, Glenda, take Wayne and go visit your mom. Or even take a mini-vacation up in the country or at the beach. Just while we check things out."

"Tony, can we cut the crap? Is this serious or not?"

"When did you start talking like that?" Joey said.

"When I started living with him," Glenda told him.

"It's really not a question of whether it's serious or not. I just want to know that you are out of harm's way while I'm finding out."

"You told me that there have been threats before, and they never came to anything."

"Glenda," Joey said, "if something were to happen, to you or Wayne, Tony could not live with that. You gotta see that. So if you stay or Wayne stays, it means you gotta be cooped up in the apartment with one of us tied up here too. Until this thing shakes down."

"Is this one of those macho things," she said, "where the women and children hide while the men go out and play with guns?"

"Yeah, if you gotta put it that way, yeah," Joey said.

"I think I'm glad I have a macho man," she said, coming close to me, "at least about this."

In bed we talked about, argued about, how to handle things with Wayne.

"Don't worry," I told her, "kids love to play hide-and-seek."

"Don't be flippant."

"Look," I said, "I know, I'm a kid."

"That's part of the problem, not a solution."

When Wayne got up and saw Unc'e Joey snoring on the couch he knew something 'citing was happening. He jumped around while I made breakfast and tried to explain, with delicacy and restraint, the way Glenda would have done it, that he and his mom were going to Grandma's because some- one had threatened me.

"Oh wow! Did they put out a contract on you?"

"Well, it's nothing as dramatic as that, Wayne."

"Wow! Wow! Wait'll I tell the kids at school," he said and ran into the living room. "Unc'e Joey, Unc'e Joey," he yelled, bouncing on top of Unc'e Joey, "we're going to the mattresses. We're going to the mattresses." He bounced off and rolled under the convertible. He came up on the other side with his hand folded in the shape of a pistol. He fired his finger at point-blank range, yelling, "Pow! Pow!"

"I'm glad," Glenda said, "that this sort of thing doesn't happen very often."

I left the building first, through the front door. Joey, Wayne and Glenda went out the service entrance. The street was quiet; nobody shot at me, threatened me or even gave me a dirty look. I walked down to the deli on the corner and bought some beer, just to look like I was doing something. Then I went upstairs and waited for Joey to get back from Grand Central. While I waited I rang Christina. I didn't leave a message on her machine. Then I put on a fresh pot of coffee.

"You got what you want? You got what you were after?" Joey said when he got back.

"Well," I said, "I meant to shake somebody up, but not to the point where they would pay to see me dead."

"Don't bullshit me. I know you better than you know you."

"What are you talking about? Are you saying I want a contract out on me?"

"Yeah, you do," he said with disgust. "You just won't be

happy until you're all the way out there on the edge, until you put it all on the line.''

"You know what's funny? This still doesn't tell us who did it. We have to find out who put this thing out, then who they did it for.''

I thought we could cover more ground moving separately. Joey thought we would survive better moving together. I yielded graciously.

We headed out to Brooklyn, looking for Johnny "Jeans" Licavollo, a small-time bookie connected to what's known as the Colombo family. Johnny used to run a scam in the garment center. It still gives me great pleasure to know that half the people strolling around in designer jeans, on which they spent anything from forty dollars to eighty dollars, are wearing five-dollar rags from Hong Kong with a forged label sewn on. Of course the other half are wearing exactly the same thing, from the same oriental sweat shops, identical except for the authentic label. We busted the operation, but we didn't bust Johnny Jeans, so he owed us one.

He was home with his family. His wife set out fresh espresso and anisette cookies, then left the men alone to do their business, in the fine old-fashioned style. He had not heard anything, but he promised to ask around. We moved on.

"Scooter" Siegal, the fence, "Butch" Dominici, who made hot cars into cool ones, and Murray Lipshitz, who converted stolen securities, hadn't heard anything. Oddly enough, our attorney, Gerald Yaskowitz, had.

We didn't get Gerry's message until late in the day, and then couldn't reach him until after nine.

Late on Friday, Gerry had talked a judge into reducing the bail on Francisco "Frankie" Montoya, dealer in heroin and cocaine, from a quarter-million down to a mere one hundred thousand dollars. Gerry and Frankie had lunch on Saturday to discuss the case. They agreed that it was open and shut, a second felony conviction that would result in a significant length of time spent at Attica. Frankie asked Gerry if, given sufficient time, the D.A.'s case might fall apart. Gerry's opinion was that that might indeed happen, given four or five years. Frankie decided, on the spot, to spend the necessary time in Mexico.

Having made that decision, Frankie felt deeply grateful to Gerry for getting the bail down to a level that he could comfortably afford to lose. As a token of his gratitude he passed along the tip that there was a contract on Gerry's favorite PI. The price was a "crummy five grand," and it came from one of the old-line Italian groups. Gerry asked Frankie if he could be more specific. All Frankie could add was that it was one of "them Godfather-type organizations, one of the families, like, you know, the Mob."

That was all Gerry knew, and by the time he reached us, Montoya was way up high, in a 747, waving good-bye.

Joey insisted on escorting me back to the apartment. There, like everywhere else we had been, he insisted on going in first with his gun in his hand. In his grim and grumbling way, he was enjoying himself. There was something in all of us, just like old Franco, that had the hots for handling a piece.

It took me an hour to get him out of there. I promised I would keep the door triple-locked, that I would not go out, that I would sleep with my gun in my hand. When he left, I gave it ten minutes, went downstairs and jumped in a cab to Christina's.

When I told her, through the intercom, who it was, she told me to go away. I leaned on the buzzer. I had been pushing all day and I was not about to stop. When she finally answered again, I said I had to talk to her.

When I got upstairs she was waiting in the hall, her door closed behind her. I could hear music from inside. I sensed that there was someone else there. "My heart lurched" is a statement with no physiological validity, but that is exactly what it felt like.

Our eyes met and they said what our eyes always said to each other, no matter where we were, no matter who else was present. Want, hunger, a rage of lust, a melting tenderness.

"Why are you here?" she asked, hurting.

"Because I can't get you out of my head. Even when there are people gunning for me or I'm falling off a cliff, I can't get you out of my head."

"Are you thinking about me when you're in bed with her?"

"I'm trying to keep my life sane. But I'm not sure I can. I did not want this to happen, but I can't stop feeling like I'm in love with you."

I took her in my arms. She turned her head from my mouth. My hand reached into the fine soft hair of her head and turned her mouth back toward me. "No. No," she said as her mouth opened to mine. The tension left her body, her body said only "Yes."

"Go home, go home," she said sorrowfully, "go home to her."

"She's away."

"For how long?" was her immediate response. Telling me again exactly what she did not want to be saying.

"At least a couple of days, maybe longer."

She stood up straight. "Not tonight. Call me tomorrow, and . . . we'll see. But . . . but I don't think so."

"Why not tonight? Is there someone here with you? Another boyfriend?"

"Yes. . . . And that's probably for the best, isn't it . . . and why not? You're not alone when you're not with me. Go home."

"I'll call you tomorrow," I said, as if it were all right.

She followed me to the stairs. "You know what," she said, "it's no damn good. Stefan is a very good lover. I used to enjoy him. But now I don't feel a damn thing, not with him or anybody else. Since I met you. I don't like that."

I turned away from the things she was saying. Then I wanted to reach out, to hold, hug, kiss her. But by the time I turned back, she had already fled toward Stefan. Who was no damn good.

Friday's storm had not cleared anything up. The air was thick and moist. I just wandered for a while until I found myself in Sheridan Square. "Hiya, Phil," I said to the statue there, "how do you like it, surrounded by all these gay blades?'' He kept morosely silent. The bookstore on the corner was open so I went in to look for Kenneth Patchen, to ask about this thing with Christina. He was there on the shelf, and I found the poem I thought about the first time:

They were wise that this man-business was just a matter
Of putting it in and taking it out, and that went all the way
From throwing up cathedrals to getting hot pants over Kathy.
Maybe there was something to get steamed about, maybe it was
Baseball to grow a beard and end up on a cross so that a lot
Of hysteria cases could have something to slap around;
Maybe the old Greek boy knew what he was doing when he
        hemlocked
It out, loving the heels who hobbled him; maybe little French
        Joan
Got a kick out of the English hot-foot; the boys at the corner
        bar
Were willing to believe it. No skin off their noses. . . .

And all things considered, it sounded about right.

When I called from the pay phone I found Laurie the stewardess at home. She was glad to hear from me, she said, but she had just flown in from the coast and her arms were tired. My old connection was just a few blocks from where I was standing, over at Perry and Fourth, so I told her I had just the thing to take care of tired. She was very interested. Excited even.

It had been a long time since I had even spoken to the man on Perry Street, but it turned out that he was still alive, still at the same address, still doing the same trade, and he was currently holding. My bank's cash machine was in equally good order, so the man was happy to see me. I got an eighth. The price was fair and the quality at least adequate.

It felt greedy and stupid, soulless and harsh. Laurie and I went at it eagerly. We did it every which way. Putting everything anyplace it would go, pushing for more than more. Long before we stopped at 4 A.M., everything was sore.

When I left, I figured it was an experience that she would cherish forever in her diary, or wherever she kept score, and be pleased if she never saw me again. It was also possible that she took it that way as a regular thing and would be ready anytime I was able.

As my cab cruised up my block, I noticed a couple of guys slouched down in the front seat of a car. I told the driver not to stop at the address I'd given him and to take it around the corner. He didn't care.

I have some neighbors, in 16B, that I don't particularly like. So when I called 911 to report a domestic disturbance and a possible gunshot, I said it came from 16B.

The response was relatively prompt. I didn't have to wait more than seven or eight minutes, hugging the shadows so I could watch around the corner for the cruiser without being seen myself. As the squad car pulled up, I made my move, timing it so that I went in the front door at the same time as the two men in uniform.

Whether or not the men slouching in their car were there for me, I will never know. If they were, I foxed them; if they weren't, at least I annoyed the folks in 16B.

I only got two or three hours sleep. Glenda called at eight, Joey a few minutes later. He asked where I had been. I claimed that I had just turned the phone off. He invited himself over for breakfast. A couple of lines and an icy shower more or less got me moving.

I asked him if he had heard anything further. Johnny Jeans had called him and confirmed what we knew, with more detail than Whelan, but less than Montoya.

"What do you wanna do?" he asked.

"I could leave town," I shrugged, "but I won't."

"I don't think we're gonna find out who, what and where too quick."

"Even if I knew who was handling the contract," I said, "what could I do about it? Go into some Don's fortress in Englewood, both guns blazing, and explain that I'm too tough to kill, too mean to die, so he better call it off?"

"Maybe," he said, "we could get Charles Bronson to do it."

"Then there's Glenda's mother. Nobody can last more

than two or three days with her. There are some sacrifices I just can't ask Glenda to make. But I don't want to bring her and Wayne back if it's not safe.''

''That's true.''

''This is the time when a guy needs a godfather.''

''Oh yeah?'' he said.

''There is really only one place to go. That I can think of.''

''Oh yeah?'' he said.

''Yeah. You know what I'm talking about.''

''No. What?'' he asked, flat.

''I'm gonna call Uncle Vincent.''

''It took you a long time to talk yourself into that,'' he said.

''Oh yeah? When did you decide I should do it?''

''The same time you did,'' he replied. ''As soon as Whelan opened his big fucking mouth.''

''Then why didn't you say something?''

''Because that's the kind of thing you have to decide for yourself.''

I still wasn't ready to call him. I still wanted to stall. I sat and sipped more coffee.

''What do you know about Vincent?'' I asked Joey. ''I mean, I've heard rumors, but I don't know much for a fact. Maybe I've avoided knowing.''

''I know what you know. He's been named in some hearings. His name has come up on some wiretaps. He's worth a lot of money, very heavy bread. Construction mostly. If he's not a made guy, he does a lot of business with them.''

''When he and my father quarreled,'' I said, ''my father ended up in the hospital with high blood pressure. Eventually, it was a stroke that killed him.''

''I didn't know that, about the hospital.''

''You know what, Joey, even if the guy is a fucking capo, he may not be able to do anything. The old Mob isn't what it used to be. Nowadays, it's like the Communist Party; half the dues-paying members are undercover cops and the other half are FBI informants.''

"You got someone else who can deal with this?"

"If it weren't for Glenda and Wayne . . ."

"Sure, Tony."

"I'm responsible for them. I mean we're not married, but . . . but it's like family. I just don't like the guy and what he stands for, Joey."

"Tony, neither do I. But right now, you're lucky he's family."

29

ROCKEFELLER LOOKOUT

LIKE A BEGGAR on horseback, I rode out to the Englewood home of my Uncle Vincent in the back of his limo. It had the bar, the television, the telephone, the everything. Like Hencio deVega's Coupe de Ville, it had real leather uphol-stery.

Uncle Vincent greeted me effusively at the door.

"You have never been to my home before, let me show it to you," he said.

"Uncle Vincent, I don't mean to be rude, but we need to talk."

"I understand," he replied, but sounded disappointed.

"I can see, just from the outside, just from the door, that it's a beautiful house." I tried to be gracious.

He led me, walking painfully, toward the back of the house, to a lovely, light, airy room done in yellow and whites, with high arched windows. It was a room that Glenda would love, or Christina. The windows looked out on a long sloping lawn that ended under the glow of three giant copper beeches. The fences on the sides were covered with roses, white and yellow. The sun shone bright though the windows.

When we sat down a middle-aged maid came out to the sun room with a steaming fresh pot of espresso, a small decanter of anisette, glass demitasse cups and a plate with garden-fresh tomatoes and cucumbers in thin delicate slices.

"Telephones, nobody can use the telephone anymore. Here I have a member of my own family, my brother's only son, visiting me for the first time in twenty-five years. Twenty-five years. The first visit, and for all I know there are federal agencies making notes about it."

It was a left-handed reprimand. A way of telling me that I should not have told him my problems on the phone.

"Well, I wouldn't have mentioned it at all, I would've let 'em come at me and taken my chances, if it weren't for Glenda and Wayne," I told him, wondering if I were bragging. I probably was, I decided. When I took the time to think about it, I was scared shitless, for myself.

"Family feeling. That's good. Do you know, the thing in my life for which I have the most regret is the quarrel with my brother. He was my little brother, I never dreamed he would be the first to go. Never. And now look at us, this stupid argument that should never have happened, it follows us beyond the grave."

"I have a problem. Can you help me or not?"

"It is almost a good thing that this has happened. Maybe it was meant to be. I do not believe that God has a hand that reaches down and guides things, no, no, I don't believe that. But sometimes . . . This has brought us together and given us the opportunity to lay to rest the problems of the past."

"Vincent, you promised to help me, no strings attached."

"Tony, Antonio, he was my baby brother," he said and it looked like there were tears in his eyes.

"Have some espresso, a sip of anisette," I said, pouring for both of us.

We each had some, while he went through the motions of recovering his self-possession.

"Look, Uncle Vincent, let's not play games. If you can help me, great. If there's something you want in return, let's get it out on the table and make whatever deal we gotta make up front. Can we do that?''

"Am I a monster? You think I am a gangster, a professional criminal. So you come to me and say, fix this thing. Then you ask me what the price is, let's make a deal, as if you were not my family.''

"I did not mean to insult you,'' I lied. "But if you can't help me with this, then you can't. I'll take care of it somehow.''

"In the course of doing business, I have dealt with people like that. It is necessary. They control the unions, they have influence with the government. I do not know what it is that your father told you, but I am a businessman and nothing more. I am not a criminal.''

"He didn't tell me anything.''

"Your father was an idealist. He wanted to fight the world. To clean it up and make everyone a saint. He didn't know what he was, a priest or a communist. I loved him for that, I did. But a business cannot be run that way.''

"So you do business with some people who might be able to help me,'' I prompted.

"Yes, yes, I do. We will have to go see somebody. If that is all right with you, if it will not stain your soul.''

"It won't be the first stain.''

"Good, you understand that when you live in the real world you must come to terms with the people in it. You understand that, you are more of a realist than he was.''

"When do we go see this guy?'' I asked.

"Soon. We only have to wait a little longer, but that gives us some time to talk.''

"Yes, I guess it does.''

"Do you ever think about settling down, Antonio?''

"I sort of think I have.''

"This so-called business of yours . . . what is it? You live from hand to mouth. When something happens, you are hurt, you die, who will care for the woman and the child? You are not even married to her and the child is not yours. What is that about?''

What it was about was none of his business, most emphatically because he was right and because I didn't know the answers and didn't like to think about the questions.

"Do you know what I am worth? Do you?"

"No, Uncle Vincent, I don't."

"More than you have ever dreamed of. My cash worth is five million dollars, without this house. All of it legitimate. All of it clean."

"That's wonderful, very impressive."

"And what is it worth? My brother died before me. My baby brother. He would have been my partner, except for that stupid quarrel. Then you would have already inherited half of it. But no. Now it is worth nothing to me. Who should I give it to? You?"

Normally I keep the wounds and resentments of not having money buried deep. The wait for the subway after an eighteen-hour day, too stinking and bone-weary to resent the people pushing me around. The apartment that was too small for three people. The one vacation in four years. The clothes I pretend to like. Telling myself that there are other measures of a man's worth in a world that doles out respect in direct ratio to cash and property.

The wonder and power of money. Ivy league for Wayne if he wanted it. A permanent muscle relaxer for the sense of financial tension that intermittently knotted Glenda's back. Getting my adrenaline rushes from skiing or skin-diving, like a normal person, instead getting off by looking down the barrel of a gun. And if it didn't buy me Christina Wood, I could rent or lease something that looked a lot like her, because women like that always seemed to end up alongside a major financial statement.

"I am going to die soon. You are intelligent enough to run the business. I just don't know if you are smart enough."

"Rockefeller Lookout" is not a political slogan or a communist threat, it is a spot to pull off the Palisades Parkway and look out from the high bluffs across the wide, wide river to the construction industry's single greatest monument,

Manhattan. It's also a fine place to chat, relatively certain you will be microphone-free.

"Do you know how blessed we are to be here? In America?" Uncle Vincent said to the view.

"America, the greatest country in the world. We are very lucky," added Michael Paley, a.k.a. Michael Pollazzio, a.k.a. Mikey Fix.

Uncle Vincent had warned me, in very emphatic and paternal tones, not to be a wise-ass with Mr. Paley. I didn't even snicker.

"This is your nephew."

"Yes, a good boy. Smart," Vincent replied.

"You look like you coulda been a fighter. Ever been in the ring, kid?"

"Just PAL when I was a kid."

"Yeah? Any good?"

"Yeah, if I was only quicker, a bit stronger, had better hands and was a lot meaner, I might have been a fair Italian middle-weight."

He laughed. "Hey, you seen that Boom-Boom Mancini fight? A disappointment, but the kid had heart, a lotta heart. You shoulda seen Marciano, wasn't one of these coloreds could have taken him. Kids, they grow up these days with money, they grow up soft. . . . How about you, you soft?"

"Compared to what?" I said.

"I hear you're pretty tough," he said. "That's good. I like the way you took care of John Straightman's problem. That was smart. Coming to your uncle with this problem. That was smart too."

Vincent nodded sagely.

"Well, I know your Uncle Vincent from way, way back. I know how much you mean to him. I'll put a stop to this thing, as much as I can."

"What does that mean?"

"It means," he said, "that the contract is canceled."

"That simple? If you want me to cover the five grand, I can. I wouldn't want anyone to take a loss," I said. And I could too, another three or four years without a vacation was worth the price of my life.

Paley laughed again, this time longer and louder. "Thanks for the offer, but I don't need that kinda bread. Besides, it's nonrefundable." Vincent chuckled with him. Even I smiled.

"Who wanted me hit?" I asked.

"That's something you're gonna have to figure out. But that should be easy, detective."

"Mr. Paley, if I don't know, what's to stop the guy from trying again, through some other avenue?"

"Nothing," he said.

"And you don't feel like telling me who? How about it, Uncle Vince?"

"Tony, I would tell you if I knew," Paley said. "This came to us from the coloreds, and I don't know if it's their thing, or someone asked them. And it's not like I can go have a chat with Ricky Sams in his maximum-security cell down in Fort Hamilton with the U.S. Army all around him."

"If you can't talk to him, how did you get involved?"

"He can get messages out. Some kinda letter code, to communicate with his people. But it's mostly a one-way thing. You understand?"

"Yeah."

"Me and your uncle, we're gonna be watching you close on this one. You handle it right, you can go a long way."

"Terrific," I said.

"Hey, hey, kid. Nothing like that. Don't get the wrong idea. I'm talking strictly legit. I got lots of things need security contracts. Construction sites, shopping centers, factories. I got union work. All kinds of stuff. It's not easy to find good people no more. Smart, tough. Too many of the kids have gone soft."

30

THE INGRATE DEAD

"THE WHOLE FUCKING bunch is as bad as I am, the whole fucking barrel is rotten . . . that super-WASP fuck Choate Haven . . . that cocksucker Goreman . . . and I'm gonna drag them all down with me," Wood screamed.

"It ain't bragging if you can do it," Dizzy Dean said. But Wood was bragging, and he couldn't. Usually bragging is merely an unattractive character trait, but when the wrong person believes the braggart, it can be a fatal flaw.

Edgar Wood never knew the secret he had died for.

But someone who had a secret believed he did. So had I, and I had spent the entire investigation looking for that as the key.

Judge McCarthy was the first one to pick up on it. If Wood had had something really hot, he would never have met the judge. He would have stopped the lawyers, if what he had was on them, or he would have forced Goreman to stop them. As a last resort he would have cut a deal with the D.A. in the process that Mel Brodsky liked to call "trading up."

It was a long chain from the man who wanted the killing done to the two men in the parking lot who had committed the execution with a tire iron. LeRoy Johnson, who had fingered Wood, led us to Alexander, Jr., who ran to Wellby. In spite of my bragging at the Goreman lawn party, I had never expected to connect the link from Wellby to . . . ?

Wellby was too well insulated and more than tough enough to keep himself that way. He had proved that by having me shoved off the cliff; when that failed, he had turned what connected him to Wood into a corpse.

But the killer had stayed in character. He fell for my bragging just like he fell for Wood's. The order went out to kill me. It started out on the same route that the order to kill Wood had taken, then diverged because of our locations. In Virginia the contract had gone to Wellby, in New York to Mikey Fix.

Paley had let me know that the contract had come from Sams. And if Sams could reach out to Paley, he could reach out to the Doctor.

But Ricky Sams didn't give a shit about Edgar Wood or me. He probably had never heard of either of us before. There was, therefore, one more link, the person who had asked Sams to do the job. There also had to be someone to tell the unknown party where Wood was, so Sams could tell Wellby to tell Alexander, so Alexander could talk to LeRoy.

I also knew who had fingered Wood. That was me.

I had given that information, at the right time, to Lawrence Choate Haven, who was also my only suspect in a position to communicate with Sams.

Ol' squash buddy, Ol' Chip, an associate in Trusts and Estates, was helping to set up Sams's estate. While an associate may do all the actual work, every case actually belongs to a partner. The most senior partner in T&E was Choate Haven, and if he wanted to go along to a meeting with Sams, Ol' Chip, living in the law-firm world of competitive paranoia, would be aware of one thing only, how Choate Haven was judging the performance of Chip Riggins.

There were two places that such a meeting was most likely to have taken place. At Fort Hamilton in Brooklyn, or in some sort of holding facility when Sams came into Manhattan to testify. In either place, there would be a record.

It was the kind of information that a judge like Stew McCarthy could ask for, and he was kind enough to do so. Choate Haven had met with Ricky Sams several times, including dates immediately before his meeting with me, at which point he may have been given a way to communicate with Wellby directly, shortly after the Hamptons party.

There was still the remote possibility that he was bird-dogging for Charles Goreman. Over & East was the sort of client that an attorney might do anything to keep. It was also remotely possible that he was acting to protect someone else at Choate, Winkler, Higgiston, Hahn & Moore, in the fear that they could not survive a scandal on top of scandal.

I had an afternoon with Christina and I told her that I was close.

"My angel, my beautiful brown-eyed angel," she said. "When I'm with you, the whole rest of the world disappears."

I understood that. There was an anger bubbling away deep inside me, waiting. The taste of fear that Whelan had roused was still fresh on my tongue, dry and foul as a lick of tobacco ash. A new fear was building, too, of what I might have to do. All of that was gone, over the rooftop and across a wide wide river, when she was there.

Everything that Laurie and I had been reaching for that angry, drugged night, pushing to the point of pain and failing even to simulate, was right there with Christina all by itself, as free and deceptive as a gift from the gods.

"Do you now how crazy I am about you?"

"Yes, I think so," she said.

"No. You don't. You have no idea. I'm crazy enough to ask you to marry me. Even though I have a notion that it's a terrible idea. I'd ask, and if you said yes, I would do it."

"That's only because you think you can trust me not to say yes."

"The thing is, you don't really believe it."

"I don't know. I know you're my angel and you shouldn't love me too much."

"What if I were free, and if I had a lot of money, then what?"

"Hush," she said, kissing me softly to close my lips. "Don't talk of things like that."

"No?"

"Just hold me, kiss me, come inside me."

Goreman had told me there were many things that Wood did not know, including what had happened in Hungary, the story of the first $80,000 that Goreman had tripled to take over Samson. I had to be sure, and when I called Goreman he reconfirmed that he had not told Wood those things.

Then I made up a story. I wove it out of wisps of information, old news clips, and what the women said: look for the overachiever.

Choate Haven was active in refugee organizations as early as '39 when it was hardly fashionable. As a side effect, or even as an ulterior and primary motive, it brought funds into Choate, Winkler, Higgiston, Hahn & Moore at a time when an ongoing depression and a Democratic administration were doing nothing to boost business at an old-line Republican Wall Street law firm. Some of those funds must have been quite substantial. Anyone in Europe who had an ounce of sense and the means was transferring cash and assets to Switzerland or America.

Only the man himself could say when it had started.

He would have heard stories of the death camps early on. He might not have believed them and waited until the end of the war when the American troops stumbled on the ovens. And on the long, carefully recorded tabulation of the numbers dead. At that point he would have been certain that many of the people who had entrusted their funds to him would not return. Neither would their spouses, children, grandchildren, cousins, brothers, sisters, nephews, nieces. No one would return to claim that money.

Maybe he began to embezzle it just because it was there

and didn't seem to belong to anyone. Maybe it was simple greed. Maybe he couldn't keep up his dues at the N.Y.A.C. and the Harvard Club. Maybe there was a golden investment he couldn't pass up or his sister needed an eye operation or his wife wanted a cosmetic mastectomy. To me, the reasons didn't matter.

Then bodies rose from the ashes. Like Charles Goreman, son of Itzhak Oberetstock. As in Goreman's case, Choate Haven denied when he could, stalled as long as he could and paid when he had to.

At some point the ratio between embezzled dollars and the number of survivors swung the wrong way and the claims of the living exceeded the amount stolen from the dead.

To cover the shortfall he went looking for clients with unreported, untraceable cash. The kind of money Ricky Sams had. I made a guess that the roots of that relationship went back in time to the forties or fifties. Sams did not pick Choate, Winkler from the yellow pages; someone had recommended the fine old firm to him.

Court clerks, particularly those working in an area as dry and dusty as probate court, remember any contact with the famous, the notorious, the glamorous. I located several old-timers; one down in Sarasota remembered Choate Haven handling crime figures.

He had been surprised, which is why he remembered it so well, to see Haven represent the estate of Philip and Vincent Mangano. Phil and Vince had founded one of New York's five families way back in '31. In '51 they made their last headline together when Albert Anastasia took over their family. He had Philip murdered, but Vincent only disappeared, presumed dead, which made for some fun probate.

I had a lot of answers. I knew who, how and understood why. I had other kinds of answers, about my own life, from Vincent, Mikey Fix, Glenda, and a confused answer from Christina.

I had answers. The more answers I had, the more problems I had. Not one was a solution. To make them mean anything, I had to do something with them.

It was funny. The whole thing had been unnecessary. The murder of Wood; the murder of Alexander, who probably deserved it; the attempt to get me, who certainly did not. For once I completely failed to see the humor in it.

31

NAKED

"How WOULD YOU like to be a big-time detective agency? Have some nice fat security contracts, all money, no work? You could do your gambling down in Grand Bahama, or even hit the casino at Monte Carlo, instead of taking that grubby bus down to Atlantic City. How would you like to set up a trust fund for your grandkids, for their college? Would you like that, Joey?"

"Is this idle chatter? Or are you talking about something? You sound like you got something eating you."

"I got an offer, two offers. Uncle Vince, he'll take me into the family business. Construction. Big money. And Mr. Paley, he says he can throw lots of business our way, strictly legit, he says. That's just in case I don't wanna go into construction."

"Is this for real?"

"Did they really say it? Or is it for real? I know they really said it. I was there."

"I don't want anything from the likes of Michael Pollazzio. I don't trust nobody who changes his name."

"Don't you ever get tired of scrounging? Being half fucking broke? Wouldn't it be nice to take a real vacation . . . I don't mean sitting at home waiting for the goddamn phone to ring because there's no work. I don't mean going down to Florida and trying to live off social security. I mean a real fucking vacation. First-class in the plane. First-class hotel. Good restaurants. Maybe you would like to take a cab once in a while, just 'cause you don't feel like riding the subway. Just 'cause you don't feel like it, and not worry about an extra five dipshit dollars.''

"Do you really feel that way?" he asked.

"Does the Pope shit in the Vatican?"

"So you're thinking about working for those kinda people," he said with contempt.

"Oh, by the way, there is a catch."

"Of course there is," he said, like I should know that there always is. I did.

"They're watching to see how I handle things with this one."

"What does that mean?''"

"How the hell do I know?" I snapped.

"How are you going to handle it?''

"How would you handle it?" I threw it back to him.

"I don' know. It's a tough one."

"Fucking A, it's a tough one. There's not word one I can prove. I can't prove Alexander took his orders from Wellby, I can't prove that Wellby got the contract from Sams, and the only connection between Sams and Haven is absolutely, perfectly legitimate. That, he can prove. Can I prove that Haven was an embezzler, forty years ago? Even Goreman, with all his money and power—and he's the one who got stung by it—didn't try. This guy is untouchable."

"So what are you going to do about it?" he asked, worried. I was sounding wound up tight, and it was more than the cocaine I was still doing. He picked up on my anxiety, but not the drug use, or he would have said something about it. He would have had a lot to say about it.

"What do you think I'm gonna do?"

"I don't know, Tony, tell me."

"Maybe when I figure it out, I'll tell you." But I don't think I was trying to figure it out. I think I had it by then, or maybe a long time ago.

"Don't do anything stupid."

"I won't," I lied to him, then I closed the door behind me as I left.

I splurged. I took a cab all the way home.

"I'll be away for a few days. Don't worry about me. Don't worry about yourself or Wayne either, I got that part of things settled. There are a few things that still need to be worked out. It's really better if I'm away while I do that. Please don't worry. I love you and Wayne very much," is what I wrote in the note that Glenda would find when she got home. I read it over, then added, "Three, four days, at the most. Promise. Then I'll see you."

When I left the house, I walked, and walked, and walked. Finally I found myself down by the water in the West Village. Down by Morton Street Pier, where Christina had put my hand to her lips and, when I asked her if it mattered that there was a woman already in my life, said, "I don't think so." I had made her a promise, that I was going to find out who did it and do what could be done about it. Christina, who called me "Angel," even when I was armed and dangerous.

The sky was muddy gray, and the muddy gray Hudson was covered with a scum. Garbage floated, but it looked like the river had a skin, and things were stabbed halfway in. When I went after Haven I would be going over the line, like him. Like going into that river in front of me, not knowing how much would cling to me when, and if, I climbed out.

I could think of reasons for diving in. The man had made me death's stalking horse, then paid me with the dead man's money. He had used Christina's pain to pay the cost of his cover-up. "Angel," she said to me, "you're the only one I can turn to." He had put my woman and my child at risk. Also, there was gold down there, under the scum. Mike Paley and Uncle Vincent had told me so. It was as if the Devil stood behind me, whispering in all his different voices, urg-

ing me on. But when I turned to look, the only thing that
stood behind me was my own shadow.

From the pier, I headed down to Wall Street, to stalk Haven.

The building with the offices of Choate, Winkler, Higgiston, Hahn & Moore, attorneys-at-law, had exits from both
ends of the lobby. An effective stakeout had to be inside. To
make myself look like I belonged, I bought a cup of coffee
in a container to go, a newspaper, picked a good vantage
point to view the elevator and leaned against the wall. From
time to time, I glanced at my watch impatiently, as if wondering, "Where the hell is she?" Had one of the security
guards questioned me, that would have been my explanation,
along with something convoluted as to why I could not be
seen with her in her office.

Associates usually leave late, anywhere from eight to midnight. Partners leave anytime they please. Sometimes after
lunch, often around four, to beat the rush. Haven came down
at ten past.

Outside the building, he headed west. He was an old man,
moving slow, and easy to follow. When he got to Broadway
he went north to Cortlandt where he turned left and headed
for the World Trade Center. I trailed him past the CNN stu-
dios and into the lobby of the Vista Hotel. He was just passing through, and I followed him as he went out to West
Street. On the other side was Gateway Plaza.

Rising out of the rubble of old warehouses and loft buildings, part of what will be Battery Park City, Gateway Plaza
is a logical idea. Housing within walking distance of the
highest density of jobs in the world, an area which otherwise
has no places to live. I had been there before, on a divorce
case. For the downtown broker, businessman or lawyer,
Gateway is heaven-sent. Nooners take place at a time that
does not have to be accounted for. Some girls work there;
more are kept there.

But Haven didn't go into the building itself. He went
around the side, to the underground garage. Slipping his
plastic card into a box mounted on a steel pole, he caused

the doors to open. There was no way to follow him in, so I waited. A few minutes later he drove out in his Mercedes.

As I watched him go, I thought that it was an odd place to keep his car. Convenient for him, but I would have assumed that the parking spots, in a town where a place to park can rent for more than entire homes elsewhere, would be reserved for tenants.

I had to endure long protestations of integrity and go all the way up to fifty bucks before the doorman at the front entrance acknowledged to me that Mr. Haven did pay the rent on an apartment there. At that price the doorman included the information that Mr. Haven didn't live there often, but that his "cutie" did.

I had some shopping to do and the time to do it in, since I couldn't make my next move until after dark. My old friend on Perry Street was home when I called and said that a quarter was no problem. We did some tasting together, and I was starting to move.

The next thing I wanted was a briefcase. Something cheap, ordinary and untraceable. Then I remembered that I had one just like that, the one that Choate Haven had given me with the initial job, the one where I fingered Wood for him. I picked it up from the office. Then I went over to Forty-second Street, and from one of many, many stores offering them, I bought a knife. I also bought a pair of panty hose.

Back at Gateway Plaza, I waited where the driveway came out into West Street. It was dark by then. What I needed was a nice lady leaving the garage to get caught at the light with her window open. It took an hour, but finally one did.

When she stopped, I stepped out. I wore a stocking mask and held the gun I had been carrying since I had chatted with Whelan at Kevin Murphy's. I told her to give me her purse. She gave it to me. I said don't yell. She agreed to that. I told her to drive away. She did.

I simply walked away in the other direction. All I wanted was the key card that opened the garage. I took it, handling everything through the stocking so as not to leave prints.

When it was all over, I intended to send her belongings back. It was the least I could do.

I wanted Choate Haven alone. Preferably at night. The garage was perfect.

The next night he worked until six. Then he went to dinner with clients. After dinner he took a cab over to the Gateway to get his car. It was eight by then and it would have been perfect, but he had one of his dinner companions with him.

The night after that, he went straight home. I was getting increasingly strained, doing more coke, worrying about stopping once it was over.

I no longer had to wait inside the lobby; I knew which way he would come out if he was going to the Gateway. At four, the day after he went home, he came out, heading west. This time he went in the front door. The time had come.

My guess was that he would take three to five hours. There would be a dinner, then some drinks. When he undressed he would hang his clothes carefully on hangers in the closet. Then it would take some time for her to get him in operating condition. But just in case I was wrong and he was going to pop her quick, I didn't want to miss him.

Using the stolen card, I let myself into the underground garage. I found his Mercedes. It was as spic and span and shiney as Edgar Wood's Jaguar had been. Sitting down in the grime and the grub to hide myself, I decided that if I had Haven's kind of money, it would be an old Silver Cloud, just to flaunt it, and I would let it go dusty, just to show I didn't give a shit.

From where I half sat and half lay, I could see the elevator door. Every half-hour I got up, did two little lines, then stretched to keep from getting too stiff. The time crept. And crept. My anger and I held each other close, like lovers, starting to breathe hard, waiting to get swept away with mutual infatuation.

Luck was with me. When the elevator door opened and Choate Haven stepped out, looking as well groomed and impeccable as ever, he was alone. As he came toward his car, I slid around the passenger side, pulled down my stocking mask and slid out my gun. As he came alongside the car, I moved around behind the trunk.

He reached in his pocket for his keys, found them and bent for the lock. I came up and around, moving fast. I had the gun in my right hand. With my left, I grabbed his hair, then smashed his face down into the roof of the car. He was an old man, weak, even frail, and it didn't take much effort. It had all the macho thrill of mugging old ladies and crips.

I lifted him up by the hair. Blood was trickling from his nose and it looked broken. I turned him around. Then I sapped him with the pistol. He crumpled. I checked his pulse. He was alive but out cold.

I had thought about confronting him. To find out why he thought he had done what he had done. Maybe just to find out if I was right, all the way down the line. But if I spoke to him, I would have seen him more and more as a person, a creature of fear and frailty. I couldn't afford that.

I picked up his keys, opened the door, then dragged him into the driver's seat. Then I heard the sound of the garage doors opening. I pushed him over so he lay flat, closed the door and scrambled around the front of the car where I would be hidden.

Whoever it was found their parking space, got out, locked up and headed for the elevator. Each sound echoed and I could follow the action easily. I kept my head down until I heard the door close.

Grabbing the briefcase, his briefcase, I came out on the passenger side. I opened that door, took my plastic bag of cocaine, worked it into the hinge until it was stuck, then pulled it until it tore. The crystalline white powder spilled over the inside of the case, as intended. Then I put his hands all over the case, leaving his prints on the case and coke on his fingertips. I scattered some more of the white lady on the seat and floor. I folded the bag down over the tear and put what was left in my pocket.

Then I closed that door and went back around the other side. He was still out, and I hauled him up. Except for the blood trickling from the smashed nose, it was a handsome patrician face. From the care he lavished on it, the perfect tan, the perfect haircut, the barber-close shave, I knew it meant a lot to him. I took the knife and began to carve a "C" in his cheek. He started twitching. I stopped; the pain was waking him up.

I sapped him again. It scared me, but when I checked, he was still alive. I finished cutting his face as quickly as I could. For good measure I blew some coke into his nose through a straw and threw a paper strip, used by banks to bind up stacks of hundred-dollar bills, on the floor.

Panic and nausea started up from my bowels. All I wanted was to get out of there. As I pushed the button that opened the garage door I heard the elevator again. I don't know if they saw me. If they had they couldn't have identified me through the mask. Still, I was only able to clamp down the control until I was outside the big metal doors. Then I ran. I ran for a long river block until what was left of my reason told me it was the worst thing I could do.

I stripped off the mask, dumped it down a drain and turned east, walking around the World Trade Center. I dropped the knife into the next drain. It was legal for me to have the gun and it had not been fired, but there would be traces of hair, blood and possibly scalp on the barrel. I wiped it as best I could with a newspaper out of the gutter, and with spit.

Then I walked into the brightly lit underground world beneath the towers. I found a fairly isolated phone booth. First I called the *New York Post*. In a half-assed Latin accent I told them that a prominent attorney had been knifed in a drug deal that went bad. I told them where it was and suggested that they get there before the police hushed it up. I gave them five minutes, then called the police. I wanted everyone to find Choate Haven before he woke up and crawled away.

They would think that the "C" carved in his face stood for cocaine.

But Haven would know better. He would know what it really said. Don't fuck with Tony Cassella. He's no better than you are. Don't fuck with Tony Cassella. He'll get right down in the dirt there and cut your face, frame you with drugs and tear your life down so that there's nothing left you care about.

Just because you're a fragile old man doesn't mean that Tony Cassella won't break your nose and leave you bleeding in an underground garage. He knows the kind of fix and frame that'll warm the hearts of aging hoods like Mikey Fix. Antonio Cassella has his devils too; he doesn't understand what they are or why they live with him, but every time you look in the mirror, you'll know.

When I got to Christina's, I didn't buzz. I slipped the outside lock. When I rang the bell to her apartment, I sensed her come to the door and I saw the light as she peered through the peephole. She unlocked the locks and opened the door as far as the chain would allow. She was lovely, in a long caftan, soft white with red and gold embroidery down the slit front.

She was distraught.

"It's done. Let me in," I said, unshaven with eyes blood-shot from too little sleep, too much coke. I could smell the stink of fear sweat coming off me.

"I have company," she said.

"It doesn't matter," I said, my voice held in neutral.

She closed the door. I heard the chain unlatch, then she opened it again. I walked past her into the living room. A slim, well-groomed young man sat there. His cotton shirt was better than anything I had, and the rep tie loose at his throat was silk. He looked like a Stefan.

"You better go now," I said to him.

"Who do you think you are?" he said.

"Tony," she admonished me.

"Get him out of here, or I will," I said. At that moment, I meant it. Cut up one, cut up two, it was all the same to me.

"Go on, Stefan, it's all right," she told him.

"Christina," he protested.

She opened her closet door and brought him his suit jacket. In spite of himself, he took it when she handed it to him. He made protesting noises as she led him to the door. She made soothing noises, then she closed the door behind him.

"He's just a friend . . . these days," she said.

"It doesn't matter."

"What's happened? You look terrible."

"I better take a shower," I told her. "I stink."

I walked into the bathroom and began to strip. I let my stinking clothes fall to the floor. I turned on the shower and stepped in. The heat felt good. Then I remembered the cocaine that was left in my pocket. There was quite a bit. I stepped out of the shower, not caring how wet the floor might get, and fumbled through the pockets. I took it back into the shower with me and held the bag open and let the rushing water flow through it. Two or three hundred dollars of cocaine washed my feet, flowed through my toes and down the drain.

Tomorrow, tomorrow I might regret it and go buy some more. For the moment, I was trying to tell at least one devil to be gone.

All the time I scrubbed, she stood there waiting. I ran it hot to make me feel clean, then I ran it cold to shut the pores and wake me. I stepped out and rubbed myself down. Half dry, I said, "Let's talk," and she followed me into the living room. The caftan was moist from the steam in the shower and clung to the shape of her body. I was naked.

We sat on the couch.

"Your father," I told her, "never knew the thing he was killed for."

The moisture gathered in the corners of her eyes. I told her, as quick and simple as I could, who, what and why. As I talked, she stayed silent, but her fist clenched and the tears streamed down her cheeks. I watched the drops fall; they fell on her breasts.

When I was done, I reached out to her. She grabbed my hand, clung to it fiercely, then held it to her cheek tightly. I put my other arm out and she came to me, sobbing loudly. Eventually, she sat up and wiped her eyes, like a very little girl trying to face adult realities.

"What will happen to . . . to that man?"

"It's already happened."

"What has?" she asked.

I told her.

"My God, Tony. Oh, my angel, what if they catch you?"

"They won't," I said flatly, then my voice turned harsh, saying, "Don't you see? What will it take to make you see? I'm not an angel."

"To me you are. And I love you."

She reached out to me, with wonder, with awe. "Nobody has ever done anything for me. Not like that. I've never known anyone who would, or could." Her lips found mine. Our kisses were fierce, biting. I held her to me, our bodies rocking, our hands grabbing, as if our bodies could fold into each other.

"My angel, my angel," she said.

I was angry. I pushed away from her and stood up. "I am not an angel. I don't know what I am, but I'm less than I should be. I'm less than my father's son."

In her eyes what I had done was wonderful. In Vince's eyes and Mike Paley's, it would have style; they would like it and be happy to offer me further opportunities. Those opportunities would pay for this woman that I loved. My father, whatever he might've thought, was dead and had nothing to say.

"What's wrong?" she asked.

What was wrong? Once there was, or somewhere there is, a world where what I had done was clean, bright, right. Maybe in Uncle Vincent's world. Or the world he had come from, old Sicily. Maybe in Haven's world, but I doubted that. Or maybe when Alan Ladd played at Shane and said, "A man's gotta do what a man's gotta do." But I didn't believe in John Wayne either. Was that what was wrong?

"I don't know," I said.

"What about us? What do you want?"

I walked over to her. I stood before her naked. I looked down at her, down into her green eyes, wide open and confused. Down at her mouth, open, moist, hungry. I wanted to take her. Perhaps she could see that; her hands reached out to hold me, settling on my hips. When she touched me, my body shook, a shiver, a tremor. My stomach turned with fear and anger, of myself, at myself, and it rose, acid and acrid in my throat. I forced it back down inside me. It showed somehow on my face, because I saw fear looking back at me.

I took her head in my hands. I wanted to kiss her, to force her to taste how foul I was, I wanted her to share the bile that was at the back of my mouth.

"What do you want?" she asked.

Did I want the short wild ride we would have? As sweet as sugar and as clear as pain? Did I want to go for the money, the gold, the girl, the everything? And pay the price that someday, somehow, Paley and Vincent and Christina would ask. My fingers curled through her hair. It was so soft, so fine. Did I want to take her? Yes, I did. I could, I could fuck my anger and confusion into her mouth.

"What do you want?" she asked.

No. I loved her, and there was something tender in me still. No, I didn't want her to be the receptacle of my fear.

"I love you, my angel, I love you."

I wanted to go home. To see Glenda and hope that she loved me enough to let me come home. Start turning the past into the memories that it ought to be, not the living, ongoing reality it sometimes is.

"What do you want?" she asked, and she was so beautiful. I hadn't realized I was sweating until a drop fell on her breast. Or maybe it was a tear. Or even something else.

"I'm going home."

HE WAS ALONE (AS IN REALITY) UPON HIS HUMBLE BED,
when imagination brought to his ears the sound of many voices
again singing the slow and monotonous psalm which was inter-
rupted by the outcries of some unseen things who attempted to
enter his chamber, and, amid yells of fear and execrations of
anger, bade him, "Arise and come forth and aid;" then the
coffined form, which slept so quietly below, stood by his side and
in beseeching accents bade him, "Arise and save what is beau-
tiful."

Come back when fog drifts out over the city
And sleep puts her kind hands on all these poor devils

Come back when the policeman is in another street
And Beatrice will let you see her thin soul under the paint

Come back to the corner and tell them what brand of poison you
        want
Ask them why your very own dear lady is always on the lay

Somebody will pick up the pieces, somebody will put you to
        bed
You're a great guy, and she's the finest broad in all the world

Take it easy, partner, death is not such a bad chaser
And you didn't mix this one anyway

They were all right, the lot of them, it wasn't up to them
And they knew it; if somebody had come along and said,
I've got a spot for a two-legged animal in the world I'm working
        on,
They wouldn't have made anything like they had been made.
They were wise that this man-business was just a matter
Of putting it in and taking it out, and that went all the way
From throwing up cathedrals to getting hot pants over Kathy.
Maybe there was something to get steamed about, maybe it was

245

Baseball to grow a beard and end up on a cross so that a lot
Of hysteria cases could have something to slap around;
Maybe the old Greek boy knew what he was doing when he
       hemlocked
It out, loving the heels who hobbled him; maybe little French
       Joan
Got a kick out of the English hot-foot; the boys at the corner
       bar
Were willing to believe it. No skin off their noses. But what was
       hard
Was when you get a snoot full and all you can think to say starts
       with s
And you know damn well you're a good guy and you'll never
       meet a dame
Who really has your address, who can really dot your t's or cross
       your i's

Come back when it's old home week in this particular hell
And you can bum enough nickels to take the fallen angels out

I sat down and said beer thinking Scotch and there by God
Was my woman just as I had always known she would be
And I went over to her and she said come home with me
Like that, raining a bit, will you get wet? no, let's hurry,
Climbing the stairs behind her, watching; what's your name?
Lorraine, don't make so much noise, the landlady; buzz her, I
       said,
Wondering how God would have gotten it all into this little tail;
Key in the lock, light; hello, you're lovely did you know that?
She was all right, all of her, it was up to me and I knew it; let's
Talk first, do you mind? I said no and she said some female stuff
Husband on the lam and I've never done this before tonight; me,
       I
Put all my cards on the table and dealt myself five aces, great
       God

I was wanting it then but she said some more things and started
To cry and I slammed on my coat and said you lousy bitch which
       shut
Her up and I put my key in the lock

And when it's open, when you've got it, when it's all yours,
When nobody else in all the world is where you are,
When your arms have really gone around something,
When your thighs know all the answers to all the questions,
Why is there always one bead of sweat that doesn't come from
    either of your faces?

Come back when sleep drifts out over the city
And the good God puts His hands on all these poor devils.

About the Author

Larry Beinhart introduced readers to Tony Cassella in *No One Rides for Free*, continuing the series with *You Get What You Pay For* and *Foreign Exchange*, both published by Ballantine Books. He lives in Woodstock, New York.